Liberation Park

Also by this author

The Lancefield Mysteries

Salvation Hall

The Redemption

Hemlock Row

St Aldate's Magick

The Rose Bennett Mysteries

Dead on Account

Dead Ringer

Death Duties

Death Benefit

Dead & Buried

Liberation Park

A Lancefield Mystery

MARIAH KINGDOM

~ Perceda Press ~

This novel is entirely a work of fiction. Any resemblance to actual persons, living or dead, or to events, locations or premises is used in a fictious manner. Salvation Hall, the Lancefield family, the Woodlands estate, Hemlock Row, the St Aldate's estate, Liberation Park and the village of Penwithen do not and have not ever existed, except in the author's imagination.

First published in digital form 2025 by WL Fowler

Copyright © Mariah Kingdom 2025

This paperback edition Perceda Press 2025

Mariah Kingdom asserts the moral right to be identified as the author of this work.

A catalogue record for this publication is available from the British Library

All rights reserved. No part of this publication may be reproduced, stored in a retrieval system or transmitted in any form or by any means, electronic, mechanical, photocopying, recording or otherwise, without the written permission of the author and/or publisher.

ISBN 978-1-8380834-9-6

Cover design by www.ebooklaunch.com

*Having seen all this you can choose to look the other way,
but you can never say again
'I did not know'*

*William Wilberforce 1759 - 1833
Politician and Abolitionist*

1

Liberation Park.

Luminous in the late-May moonlight, its four-pillared portico rises up to meet the silent, uncluttered night sky. Cast in a honey-coloured stone, its simple lines and modest windows stand testament to the timeless, understated elegance of its age. Here and there, a chandelier glints through Georgian glass, hinting at interior luxury; along the roofline, a steady stream of smoke from plain, utilitarian chimney pots hints at the warmth and comfort provided by fires burning beneath ornate, exquisitely appointed fireplaces in the rooms below.

Once heartlessly neglected, the house has blossomed under diligent care. Rotting floorboards have been replaced with oak and crumbling walls restored to their former, stuccoed glory. Indulgence oozes from every interior pore: damask drapes keep out the cold while gilt-edged chairs vie with sumptuous sofas for the privilege of affording a place to sit; antique books adorn mahogany cases and lavish artworks jostle for prominence on the vast expanse of space above the magnificent central staircase.

On the first floor of the house, the grand reception room carries all the trappings of an elegant wedding supper: twelve tables furnished with silks and silver; the finest bone china for serving and crystal flutes for raising a toast to the newlyweds. Two hundred roses, white and pure, fill silver buckets that line the walls, their fragrance mingling with spikes of rosemary and fronds of delicate flowering jasmine. And what remains of a hundred and twenty guests – those not dancing in the ballroom below, or retired already to a sumptuous bedroom on the floors above – mingle and gossip over vintage ports and expensive liqueurs, their appetites assuaged by endless platters of cheeses, fruits and petit fours.

Outside in the darkness a slender, solitary figure sits calmly on a cool, stone bench. Entranced by the scene, she casts her eyes across the front elevation of the house, her gaze drawn slowly from window to window to window: here, the rosy glow of the library fireplace just visible through the panes of handmade glass; there, the sight of wedding guests chatting quietly in the dimly lit drawing room; above, the welcoming glow of bedside lamps lit early to guide the somnolent to slumber. For a moment, captivated by the vision, she holds her breath. And then, reluctant but accepting, she rises: the time has come at last for her to turn and walk away.

The distance to her future is a short one: along the front of the house and across a short, precisely manicured lawn to the gatehouse. Beyond its heavy, black-panelled door that future will be waiting for her, and she pushes on it eagerly, gliding through the hallway to the bedroom to find him stretched from east to west across the bed.

The room is dimly lit, the light too low for her to see much beyond the stillness of his body, and without another moment's thought she drops her shawl to the floor and slips off her shoes, clambering carefully up beside him with a smile. Though the bed begins to shift beneath her weight he doesn't stir, and she nudges at his arm to awaken him with a playful, loving hand. But the hand rebounds unexpectedly against his unresponsive flesh; her pulse begins to race as she realises that the arm she touched is flaccid, the once-firm muscle slack, and she narrows her eyes against the darkness, turning them up towards his face.

For twenty heart-stopping seconds her mind simply refuses to accept the truth of what she sees: his head thrown back in a spasm of pain; the deep blue eyes wide and unseeing; the skin pallid and clammy from the sudden shock of death. Then she grasps at his limp and lifeless hand; presses it to her lips; feels burning tears of heartache begin to blister down her cheeks as her body suddenly heaves, unbidden, with the shock.

Her shoulders tremble, her mouth runs dry, her breathing stumbles in fits and starts. And then she pushes herself to her knees, all sense of reason suddenly paralysed by the unimaginable pain of loss, and she throws back her head to howl wretchedly into the pitiless, unforgiving shadows.

*

Ennor Price watched as Kathryn Clifton hitched up the sleeves of her soft, silk dress and rested her forearms on the table. There was a hint of mischief in her warm hazel eyes, a look that he was growing all too fond of, and he knew that any moment he would be called upon to defend himself.

'Well, I think it's been a relative success, all things considered.' She bent her head forward until it was almost touching his. 'I won't deny that I had my reservations, but your behaviour has been impeccable.'

'*My* behaviour?' His tone was teasing, his usual reserve softened by the joy of the occasion and a surfeit of quality wine. 'What did you expect me to do? Frisk each wedding guest as they arrived at the church? Why would I do that if I wasn't on duty? As I recall, Laurence and Jennet invited me to be your plus-one, so that makes me a guest.'

'And you don't think that was just a ploy, so Laurence could keep you close by?'

Perhaps she had a point. But whatever the hosts' motivation, Ennor had been only too happy to accept. 'I suppose Marcus is only here under sufferance?' He turned his head to cast a subtle glance across the room. 'Do you think he's actually drunk, or just pretending?'

Kathryn followed his gaze. 'Pretending.' The subject of their conversation was sprawled in a velvet-covered carver chair, his silk tie slackened and askew beneath the unbuttoned collar of his shirt, his fingers wrapped loosely around an almost-empty whisky tumbler. 'I can't help wondering if it was a little unkind of Richard to insist that he attend. It would have been quite enough for David and Nancy to represent the Lancefield branch of the family.' She stretched out a hand to retrieve a bottle of Chablis from the solid-silver cooler on the table. 'Richard and David have done everything they can to encourage Marcus and Laurence to bury their grievances and be friends, but I've seen no sign of it yet.' She topped up Ennor's glass as she spoke. 'I suppose it's only been ten weeks since Eva died. And some people just need more time to grieve and forget.'

And some would never get there. Two and half months had passed since Eva McWhinney's fateful journey to London to meet Laurence Payne for dinner. Less than twenty-four hours after arriving, her lifeless body had been dragged from the north dock at West India Quay. Ennor suspected that Marcus would probably always blame Laurence for her death: for failing to walk her safely back to the door of her hotel, and for letting her wander into the path of the serial killer so intent on taking her life.

As for that killer meeting his own untimely end in the

potting shed at Salvation Hall…

Ennor shivered and picked up his glass. The complexities of the case were enough to tax the skill and patience of a better man than him. Smith's sister claimed that he murdered Eva in return for forty thousand pounds promised to him by Marcus Drake: a claim which Marcus, unsurprisingly, refuted. Just as he denied any involvement in Smith's own death barely forty-eight hours later. Lacking any substantial evidence to support a murder charge for either crime, Ennor had been left with no choice but to let the young man walk free. But doubts about his innocence lingered in the detective's mind like a disease that refuses a cure. 'If Marcus still blames Laurence for Eva's death, there's no wonder he didn't want to come here. I suppose I should be grateful, at least, that he's been civil to me.'

'I made it very clear to him that you were here as my companion, not in any official capacity.' Kathryn, suddenly pensive, ran a manicured finger around the rim of her wine glass. 'And whatever the reason for the invitation, that *is* why you accepted, isn't it? Not because it gave you the opportunity to keep Marcus under surveillance?'

The hint of disappointment in her voice was unmistakeable and he put down his glass to take hold of her hand. 'I came to be with you and to share the enjoyment of the day.' The time had come to change the subject. 'Laurence and Jennet make a lovely couple, their family and friends couldn't have been more welcoming, and this place' – he flicked his eyes upwards and around the room – 'is spectacular. I didn't expect it to be so grand. I thought Salvation Hall was impressive but Liberation Park makes it look like a country cottage. Does it really belong to Jennet's family?'

'Yes, it was left to her father by a distant cousin. I'm told they invested a small fortune in restoring it. It was Jennet's mother who saw the potential for it to be turned into a hotel. I suppose it was her way of making the place pay for itself.'

'Salvation Hall doesn't have to pay for itself.'

'No, but then the Lancefields have always been shrewd in business. Their other assets yield enough income to support the running costs of the house. Perhaps Jennet's family aren't in the same league when it comes to family wealth.'

'You mean their family didn't manage to make millions from the slave trade?'

Kathryn's lips puckered. 'How many times do I have to tell you? The Lancefields didn't make their money from the trade, they made it from sugar production.'

As if it made a difference. 'So, where did the money come from to build Liberation Park?'

Her cheeks dimpled. 'From sugar production, of course. I can't believe it's taken you so long to ask me that.' She leaned a little closer to him. 'The house was built in the eighteenth century by the Huntsford family with the profits from their sugar plantation in Jamaica. But at the beginning of the nineteenth century the family found themselves with no male heir to carry on the line. Their only daughter married a man called Ezekiel Taylor, a clergyman and abolitionist, and he changed the name from Huntsford Hall to Liberation Park, to signify his support for the abolition of slavery.'

'Then the house passed from a slave owner to an abolitionist?'

'Ah, not quite. It passed from a slave owner to an abolitionist, who also happened to be a slave owner.'

*

Sadie Smith cradled the sobbing toddler in her arms, resting her chin atop the little girl's head as she gently rocked her shoulders to and fro.

But the child was not to be pacified. Writhing in her

agony, she arched her back and lashed out wildly with a sticky, snot-covered hand. The blow caught the unsuspecting grandmother sharply on the cheek and she grabbed the tiny fingers between her own and held them tight. 'Now you stop that, Frankie, d'you hear me? Your mummy will be back soon enough. There's no need for all this nonsense.'

Just as there had been no need for Becca Smith to do a disappearing act. "Just overnight", she had said the previous morning, as she sweet-talked Sadie into looking after her daughter. "I've got the chance of a night out with the girls and I don't want to miss it."

It had been no hardship to agree, of course. Sadie was as fond of Frankie as she was of all her other grandchildren, and it was a joy to spend time with any of them – providing their parents kept to their own side of the bargain. But Becca had a habit of pushing her luck and this time she had overstepped the mark. Six o'clock on Friday evening, the promised time of collection, had come and gone. And seven calls made to Becca's mobile phone had failed to yield a result.

Sadie looked down again at her snivelling grandchild and lowered her head to kiss the girl's forehead. 'Now, you be a good girl and stay quiet for a minute.' She held the child firmly with her right arm and stretched out her left hand to retrieve her mobile phone from the arm of the sofa, jabbing briskly at it with her thumb and pressing it to her ear with an impatient flick of the wrist.

The call diverted immediately to an answering service and Sadie, indignant, swore silently under her breath. 'Becca, it's me again.' She bit off the words. 'You're four hours late now and Frankie needs to go to bed. I'm going to have to put her down here for tonight. It wouldn't do you any harm to pick up the phone and tell me where you are. The poor little mite has been through enough.' She flicked a thumb at the phone for a second time, disconnecting the call, and dropped the device onto the cushion beside her with a sigh.

Little Frankie had been through enough, alright. Her father, Philip, murdered by that Marcus Drake. Her Uncle Zak murdered by heaven knows who. Her mother facing charges of assisting an offender for helping Zak to stay on the run, her only chance of escaping imprisonment hanging by a thread on Richard Lancefield's willingness to fund her legal representation. Sadie had never been comfortable with the idea of the lord of the Lancefield manors being godfather to her precious youngest granddaughter. But God knows it had turned out for the best – at least the man understood what it would do to the fatherless child if a prison sentence rendered her motherless into the bargain.

Sadie heaved out a sigh and slumped back against the sofa's curves. 'Well, pet, it looks like you're here for another night.' The child had calmed and Sadie stroked her curls with a gentle hand. 'You know I don't mind you being here. Truth be told, I didn't mind at all that your mummy wanted a night out to herself, if it finally puts a smile on her face. I just hope that when she turns up with her excuses, she manages to make them good ones.'

2

'The call was passed to us just after two o'clock this morning.' Detective Sergeant Jim Collinson, fresh-faced and eager despite the early hour, consulted his notebook as he spoke. 'The wife found the body and just sat with him for the best part of an hour before she called for help.'

'And what did we do at two in the morning? Sit on our hands and wait for the day shift?' Detective Inspector Steph Hall leaned over the bed and a faint scent of sandalwood and bergamot met her nostrils. 'Expensive cologne.' Her eyes swept slowly across the body, taking in the quality of his clothing as they went: the fine Egyptian cotton of his shirt, the worsted herringbone trousers, the silk socks. 'It looks as though he kicked off his shoes, undid his belt, took off his tie and just lay down to go to sleep.' She straightened her back and turned to look at her colleague. 'We should have been here from the off. Why didn't his wife go for help straight away?'

'She told Terry Bradley it was the shock.'

'Terry was the first officer on the scene?'

'Yes. She told him that after she pulled herself together, she went back into the hotel to find her mother. Then there was a further delay before they involved the hotel staff. The manager called for an ambulance and that took nearly ninety minutes to arrive.'

'Prioritising the living over the dead?'

'Give them a break, Steph. You know what Friday nights are like. Anyway, it was the ambulance crew who called us in. It looked like heart failure but they weren't convinced it was natural causes.'

'And I suppose they had their hands all over him while they were coming to that conclusion?' It wouldn't have occurred to them that he was a potential crime scene. At least, not until it was too late and they'd contaminated half the evidence. 'Has Doctor Philips seen the body?'

Collinson flipped the page in his notebook. 'Yes. He estimates the time of death between ten o'clock and midnight, which fits with the wife's story.'

'Any idea of the cause?'

'He thinks it might be poisoning.'

'Poisoning?' Hall bristled, and arched a carefully pencilled eyebrow above the thick, black frame of her spectacles. 'From what?'

'He doesn't know yet. There's an empty whisky tumbler on the bedside table.' Collinson flicked a chubby finger towards the offending item. 'He left it there so we could see it in situ before it gets bagged up for analysis. There's no decanter or bottle in the room, so he must have brought it from the bar.' The sergeant ran his tongue around his teeth. 'What's your initial view?'

'That we need to speak to his wife.' Hall winced. 'His widow.' She stepped back from the bed, pushing her hands into the pockets of her raincoat. 'We only have her word for it that she found him dead. She could have brought the whisky tumbler with her. She also, by her own admission, waited an hour before she raised the alarm, so how do we know she hasn't tampered with the room in some way?'

'We don't.' Collinson flipped his notebook shut and slipped it into his pocket. 'She's over in the main hotel building if you want to speak to her now. I'll get the glass sent off for analysis.' He began to move towards the door.

'I'm not sure how to break this to you, but there were a hundred and twenty wedding guests in the hotel last night, plus hotel staff. If we need to conduct interviews…'

'Only a hundred and twenty? Well, I suppose it could have been worse.' Hall's shoulders drooped under a sigh. 'Are people in the hotel aware of what's happened?'

'Terry said he framed it as a medical emergency. The wife, her mother and the hotel manager are the only people who know about the death. The staff are gossiping and one or two guests have enquired about the patrol car and ambulance that arrived during the night, but they've all been reassured there's nothing to worry about.'

'Then let's try to keep it that way until we have a cause of death.' The inspector nodded to herself and turned her eyes around the room. 'It's a bit fancy for a gatehouse, isn't it? Antique furniture, oil paintings' – she flicked her eyes upwards – 'chandelier lighting?'

'It's the bridal suite.' Collinson almost whispered the words. 'They do a lot of weddings and the manager says it gives the newlyweds a sense of privacy from the guests if they're staying here for their wedding night.'

'It certainly gave the victim's bride the privacy to sit with the groom's body before she raised the alarm.' Hall's eyes narrowed as the cogs in her brain began to turn. 'Let's hope for her sake she has a convincing explanation for the whisky glass.'

Collinson hesitated beside the door, his hand halfway to the doorknob. 'Steph, you don't think there's a possibility that any poison might have been self-administered? That he came over here to end his own life?'

'On his wedding night?' She spluttered a laugh. 'You really don't have a very high opinion of matrimony, do you? Has Yvonne been badgering you about commitment again?'

'She never stops badgering me about it.' His youthful cheeks blushed. 'I just don't pay any attention.'

'Then maybe you should. Yvonne's a catch and she

won't hang around forever.' Hall frowned and turned back to look at the body lying prone across the bed. 'On the other hand, if she hears what happened here in the bridal suite last night it might put her off the idea of marriage for good.'

*

David Lancefield lifted a slice of toast from the silver rack on the table and set about buttering it. 'I know the hour is still early, but I thought Marcus and Nancy might have made an appearance by now. They're well aware that I want to head off as soon as possible after breakfast.' He glanced up at Kathryn as she pulled a chair away from the table and sat down. 'Will Inspector Price be joining us?'

'Is that why you think Nancy and Marcus are dragging their heels? Because they don't want to share a breakfast table with Ennor?'

'The thought had occurred to me.' David waved the knife in her direction before digging it into a small pot of marmalade. 'And is the reverse of the hypothesis the reason Inspector Price hasn't made an appearance yet? Because he is avoiding Nancy and Marcus?'

'Not in the least.' Kathryn lifted a napkin from the table and shook it out, draping it across her lap. She stretched out a hand for the teapot and set about pouring Earl Grey into her cup. 'Do you think you'll ever be able to call him Ennor, or will he always be Inspector Price?'

'I fear he will be Inspector Price until he has caught Zak Smith's killer and the family is no longer under his scrutiny.' There was no malice in David's voice but the sentiment was clear enough. 'I have a great deal of respect for him, of course. And I know the two of you have grown very close. But he will always be a police officer first and foremost, at least to me.'

'Then let's hope he catches Zak's killer soon, for all our

sakes.' She took a slice of lemon from a small bowl on the table and dropped it into her cup. 'He'll be joining us shortly. We were just on our way down to join you when Sergeant Parkinson called him. It's police business, so he's gone back to his room to take the call.'

'I rest my case.' A wry smile pulled at David's lips. 'Nothing troublesome, I hope?'

'I wouldn't have thought so.' At least, she hoped not. 'Is it my imagination, or is there an odd atmosphere in here this morning? The place feels very subdued. Had you noticed?'

'It would have been difficult *not* to notice.' The hotel's breakfast room was almost empty, and the handful of guests around them were talking in hushed and furtive tones. 'I wondered if people were just nursing their hangovers. The party did go on until the early hours.' David looked over his shoulder as he spoke. 'I was hoping to see Laurence and Jennet before we leave, though perhaps it was a tad foolish of me to think they would make an appearance so early in the morning. I shall have to leave our best wishes in a message at the reception desk when we check out. I'm sure I'll have the opportunity to speak to them before they fly out to St Felix for their honeymoon.' He placed his knife down on the table and licked a smear of marmalade from his fingers. 'Does Inspector Price know that Marcus is planning to fly back to St Felix on Monday?'

Knew it, was frustrated by it, and could do nothing to stop it. 'I think I did mention it to him.' She tried to make it sound unimportant. 'But it doesn't really impact his investigation.'

'He's still looking at Marcus as his primary suspect for Zak Smith's murder though, isn't he?'

'He doesn't have many other options. Ennor always says that solving a crime comes down to motive, means and opportunity. I'm afraid that approach puts several people in the frame.' She might have said "including you,

David" but she would spare him the embarrassment. 'Zak's body was found at Salvation Hall, so in a broad sense every member of the household had the opportunity to kill him.' The police had certainly found forensic evidence showing that every member of the household had been in the potting shed at one time or another. 'Anyone could have picked up the spade and hit him with it, so the means were readily available.' But as things stood, she knew Ennor didn't believe anyone else had quite the same grudge against Zak. And he had to take into account that Marcus had already shown he was capable of killing. 'You do know that he will find the killer, David? That he won't stop until he does?' She placed a hand on David's arm. 'And I don't believe you would want him to stop, whatever the outcome?'

David's grey eyes softened beneath a furrowed brow. 'You know me too well. And although it pains me to say it, I share his opinion. It's too fantastic to think Smith met his end at the hands of some random stranger who just wandered into our potting shed. I just wish this whole, sordid affair was over so that we could pick up the pieces of our lives without living under its shadow. But for now, all I can do is speed Marcus back to Salvation Hall, away from the inspector's watchful eye. The two of them have been glowering at each other since we arrived at Liberation Park on Thursday evening and, quite frankly, my poor nerves won't stand another minute of it.'

*

'We were just on our way down to breakfast and I thought it would be better if I called you back from the hotel room.' Ennor Price sat down on the edge of the bed and pressed the mobile phone to his ear with a sigh of resignation. A whole uninterrupted weekend with Kathryn had probably been too much to hope for, as had the chance to put some distance between himself and the unspoken obligation he felt to put in never-ending amounts of unpaid overtime. But he knew that DS Parkinson wouldn't disturb him without good reason. 'What couldn't wait until Monday?'

'Hopefully something and nothing.' Parkinson sounded subdued at the end of the line. 'Dare I ask how things are going up there?'

'Oh, dare away.' Price laughed softly at the question. 'The hotel is spectacular and dinner on Thursday evening was well up to scratch. As was the wedding itself: I wasn't sure what to expect, but Laurence's wife is charming.' He wanted to say *far too normal* to marry an Obeah-loving weirdo like Laurence Payne, but he resisted the temptation. 'In fact, it was almost the perfect weekend away.'

'Do I have to ask what spoilt it?'

'Probably not: thirty-six hours in a social setting with Marcus Drake, trying to act casual and remember that I wasn't on duty.'

Parkinson grunted. 'How is Kathryn dealing with it?'

'Stoically.' Price knew her patience had been tested but she had made little attempt to complain. 'Things have changed since Smith's body turned up at Salvation Hall. The family had always been accepting of her friendship with me, but now they're more guarded with her. They think she's spying on them and passing information back to me.'

'I thought that was the idea?'

'No, the idea was for her to help me bring Zak's killer to justice, whoever that is.' It wasn't quite the same thing in Price's book but he wasn't in the mood to argue the point. 'Anyway, Tom, what's so important that it warranted a call?'

The sergeant hesitated. 'I'm not sure if it *is* important, but I thought you'd want to know. Becca Smith has been reported missing.'

It took a few seconds for the news to register. 'When did this happen?'

'The call came in from her mother about an hour ago. Becca left little Frankie with her on Thursday morning so she could go on a night out with some friends. They were former colleagues from her hospital job in Truro, and she was planning to sleep over with one of them to save the cost of a taxi home. She dropped Frankie off in the morning and was due to pick her up from Sadie's at four o'clock on Friday afternoon. But she didn't turn up. Sadie's made multiple calls to her mobile phone but none have been answered.'

'Why didn't she call us on Friday?'

'You know what the Smith family are like when it comes to the police. Anyway, I've tried Becca's mobile number myself and there's no answer.' Parkinson's voice wavered. 'I have a bad feeling about this, boss. Apart from anything else, she's broken her bail conditions. She's supposed to check in every Friday morning and I find it hard to believe she'd skip that without good reason. There's too much at stake.'

'Has Sadie contacted any of the friends Becca was out with?'

'She doesn't have their contact details. At this point we're assuming Becca turned up for the night out and went missing afterwards.'

Price pressed his fingers to a greying temple. 'Okay, you need to start with Thursday morning. Where did she go after dropping Frankie off?'

'Sadie said she was going shopping. She wanted a new outfit for the evening.' The sergeant cleared his throat. 'I'm sending someone over to Sadie's now to take a statement. I'm heading to the hospital myself to see if I can track down the girls she was meeting. Sadie said she mentioned someone called Maddie, but that was the only name she had. I know we need to nail the last sighting of her, but...' Parkinson's voice trailed off. Then he said, 'It's too much of a coincidence, isn't it? For Becca to disappear on the day Laurence Payne was getting married?'

'For pity's sake, Tom, of course it is. So far, Becca's managed to avoid prison for assisting Zak when he was on the run. Richard Lancefield is throwing money at her again and she still has her new home in Truro, even if she did lose her job at the hospital. Lancefield will help her to find another job after her case comes to trial. She's hardly likely to mess all of that up deliberately, is she? Even Becca couldn't be that stupid.'

'No, I don't suppose she could.' Parkinson didn't sound convinced. 'So, what do you think has happened to her?'

'I think she enjoyed her night out on Thursday so much she decided to try it on with Sadie and spin another night's freedom out of it. Frankie isn't going to come to any harm with her grandmother, is she? And Sadie's used to being trampled on by her ungrateful kids. She seems able to forgive them anything.' Price paused, and then said, 'If it turns out Becca met a man on Thursday evening, that scenario will look even more likely.'

'Then I suppose we just have to keep an open mind for now, until we have a better idea of her movements on Thursday. Do you want me to keep you up to date, or would you rather I left you in peace for the rest of the weekend?'

'Keep me in the picture, if it makes you feel any better.' Price stood up from the bed, the phone still pressed to his ear. 'And try not to worry. I know you've got a soft spot for Becca, but she's as tough as old boots. She'll turn up when she's ready. I'd stake good money on it.'

3

The large, private drawing room to the rear of the hotel's first floor reeked of luxury: furnished with fine antique furniture and original artworks, its tall sash windows framed by elegant velvet drapes, it was a far cry from the grubby industrial estates, concrete tower blocks, and drab back-to-back terraces where DI Hall and DS Collinson usually plied their trade.

They found Jennet Payne already waiting for them. A petite doe-eyed brunette, she was sitting calmly on an enormous russet-coloured Chesterfield beside a slim, elegant woman dressed in blue. The woman smiled as they approached and gestured to a matching sofa opposite. Jennet, her pretty face pale and drawn, didn't stir.

'Mrs Payne?' Hall began to pick her way across a striking Chinese rug. 'I'm Detective Inspector Stephanie Hall and this is my colleague, Detective Sergeant Collinson.' She pulled out a warrant card and showed it to Jennet before sitting awkwardly on the edge of the sofa. 'I know you gave a statement to our colleagues during the night, but we'd like to understand a bit more about the events surrounding your husband's death.' She looked up at Collinson as he sat down beside her, the tilt of her head almost imperceptible.

He took the cue with practised ease. 'Please don't be

concerned, it's just a matter of routine in the case of an unexpected death.' He turned warm, encouraging eyes to the elegant woman in blue. 'If you have anything to add, Mrs Taylor, please feel free.'

Rosemary Taylor responded by taking hold of her daughter's hand. 'Jennet's been through a great deal in the last few hours.' Her voice was rich and smooth. 'But we'll do our best, won't we, darling?'

Collinson pulled a pen and notebook from his pocket. 'The wedding ceremony was at four o'clock, wasn't it?' He directed the question at Jennet. 'Can you tell us what happened after that?'

'Yes, of course.' The girl was softly spoken, her voice surprisingly controlled. 'The ceremony lasted for around thirty minutes and then the wedding party went out into the grounds for the photographs to be taken. That took about an hour. And then we moved back in to the hotel to greet the guests for dinner.'

'And how many people were present?'

'Eighty for the ceremony and dinner, and then another forty joined us after eight o'clock for a supper party.'

'Was Laurence feeling okay when you greeted the guests for dinner?'

'Yes, he was in good spirits. We were all very happy.'

DI Hall leaned forward. 'Can you remember what he had to eat and drink?'

Rosemary frowned. 'Everything was prepared fresh on the premises.'

'I'm sure it was. It's just a routine question, Mrs Taylor. We're not suggesting there was anything wrong with the items served.' Hall turned a gentle smile to Jennet. 'Can you remember?'

'Of course. There were two choices for each course – melon or prawn bisque, lamb cutlet or wild mushroom risotto, and crème brûlée or lemon sorbet to finish. Laurence had the melon, the lamb and the crème brûlée.'

'And what about drinks?'

'Soft drinks were served while the photographs were being taken. I think Laurence had homemade lemonade, served from a pitcher that everyone shared. We had red and white wines with the meal, and champagne for the toasts.' Jennet's brow creased in concentration. 'After the meal, we went back to the gatehouse to change for the evening party. He was fine at that point.'

'You said there was a supper in the evening?'

'Yes. But that was for the evening guests. We didn't eat anything else because we'd had a three-course meal. Except,' she hesitated, 'I think Laurence had some cheese.' She turned to her mother. 'He shared it with you.'

Rosemary nodded. 'It was roquefort. He never could resist it.'

DS Collinson's pen halted. 'Did he drink whisky with the cheese?'

'Heavens, no. That wouldn't pair at all.' Rosemary's nose wrinkled. 'I think he was drinking Sauterne. Why do you ask?'

'There was a whisky glass in the gatehouse. We thought he might have carried it over from the party.'

'Then I would think he picked it up from the bar before he left.'

Hall and Collinson exchanged a glance and then the inspector, uneasy, uttered a sigh. 'Can either of you remember when Laurence began to feel unwell?'

His widow's face paled a little further at the question. 'It was around nine thirty. He said he felt cold and shivery, but it was very warm in the room.'

'Which room was this?'

'The grand reception room upstairs.'

'And did he look unwell to you?'

'A little. He was pale, and he looked tired. It was my idea for him to go back to the gatehouse. He didn't want to leave me alone at the party but I managed to persuade him. I told him I'd stay with the guests for around an hour, and then take my leave.'

'And you can't remember if he had a whisky glass with him when he left?'

'No, I'm afraid I can't. Is it important to know where the whisky glass came from?'

'It might be.' Hall looked down at her hands. 'The thing is, Mrs Payne, the doctor who examined Laurence earlier this morning doesn't think his death was from natural causes. So, I'm afraid there will have to be a post mortem.'

'But Laurence died from a heart attack. I was told that last night by one of the paramedics.'

'I can only apologise, and assure you there was no intention to mislead. Further examination has confirmed that Laurence died from heart failure. It isn't necessarily the same thing as a heart attack. I'm afraid the circumstances of his death may have to be investigated further.'

For a few seconds, Jennet's face remained impassive. And then her lower lip began to tremble and she slumped forwards, bowing her head until her face was no longer visible. 'So, what happens now?' Her words were barely audible.

"We would appreciate the contact details for all guests and hotel staff who were in attendance at the wedding. We'd also like to speak to your bar staff today, to see if anyone can remember serving Laurence with the whisky he took back to the gatehouse.'

'If Laurence's death wasn't from natural causes then…' Jennet slowly raised her head to turn tear-soaked eyes from Collinson to Hall, and back again. 'Are you trying to suggest that he took his own life?'

Either that, or someone else took it from him. Hall's heart sank. How did you break that sort of news to anyone, let alone a woman widowed after barely seven or eight hours of marriage? 'We're not drawing any conclusions at this stage. But we're very grateful for your help so far.' She stood up and stepped forward to crouch down in front of the newly widowed girl. 'And I give you my word that the minute we have any further information, you will be the first to know.'

*

'You do know it will take us the best part of eight hours to drive home?' Ennor let the heavy wooden door swing shut behind him. 'I thought the whole point of checking out of the hotel was so we could be on our way.'

'I know. But one more walk around the rose garden won't hurt, will it?' Kathryn set off slowly along a tidy gravel path. 'It will do us good to have some fresh air before spending all that time cramped in the car.'

'And that's the only reason you don't want to set off yet? There's no ulterior motive: like wanting to hang around to speak to Laurence?'

'Now, why would we want to speak to Laurence? I'm sure he's got far more important things to do this morning than speak to us.' She sucked in her cheeks. 'Do *you* think we need to speak to Laurence?'

What sort of a question was that? 'Please tell me you're not hanging around to make sure he survived the night.'

'No? I thought that was why he invited you to the wedding? To make sure he was safe while Marcus was at Liberation Park?' She took hold of his arm to guide him through a fragrant arch of early-flowering honeysuckle. 'Don't you want to know it was worth your while being here?'

'Kathryn, are you making fun of me?'

'Only a little.' She pulled playfully on the sleeve of his shirt. 'Anyway, Laurence won't need to worry about Marcus after today, will he? Assuming you're still okay with Marcus going back to St Felix.'

'I don't have much choice, do I?' It would be pointless to go on bemoaning the fact that he couldn't prevent it.

'So, why *are* we still here?'

'Because of something Jennet mentioned to me yesterday evening, when we were chatting. I told her I'd done a little research into the history of Liberation Park, and she said when they were restoring the house they found a Bible that might have come from Ezekiel Taylor's plantation in the Caribbean. They considered it a curiosity and thought that one day they might make a feature of it for the hotel. She asked if I'd like to see it before we left for Cornwall, so I'm just waiting for the hotel manager to bring it out of storage.'

Ennor shook Kathryn's hand away from his arm. 'We're making a late start on an eight-hour drive so you can see another piece of dusty old history?' He sank his hands into his trouser pockets. 'I suppose that's something I'll have to get used to, isn't it?'

'Only if you want to.'

There was no question of that. He'd already learned that displaying an interest in dusty old documents was one way of keeping Kathryn happy. Just as he'd realised how much Kathryn's happiness was crucial to his own. 'You still haven't explained to me how a clergyman and abolitionist could also be a slave-owner.'

'As if you're really interested.' She paused beside a towering Bourbon rose. 'But if that's the game we're playing, I'm more than happy to participate.' She leaned forward to examine the tightly furled, carmine-coloured rose buds as she spoke. 'Ezekiel Taylor was a clergyman but he came from a slave-owning family. His father owned a sugar plantation on St Felix and he inherited the estate when his father died. I know it seems unthinkable to us now, but at the time slave ownership was a fairly commonplace thing. And not always the preserve of wealthy people.' She stepped back and turned on her heel, continuing her way along the path. 'There are plenty of recorded cases of quite modest individuals owning slaves, often through marriage or inheritance. And, of course, the

Church itself was a significant slave-owner.'

'The Church profited from slavery?'

'And from the slave trade. Religion doesn't always guarantee integrity, does it? Plenty of clergymen have viewed their role as a career and a living, rather than a spiritual vocation.'

Ennor followed slowly in her wake. 'I suppose now you're going to tell me not all clergymen were in favour of abolishing slavery.'

'And you'd be right. Ezekiel was, though, and perhaps he must have battled with his conscience. But he wasn't alone in that. William Wilberforce was one of the most famous names associated with the abolition movement, and instrumental in abolishing the slave trade, and yet his daughter was briefly engaged to the son of a wealthy plantation owner. It was almost impossible at the time for abolitionists to avoid being caught up in connections with traders and plantation owners, because the practice of slavery was so embedded in society.' They had reached a small iron bench and Kathryn sat down on it. 'Anyway, Ezekiel did very well financially out of the thing he claimed to oppose. He inherited his own family's plantation on St Felix and his new wife's estate in Jamaica, as well as Huntsford Hall. And he will have benefitted from the compensation paid to all slave owners when slavery was abolished.'

Ennor sat down beside her. 'Compensation?'

'Certainly. The commercial implications of abolition were huge. When slavery was abolished in the British colonies, the government paid compensation to all slave owners to cover their losses. So Ezekiel would have been compensated for the loss of his slaves on both plantations.' Kathryn frowned. 'He did sell off both estates, of course, to concentrate on developing Liberation Park and the farmlands around it.'

'Even though the place was built with money from the sugar trade?'

'I don't think that would have worried him, any more than it would have worried him to inherit his wife's property. At that time, a married woman couldn't own property in her own right. Isobel Huntsford must have loved him very deeply. I think if I stood to inherit a plantation estate in Jamaica and a grand house in England simply by remaining a spinster then marriage would have been the last thing on my mind.'

Ennor folded his arms and looked away across the neat, rose-filled beds. 'It's funny, isn't it, how easily people can be tempted to do the wrong thing when obscene amounts of money are involved?'

'Whatever made you say that?'

'It's the policeman in me. I can't stop thinking about people's motives. Take Jason Speed, for example. He murdered his father because he hoped to inherit wealth from the Lancefields, and he murdered his partner because she threatened to expose the truth and stop him.'

'That's not really what you're thinking about though, is it?' Kathryn turned probing eyes towards him. 'What you're really thinking is that when Eva died, Marcus inherited her fortune.'

*

Amber Kimbrall watched as DS Parkinson navigated his way through the throng of lunchtime drinkers in the lounge bar of The Lancefield Arms. 'I wondered how long it would be before you called in to see me.' She reached up to the rack above the bar and pulled down a pint glass. 'The usual?' She jammed the glass under a tap without waiting for an answer. 'And before you ask, I have no idea where she is.'

Parkinson slipped off his jacket and draped it over a bar stool before loosening his tie. 'You look as weary as I feel.' He leaned an elbow on the bar, watching as she topped off the pint of Cornish ale and slid it across the counter. After the morning's disappointments, it looked to him like nectar. 'You didn't ask if I was on duty.'

'I didn't need to. You just look like a man who needs a drink.' Amber folded her arms on the counter top, enveloping him in a cloud of familiar musky perfume. 'She hasn't turned up yet then?'

'Would I be here if she had?' He lifted the pint and took a long, sustaining drink. 'When did you hear she was missing?'

'Sadie called me yesterday evening. I told her to call you but she was adamant that Becca was just being Becca. She wasn't unduly worried at that point, just annoyed Becs was taking advantage of her again.' Amber sniffed. 'Do you think there's anything to worry about?'

'Yes, unfortunately.' Parkinson balanced his glass on the edge of the bar. 'I managed to track down one of her hospital friends this morning. Becca didn't show up to meet them on Thursday evening and she isn't answering any calls or messages. So we have no idea what happened to her after she dropped Frankie off with Sadie.' He pushed out his lips and puffed out his frustrations. 'Unless you heard from her at any point on Thursday?'

'As it happens, I did.' Amber slipped a hand into the back pocket of her jeans and pulled out her mobile phone, skimming a thumb across the screen. 'She sent me a text to say she'd dropped Frankie off, and asking if I could meet her for lunch. See?' The landlady turned her phone towards him. 'I can't just skip off now I'm running this place. I was expecting a delivery from the brewery so I asked her to come here for lunch, and she said maybe.'

'Did you hear from her again?'

'No, but I didn't think anything about it. You know how fickle she can be. Not that many weeks ago she wouldn't even speak to me.' Amber leaned a little closer to the policeman. 'You will find her, won't you, Sergeant Parkinson? I wasn't worried before, but I am now. She wouldn't just stand those girls up without letting them know. She's proud of herself for making a new set of friends, even if she doesn't work with them anymore. And there's no way she would just go off and leave little Frankie like that.'

'I suppose you've tried calling her?'

'We've all tried. Me, Sadie, Robin…' She slipped the phone back into her pocket with a shrug. 'So, what happens now?'

Parkinson wasn't sure he had the answer. At least, not one that would definitely yield a result. 'She left Sadie's at about nine forty-five on Thursday morning, and she didn't turn your invitation down flat. So I have to ask myself what she did next. Given that she said "maybe" to your lunch invitation, did she just catch a bus and head for Penwithen anyway?'

'I doubt it. She would have sent another text to tell me. I think it's more likely she made her way back to Truro to go shopping. The walk from Sadie's back to the train station would have taken her around fifteen minutes. There's bound to be a CCTV camera there, isn't there?'

The policeman couldn't hide his amusement. 'You know, you're wasted behind a bar, Amber. You could go a long way with those detective skills.' He swigged again on his ale, thinking. 'As it happens, there isn't a CCTV camera at the station. But there's one nearby. If we can get a confirmed sighting of her we can probably assume she went back to Truro.' He put the glass down on the bar and picked up his jacket. 'I don't suppose there's any way you could come over to Truro now, is there? Sadie has a key to Becca's house and she's agreed to meet me there to check the place out. I'd feel a lot more comfortable if you were there to keep her company.'

4

DI Hall slipped her mobile phone back into the handbag on her lap.

She was sitting in the passenger seat of Collinson's BMW, parked discreetly behind the gatehouse, and she turned her head to look at him over the top of her heavy, black-rimmed spectacles. 'That was Dr Philips. There was nothing in the whisky glass except evidence of a good single malt.' It was hard to keep the disappointment from her voice.

'Has he confirmed the cause of death?'

'Yes, taxine poisoning.' She removed her spectacles and examined them. 'It's an alkaloid derived from yews.'

'As in yew trees?'

'Apparently so.' She rubbed with her thumb at a smudge on the right-hand lens. 'A large dose can kill within a few hours of consumption. But it can take up to forty-eight hours with a smaller dose.' Suddenly her decision to let all the hotel guests leave didn't look like such a good idea. 'Dr Philips said there are often no obvious symptoms until the heart stops.'

Collinson exhaled a long, slow breath. 'If there *are* symptoms, how do they manifest?'

'Weakness, low blood-pressure, maybe nausea and vomiting. Jennet said he complained of feeling unwell, didn't she? Perhaps that was the onset.' Hall lifted her spectacles up and examined the lenses for clarity. 'He's going to try to narrow down the timeframes, but he can't promise much more in the way of accuracy. Which means we'll have to look at Laurence's movements for up to forty-eight hours before the time of death. Where he was, who he was with, what he ate and drank.'

'You still don't think he might have taken the stuff himself?'

'No, I agree with Jennet. He had no reason for suicide.' Hall shot a sideways glance at Collinson. 'Do you think she could have administered it to him, and left the whisky glass in the room to throw us off the scent?'

'A decoy glass with nothing in it other than whisky?' The sergeant puffed out his cheeks. 'I suppose it's possible. But she looks to me as though she's genuinely grieving. She's bearing up well, with that stiff upper lip and calm demeanour. But you can tell it's hit her very hard.' His blue eyes softened and he blinked at Hall. 'Don't you agree?'

'I suppose so.' Hall balanced her spectacles back on her nose. 'But I reserve the right to change my mind if we come up with a motive.' She sank deeper into her seat. 'What would she stand to gain by killing him?'

'Financially, whatever she inherits from him. But she's hardly the black-widow type and if she's a co-owner of Liberation Park I can't imagine she needs the money. In any case, she would have benefitted just by marrying him, wouldn't she?'

'What about other motives? Something that cropped up after the marriage had gone ahead – another woman, maybe, or discovering he wasn't the man she thought he was?' They needed to know more about Laurence Payne: who is was, who he knew, what made him tick and, above all, who might have wanted him out of the way. 'Do you think she's up to another round of questioning today?'

'I don't know. And her mother's view might not

necessarily be unbiased, so what about trying the hotel's manager?'

'Is the manager likely to know much about Laurence?' Hall didn't think she would. 'What about the wedding guests? Is there anyone still here at the hotel?' She offered her colleague a rueful smile. 'There's no need to remind me, by the way, that I said they could all go home.'

'As if.' Collinson met the confession with a grin. 'We can ask at the reception desk. Check-out time was eleven o'clock, but it's possible one or more guests might have stayed for lunch, or is staying another night to make a weekend of it.' He tapped a chubby finger on the steering wheel. 'How do you get taxine from a yew tree?'

'I've no idea.' But the information probably wouldn't be difficult to come by. Hall retrieved her mobile phone from her bag and swiped at the screen. 'Yew tree — taxine — poison.' She spoke softly as she tapped the words into a search engine. 'Here we are: the yew tree. Taxus Baccata. Commonly used in landscaping. Good for specimen trees or hedging. Evergreen, needle-like leaves, reddish-brown bark. Can reach a height of twenty metres. All parts poisonous, apart from the flesh of the berries. Fatal to humans and livestock. Frequently reported for fatal outcomes when taken by accident or'– she flashed a look of mild irritation at Collinson – 'when used as a means to suicide. Death usually occurs after consuming leaves or bark, or a decoction made from either.' She furrowed her neatly drawn brows. 'So, he could have taken the stuff himself, assuming he had access to a yew tree. But it's more likely someone fed it to him, either raw or made into an infusion?'

'The infusion is more likely, wouldn't you think? Easier to slip into his food or drink?'

'I would guess so. That's another question for Doctor Philips.' Hall shut down the search engine and returned the phone to her bag. 'Right then, Jim. Let's go back into the hotel and break the news to Jennet. Then we can look for a stray wedding guest or two. Someone who might be able to give us the lowdown on Laurence.' She opened the car door and then turned back to look at her colleague. 'What did you make of Rosemary Taylor? All that guff about pairing whisky with cheese, when her daughter's just been widowed?'

'I wouldn't exactly call her empathetic. But it could be down to the shock. Perhaps the penny hasn't dropped yet.' Collinson pulled his car keys from the ignition and slipped them into his pocket. 'Do you want her there when we break the news to Jennet?'

*

'So, Marcus, what did you make of the lovely bride?' Nancy Woodlands, lounging in the back of David Lancefield's Mercedes, tossed the question mischievously into the front of the car. 'Do you think she and Laurence are well-suited?'

'How can I possibly say?' Marcus, one hand loosely on the steering wheel, kept his eyes on the road ahead. 'I hardly met the woman. She seemed pleasant enough. And it makes no odds to me whether she and Laurence are well-suited or not.' He raised inquisitive eyes momentarily to the rear-view mirror. 'What did you make of her?'

'I thought she was rather pretty in a bland sort of way. A little meek for someone as charismatic as Laurence. But perhaps that's why she appeals to him. Isn't that the point of the old cliché: opposites attract?' Nancy leaned forward and rested her chin on the edge of the passenger seat in front of her. 'What does David think?'

'Apart from thinking it irresponsible of you not to be wearing your seatbelt?' David, irritated, shifted sideways in his seat. 'I think Jennet is positively charming and they make a very handsome couple.' He turned his head to look out of the window but it was a perfunctory manoeuvre and his soft grey eyes barely registered the passing scenery. 'It was generous of them to invite us to their wedding on the back of such a relatively short acquaintance.'

'Was it?' Marcus bridled. 'I might call it insensitive.'

'Insensitive? A wedding is a joyous occasion. On what level could an invitation to one be construed as insensitive?'

'You don't think it was insensitive to invite me to witness his "happy ever after" when his negligence led to Eva's death?'

Was the bitterness never to subside? The losses to David's own heart over the past few months had been painful beyond measure, but they hadn't robbed him of the ability to share in another man's joy. And he hoped they never would. 'Haven't you ever heard it said that resentment is akin to drinking poison and expecting the other man to die?' He turned pitying eyes to his stepson. 'I hope you're not going to behave like this when they travel to St Felix.'

'I have no intention of seeing them when they travel to St Felix. Honeysuckle has agreed to look after them.' Marcus flicked his eyes back up to the rear-view mirror. 'Do *you* think it was generous of them to invite us to the wedding, Nancy?'

'I think it was generous of them to invite Kathryn and Inspector Price.' Nancy smirked and leaned back against the cool leather of the car's seat. 'Or perhaps Laurence was just being cautious. Perhaps he thought the presence of a detective chief inspector might deter any would-be assassins from taking a potshot at him.'

'For pity's sake, both of you, just stop.' David banged a fist against the car's door. 'Just stop and think about what you're saying. My beloved Stella died because Zak Smith took a potshot at her. Do you understand that, Nancy? My wife *died.*' He felt an angry tear sting at the back of his eye, and he struggled to suppress it. 'Stella *died*. Eva *died*. Geraldine Morton *died*.'

'Well, if it comes to that, Zak Smith *died*.' Nancy lifted her gaze and locked challenging eyes with Marcus in the rear-view mirror. 'Didn't he, Marcus?'

'Nancy, you are unspeakable.' David folded his arms tightly across his chest. 'I don't know what's got into you today, but I think it's high time you were back in St Felix. Your manners are no longer becoming of the position you hold within this family. And I don't want to hear any more about it.'

A brittle silence filled the car until, eventually, Nancy placed a hand on David's shoulder. 'David, forgive me.' She spoke softly. 'I shouldn't have made light of the situation. But you must admit there was something odd about extending the invitation to Inspector Price. He isn't a member of the family. And it does rather suggest that Laurence didn't trust us.'

'And is that what you think, Marcus?'

'Does it matter what I think? Everyone seems to have made up their minds that I'm guilty of something: bribing Smith to murder Eva, killing Smith to keep him quiet… is there anything else you would like to add to the tally?' Marcus pulled gently on the steering wheel, easing the car into the inside lane, and depressed the brake to lower its speed. 'It isn't that Laurence doesn't trust *us*, is it? It's that Laurence doesn't trust *me*.' They were approaching the slip road to a service station and Marcus pressed down on the car's indicator. 'I'm going to pull in here. I need some fresh air and a coffee, and for someone else to take a turn at driving. And when we get back into the car, I'd like to talk about something else. Anything else. Just not Laurence, or Inspector Price, or whether or not it was one of us who murdered Zak Smith.'

*

DI Hall stared at Ennor Price through the heavy, black-rimmed spectacles. 'When the receptionist told me you might be able to help, I wasn't prepared for this. How do I know you're not exaggerating?'

Could his imagination ever have stretched that far? 'I'll give you the contact details for Andy Drummond in Liverpool, Alyson Grant in Edinburgh and Chris Greenway in London. They're all DCIs and all acted as SIO in their respective investigations. They'll all corroborate what I've told you.' She might only have asked for five minutes of his time, but he had been determined to give her the full story. 'I know it's a lot to take in. Maybe I should leave you to reflect on it. Kathryn and I will be setting off for Penzance soon but you have my number if you want to pick up the thread.'

They were sitting at a small corner table in the hotel's bar and Hall picked up a cardboard beer mat from the table and began to twist it around between her fingers. 'Just to be clear' – she tapped the mat gently on the table – 'Laurence was distantly connected to a family called Lancefield, and in the last nine months they've endured a hate campaign and multiple murders. And Laurence himself was recently implicated in one of those crimes.'

'He wasn't implicated. He was briefly a person of interest and he was quickly eliminated from the enquiry.'

'But he felt his own life was at risk, and that's why he invited you to the wedding.'

'He didn't spell it out like that. The official line was that I was Kathryn's guest. But I don't think he felt comfortable when Marcus was around.'

'Then why invite Marcus to the wedding?'

'It's complicated.'

'Complicated?' Hall ran her tongue slowly around her lips. 'Marcus Drake is a convicted killer, suspected of committing another murder in February, though you don't have enough evidence to charge him. And you thought it was a good idea to let him come to Laurence's wedding?'

'How would I have stopped him? His conviction is

spent and he's not facing any further charges. He's free to come and go as he pleases until I can scrape up enough evidence to make a case.'

'Or until I can scrape up enough evidence to prove he poisoned Laurence Payne with taxine?' The thought seemed to amuse her. 'When did Marcus arrive at Liberation Park?'

'On Thursday evening, just before eight o'clock.'

'Did he spend any time with Laurence, either alone or with others present?'

'Yes. We all had drinks together after dinner on Thursday evening, here in the bar: Laurence, David, Marcus, Nancy, me and Kathryn.'

'But not Jennet?'

'She'd gone out with her mother for the evening, though she did stop by briefly to say hello when they returned.' Price leaned back in his chair and folded his arms. 'The six of us chatted until around ten thirty, then we all turned in. To the best of my knowledge, Laurence went straight up to his room alone.'

'To the gatehouse.'

'No, to a room in the main building. He and Jennet had agreed not to see each other again until the wedding ceremony.'

'I didn't realise people still went in for that sort of superstition.'

If only she knew just how much superstition had figured in Laurence Payne's life. 'Superstitious or not, the decision might remove Jennet from your list of possible suspects, depending on when you think the taxine was administered.'

'Ah, well, that's a bit problematic. Our pathologist thinks anything up to forty-eight hours before the time of death, depending on the dose. Which means it could have been slipped into his food or drink at any time from nine o'clock on the Wednesday evening. And that, unfortunately, leaves Jennet partly in the frame.' Hall dropped the beer mat onto the table. 'Do you know much about her?'

'I'm afraid not. I didn't meet her until we arrived on Thursday. I've been told she owns Liberation Park jointly with her parents, and had a hand in turning it into a hotel. Kathryn told me Laurence and Jennet met around four years ago, and that their relationship had been stretched over some distance – she was based up here in Yorkshire and he divided his time between homes in Hertfordshire and Canary Wharf.'

'Now, that *is* interesting. What were they planning to do after the wedding? Live together in one location or carry on a long-distance marriage?'

'You would have to ask Jennet. I do know they planned to spend their wedding night here in the gatehouse and then drive to Hertfordshire for a few days to themselves.'

'They hadn't planned a honeymoon?'

'Yes, but not immediately. The Lancefields own property in the Caribbean and Richard Lancefield had offered them the use of a cottage out there as a wedding gift. They were planning to travel out in early June.'

Hall exhaled. 'Jennet owns a share of Liberation Park and the Lancefields are obviously not short of a bob or two. Was Laurence wealthy in his own right? You said he owned two properties.'

'Laurence was descended from a line of the Lancefield family that made its fortune trading in sugar and other commodities. The property in Hertfordshire is a Georgian manor house with extensive grounds, and he also owned a penthouse flat in Canary Wharf. I think he had a significant private income, but I don't know exactly where it came from.'

'Is it possible he was murdered for his money?'

'I doubt it. I'd be more inclined to consider jealousy or revenge.'

'Revenge? Revenge for what?'

'For murders already committed. I think Marcus still

blames Laurence for Eva's death.' Price rested his elbows on the table. 'And then there's Zak Smith's family. We believe Smith murdered Eva McWhinney in order to punish the Lancefields. Murdering Laurence would just be another twist of the knife.'

'But you told me Smith was dead.'

'Sure. But his sister isn't. And just a couple of hours ago I was told that she's gone missing. In fact' – Price pulled thoughtfully on his ear – 'she hasn't been seen since early on Thursday morning.'

5

'I'm so glad you're still here, Kathryn.' Jennet looked up with a wan smile as Kathryn made her way across the drawing room. She was sitting alone, a small and lonely figure adrift on the oversized russet Chesterfield, and she patted the seat beside her as Kathryn approached. 'Is Inspector Price with DI Hall?'

'Yes. Did you want to speak to him?'

'No, I'm just thankful he'll be able to tell her what he knows. It would have sounded so implausible coming from me.' Jennet moved along the sofa a little and waited for Kathryn to sit beside her. 'I've been told Laurence didn't die from natural causes, and I can't help wondering if he died because of his connection to the Lancefields.'

'Because of what happened to Eva?'

'Because there was never any trouble until he agreed to meet with her. And because I feel he didn't tell me everything I needed to know.' She dabbed at her cheek with a small cotton handkerchief, brushing away a tear. 'I thought you might be able to fill in the blanks. You know the family so well.'

Not only the family, but everything that had befallen them. 'What *did* Laurence tell you?'

'That he was very distantly related to Eva and the Lancefields and the connection goes all the way back to the eighteenth century.' Jennet twisted the sodden handkerchief around between her fingers. 'I've always known about Eva: the first Christmas Laurence and I spent together, he received the most beautiful Christmas card from her, and I asked who she was. I was so besotted with him, I was afraid there was another woman lurking around in the background.' Jennet's eyes creased at the thought of her own foolishness. 'He explained he didn't really know her, they just kept up the connection because their parents had done so.'

'When did he first mention the Lancefields to you?'

'When Eva contacted him in February. He told me she'd asked for a meeting, to discuss the family's history so she could share it with Richard Lancefield. He asked me whether he should accept the invitation and I said why not? What harm could it do?'

More harm than anyone could have guessed, with the benefit of hindsight. 'But you knew about his connection to St Felix?'

'Yes, of course. He was very proud of his Caribbean heritage, and he told me all about his ancestors and how they owned the St Aldate's plantation. He didn't hide any of it. Not even that dreadful story about them selling it to a man who was murdered by his slaves.'

'Edward Mason?'

'Yes. That's the connection to the Obeah garland, isn't it? The thing that was hung around Eva's neck when she was murdered.' Jennet shivered. 'He took Eva's death very badly and felt the garland had been used to point the finger at him.'

'But it didn't stop him from travelling to Penwithen to seek a conversation with Richard and David.'

'Why should it? He asked my opinion about that too, and I told him to do whatever he had to do to square things for himself. He knew he had nothing to do with Eva's death, why shouldn't he have the right to put his side of the story across?'

No reason that Kathryn could think of. 'What do you think he didn't tell you? About the Lancefields, I mean?'

Jennet sniffed into the handkerchief. 'He told me the man who murdered Eva had a grudge against the family, and that the man himself was found murdered at Salvation Hall just a few days after Eva died.' She scrunched the handkerchief into a ball, holding it tightly in her fist. 'What was the grudge?'

'Oh, Jennet.' Kathryn's heart sank. She didn't want to repeat the story but the girl had a right to know. 'Marcus was engaged to David's daughter, Lucy, but she was having an affair with Philip, the gardener at Salvation Hall. Lucy was murdered and Marcus believed Philip was responsible, so he killed him in revenge.'

'Marcus murdered someone? Did he go to prison?'

'No. The story is a rather complex one. Philip's partner, Becca Smith, was the housekeeper at Salvation Hall. She was heartbroken when Marcus received a light sentence for Philip's murder and avoided prison. It's believed that her brother Zak targeted Eva as a way of getting back at the Lancefields, but his first attempts on her life didn't succeed.'

'Attempts, plural?'

'Yes. Along the way he murdered a friend of Eva's by mistake and...' Kathryn bowed her head. 'I'm afraid he broke into the grounds of Salvation Hall with a shotgun, but he missed Eva and hit David's wife instead. Stella didn't survive the night.'

'Then David has lost his daughter and his wife?' Jennet's voice sank to a whisper. 'The poor man, I had no idea.' She closed her eyes for a moment. 'How did Eva's killer know she would be in London with Laurence?'

'We don't know. Someone must have told him, but we don't know who.'

Jennet opened her eyes. 'Surely they didn't think it was Laurence?'

'It was a possibility, but no link between Zak or

Laurence was ever found.'

'He didn't tell me.' Jennet's face contorted and she twisted her lips inwards. 'He told me they initially suspected him of Eva's murder because he was the last person to see her, but he didn't tell me…' A single tear rolled down her right cheek. 'Who else knew she was going to London?'

'She kept the meeting a secret from the family, because Richard didn't want her to go through with it. She did tell a couple of friends in Edinburgh, but they have no links to the Lancefields.'

Jennet released the handkerchief from her fist and dabbed at her eyes with it. 'Eva was in a relationship with Marcus wasn't she?'

'Yes.' Kathryn knew what the next question would be, and decided to head it off at the pass. 'Marcus denies knowing that Eva was travelling to London. But I'm afraid he did initially blame Laurence for her death.'

'I know. Laurence said he tried to get on with Marcus to please David and Richard but Marcus didn't make it easy. For what it's worth, I didn't want him to invite Marcus to the wedding but he insisted. And he said it would be okay, because he was also inviting you, and you would bring Inspector Price with you.' Jennet leaned towards Kathryn. 'He was afraid, Kathryn. He wanted Inspector Price as a witness, didn't he? To keep an eye on Marcus?'

There would be little point in denying it. 'No one knows how Zak found Eva that night. Blaming Marcus seems to be the obvious answer, but Marcus insists he's innocent.'

'Do you believe him?'

'Yes, I do.'

'Do you think he murdered Zak Smith? The way he killed his fiancée's lover?'

'To be honest, I'm not sure what to think about that.' Kathryn looked down at her fingers. 'Do you suspect

Marcus was in some way responsible for Laurence's death?'

'I think it's possible, given what you've told me.' Jennet's voice was growing stronger. 'Can I trust Inspector Price to get at the truth?'

'I sincerely hope so, Jennet. Because if Ennor can't get to the truth, then I don't think anyone can.'

*

DS Parkinson stared at the tall chest of drawers and then pulled on the handles of the top drawer to reveal a jumbled collection of ladies underwear, socks and pyjamas. He winced at the sight and then dug a reluctant hand in amongst the garments, feeling around for some unexpected item that might surrender a clue to Becca Smith's whereabouts.

'Nothing in there.' He turned his attention to the drawer beneath. 'Jumpers and T-shirts in here.' He rummaged amongst the contents, grumbling under his breath. 'Nope, nothing.' He slammed the drawer shut and straightened his back. It had been a relief when Sadie Smith had agreed to give the police access to the house, and an even bigger one when Amber had agreed to assist with the proceedings. But too much to hope, perhaps, that they might find anything of any use.

He stepped across the room and out into the hallway. In the small bedroom opposite, a uniformed policewoman was searching through little Frankie's wardrobe, her neck craned upwards as she examined the contents of a shelf above the clothes rail. Parkinson tapped lightly on the open door. 'There's nothing in the bedroom, I'm going downstairs to take a look in the kitchen.' The policewoman turned her head and nodded as he backed out of the room, her attention barely drawn away from the task in hand.

He walked slowly down the narrow staircase and

headed towards the lounge. Through the partially open door he could hear the quiet murmurings of a conversation between Amber Kimbrall and Sadie Smith as they sat, heads close together, on the small grey armchairs that flanked the fireplace. For a moment he considered joining them, and then he thought better of it and continued on his way into the kitchen.

The room was neat and clean, tidy in a way he found difficult to associate with Becca Smith. There was no question the girl had worked hard to hang on to her fresh start in Truro, and no way she would walk away from her new life and her new home.

No way that she would walk away from little Frankie.

Parkinson felt a sinking feeling in the pit of his stomach and he mumbled under his breath. 'So help me, Becca, if you're just playing around and this turns out to be a wild goose chase…' He pulled on the handle of a nearby drawer and it slid open to reveal nothing more interesting than cutlery. The drawer beneath it was stuffed with tea towels and aprons, and the one below that held a collection of shiny new baking tins which clattered noisily as the drawer slid shakily forwards on its runners.

He slammed the drawer shut and turned his eyes around the room. Oven, microwave, fridge freezer: none of those were going to surrender any clues. A handful of envelopes rested on the worktop – unopened mail Amber had rescued from the doormat when they had let themselves into the property. He could check the upper run of cupboards, but it was unlikely that…

The thought process halted and his eyes returned to the small pile of unopened mail; his curiosity piqued, he stepped forward to examine it. 'Gas bill, bank statement' – he pushed the envelopes to one side – 'And what's this?' He picked up a third envelope, large and white, and ran his eyes over the front of it. 'Well, it's addressed to Becca. And postmarked…?' His mouth felt suddenly dry and he turned the envelope over to run a fingernail along the flap before tipping it up. A slim glossy brochure fell out onto the kitchen counter and he bent his head to look at it, running his eyes across the typewritten letter that had been paperclipped to the cover.

Dear Ms Smith, We thank you for your enquiry and have pleasure in enclosing...

He didn't need to read any further. He slipped the brochure back into the envelope and stepped briskly back across the hall to peer through the open doorway into the lounge. 'Amber, can I borrow you for a minute?'

The girl blinked in surprise. 'Of course.' She had been holding Sadie's hand for comfort and she let go of it as she stood up. 'I'll be back in a minute.' She followed Parkinson out into the hallway and let the door close gently behind her. 'Have you found something, Sergeant Parkinson?'

'I think so.' He held up the envelope as he spoke. 'Have you ever heard Becca talk about a hotel called Liberation Park?'

*

'So, we've got an unexplained death that looks like murder: a suspected heart attack that turned out to be heart failure due to taxine poisoning; the taxine administered sometime in the last forty-eight hours. We still don't know in what form it was taken, but at this stage we have no reason to believe it was self-administered. We have a grieving widow who will most likely benefit significantly from the death. I'm guessing here that yesterday's wedding will have rendered any existing will null and void, leaving her to inherit.' DI Hall tilted her head towards Collinson. 'And we have a recent connection between Laurence and a family from Cornwall that death follows around as fervently as seagulls follow the herring fleet.'

'I'm still trying to get my head around this Lancefield

business.' The car was still parked beside the gatehouse and Collinson stared blankly through the windscreen. 'Did you say eight murders in the last nine months?'

'Yes. But only six of them are relevant to our case.' She made it sound like an everyday occurrence. 'Look on the bright side, Jim. We might have a head start with this one thanks to DCI Price. And he's keen to work with us, so we can view him as an extra pair of hands that's already up to speed.'

'It doesn't bother you that he let a potential suspect in a murder investigation come to the wedding? Someone who already has a criminal record for manslaughter; someone who, it appears, didn't get on with the victim?' Collinson cast a bemused glance at his senior officer. 'Only this is beginning to sound so farfetched that I'm struggling to keep up.'

'I'll admit it all sounds a bit fanciful and yes, it does bother me. But he's given us the contact details of three other DCIs who will back up his story.' Hall turned her head to glance out of the window. 'I think we'll start with these two fairly obvious lines of enquiry – the widow and the unfriendly wedding guest. Both had the opportunity to administer the taxine in the timeframe we're looking at.'

'Along with a hundred and nineteen other wedding guests that have scattered to the four corners of the country. And any member of the hotel's staff who worked a shift between Thursday morning and Saturday evening. Including agency staff.'

'A hundred and seventeen wedding guests. I think we can discount Price and Kathryn Clifton.' Hall presented the sergeant with a withering smile. 'Both Jennet and Marcus Drake could have had had a motive: Jennet for the money and Marcus Drake for...' Her words trailed off and then she nodded to herself. 'We'll go with Price's opinion on that and say revenge. Some sort of payback. Either way, I'd like to talk to Price in more detail, to see if we can get a broader explanation of what's going on with the Lancefield family.'

'And what about the missing girl? Becca Smith?'

'I don't think we need to take that suggestion too seriously. She might have had a grudge, but she didn't have an opportunity. Even if she'd travelled all the way up from Cornwall, how could she have administered the taxine? She wasn't a guest at the wedding.'

'Could Jennet and Marcus both have had access to taxine?'

'I suppose it depends on what form the taxine was in.' She ran her tongue thoughtfully around her teeth. 'I'm still not sure if Dr Philips will be able to confirm that.' And that was a problem. 'Who can we ask about yew trees here at Liberation Park?'

'There are formal gardens and acres of parkland, so there must be some sort of gardener or groundsman. When we've finished this conversation, I'll go back to the reception desk and ask.' Collinson tapped his fingers on the steering wheel. 'Where would Marcus Drake find taxine?'

'That sounds like a question for DCI Price.' Hall brightened. 'Drake will be halfway back to Cornwall by now but Price has offered to speak to him tomorrow on our behalf. In the meantime' – she leaned her head against the seat's headrest – 'we can start with Jennet. I haven't heard anyone talk about Laurence's family yet – no mention of parents or siblings. If he had any close relatives, why weren't they at the wedding? We need to understand whether he had a will in place and whether it was changed in anticipation of marriage. If it wasn't, then we need to find out if any beneficiaries would have been disadvantaged by the marriage.'

'Jennet seemed badly shaken when I broke the news to her that it was taxine poisoning. Do you think we're piling too much pressure on too quickly?'

The inspector screwed up her nose. 'Not if she shares our desire to find out who murdered her husband.'

6

'I've spoken to both of them: DI Hall and DS Collinson.' Price, sitting alone at a small corner table in the hotel bar, stared straight ahead as he spoke into his mobile phone. Behind the bar, directly in his eyeline, was a large, gilt-edged mirror and he found the sight of his own reflection unnerving. There was no question he'd aged in the last nine months, since first encountering the Lancefield family. Or, perhaps, because of it. 'I'm not sure either of them grasped the gravity of the situation.'

'I suppose you can hardly blame them.' Tom Parkinson sounded weary. 'Does DI Hall look like a safe pair of hands?'

'Come on, Tom, you know I don't like to stand in judgement of a fellow officer.' But there was always an exception to the rule. If pushed, he might have said she was out of her depth. But it was still early in the investigation, and in fairness she didn't have a great deal to go on. 'She thinks Laurence was murdered for his money. I think she's eyeing Jennet Payne as some sort of black widow.' He turned his eyes away from the mirror. 'I went through the full Lancefield story with her, and then again with Collinson. And I told them about Becca's disappearance, although I think we're all agreed it doesn't bear any relevance to Laurence's death.'

Parkinson was silent at the end of the line. Eventually he said, 'You might want to reconsider that decision when you hear what I have to tell you.'

'You've got a lead?'

'I don't know. But I'm fearing the worst. When I went over to Truro to search the house, I found an envelope addressed to Becca. That envelope contained a hotel brochure and a covering letter saying it had been set in response to her enquiry.' The sergeant inhaled a noisy breath. 'The hotel was Liberation Park.'

'Then it *is* possible that she…?' Price could hardly take in the news. Truth be told, he'd convinced himself her disappearance was nothing more than a timely coincidence. But even he couldn't have foreseen this turn of events. 'Did Amber or Sadie know anything about it?'

'No.' Parkinson sounded suddenly uncertain. 'I know her hatred of the Lancefields runs deep, but I can't believe she would risk jeopardising her life with Frankie.'

'But you've found a link between her and the location of Laurence's death.'

'I know, but you said it yourself: it's too ridiculous to contemplate.'

'Not if she was still hellbent on revenge.' And not if they took into account Price's number one rule – until the truth comes out, consider everything, discount nothing.

'She accepted Richard Lancefield's help to avoid a prison sentence.'

'Of course she did. She couldn't go on to cause more trouble if she was in prison, could she?' Price raised his eyes and scowled at his own reflection in the mirror. 'Do we have anything yet on her movements after she left Sadie's?'

'No. I've requested CCTV footage from the nearest camera to Hayle train station, but that's a long shot so I've sent an officer down to question the station staff. Someone must remember seeing her. For what it's worth,

Amber thinks it likely she would have caught the train from there back to Truro.'

'Unless she was coming up to Yorkshire. In which case, what route would she have taken?'

'Still back to Truro, either to the house to collect something or straight to the railway station, and then by train to Yorkshire.'

'How long would it take for her to reach Liberation Park?'

'I don't know. The nearest mainline station would be Hull, so my guess would be eight to nine hours, depending on which service she boarded. She dropped Frankie off before ten o'clock and the journey back to Truro would take around an hour, including a walk at both ends. Even if she'd gone home first she could have caught a lunchtime train for the north. With a couple of connections she would reach Hull around eight or nine in the evening. How would she get to Liberation Park from there? By bus?'

'By taxi. It's too remote for a bus service, about four miles off the main road.' Price felt his pulse begin to quicken. 'We have to consider every possibility. Does Becca have a driving licence? Could she have hired a car and driven up to Yorkshire?'

'I suppose it's possible. I'll add a sweep of the local car hire firms to the list. And Amber's given me a couple of photos of Becca, head and shoulders shots. I'll send them over to you after we finish the call.'

'Thanks, Tom. You've gone above and beyond.'

'I did it because it was Becca.'

And because he'd always had a soft spot for her. Price had always suspected as much. 'You don't want to believe she's involved, do you?'

'Is it that obvious? I've felt sorry for the girl since we fished Philip McKeith's body out of the lake at Salvation Hall. She really loved him, you know, in spite of everything. And we let her down. We let Marcus Drake walk free.'

'You seem to forget she assisted Zak when he was on the run, and that if she'd turned him in Eva McWhinney might still be alive.' Sympathy for the loss of her lover was one thing, but two wrongs didn't make a right in Price's book. 'You sound all in, Tom. Let's pick this up again in the morning. I'll have a word with the hotel manager before I leave, to see if they have a record of Becca's request for a brochure. And I'll try to catch a minute with DI Hall to let her know what you've found.'

'I suppose this lets Marcus Drake off the hook now?' Parkinson could barely hide his disappointment.

'Unless he was working with Becca.' Price turned his eyes back to the mirror and regarded his reflection with scornful eyes.

Marcus Drake collaborating with Becca Smith? Now that *was* just too ridiculous to contemplate.

*

The drive back to Salvation Hall had been a long and tiring one. Now, sitting quietly with his father in the Dower House lounge, David Lancefield couldn't help wondering what the last couple of days had been about. He had travelled four hundred miles north to attend the wedding of a distant cousin, a man he hadn't even known existed until a couple of months earlier. And now, thanks to a cruel and unpredictable twist of fate, the man *didn't* exist. He was gone from their lives as quickly and as unexpectedly as he had arrived.

'It was good of Kathryn to call and let us know as soon as possible. And of course, Laurence's death is to be lamented. He was a decent individual and a credit to the family. But I cannot see it has anything to do with us.' Richard Lancefield had taken the news with a weary resignation. 'I have come to accept a degree of responsibility for Dennis Speed's death, since our invitation to connect led Jason to discover the unfortunate truth about his parentage. And, though painful to admit, I cannot deny Eva and Stella both died because of Smith's desire to take revenge on the family. But Laurence was not invited to connect with us. He made the decision to seek us out. We cannot be held responsible for that.' The old man was nursing a mug of coffee and he raised it carefully to his thin lips to drink. 'In any case, Smith cannot take revenge from beyond the grave, can he?'

'It wasn't Smith I was thinking of.' David dropped a hand to the side of his chair where Samson, his father's fox terrier, was quietly dozing. 'I'm concerned that the police may look at us.' He ruffled the dog's fur. 'At the family.'

'Nonsense. What possible motive could one of us have for killing him? Laurence asked nothing of us other than friendship, and we gave him what he asked for. We know he had nothing to do with Eva's death. We cannot blame him for that, however hard Marcus might try. Are the police absolutely certain his death was suspicious?'

'I very much doubt they would have confirmed the fact to Inspector Price unless they had the evidence to back it up.'

'Then they must search amongst Laurence's other friends and family for their killer: another wedding guest, or someone who worked at the hotel. Someone who knew Laurence far better than we did and bore him a grudge. My heart goes out to his widow. Of course it does. But this is not a crime that can be laid at our door.' Richard drained off what was left of his coffee and stretched out an unsteady hand to place the empty mug down on the small walnut table beside his chair. 'Once the arrangements have been finalised, we must be represented at the funeral to show our respects. But you must resign yourself to this being nothing more than an unhappy coincidence. We must focus our attention on our own affairs.' He rested his elbows on the chair's arms and steepled his fingers. 'While you were in Yorkshire, Barbara and I finalised the details of my return to St Felix. We have agreed Samson will stay here to see out his days, though I shall miss my old friend beyond measure. He is too old now to acclimatise to the heat and change of environment, I would not subject him to the distress.'

'And might the same not also be said of you?'

'Tush.' Richard dismissed the suggestion with a flick of his fingers. 'The climate is the least of my concerns. Marcus and Nancy will return to Woodlands on Monday. That will give them plenty of time to settle back in before I arrive in July.'

'July? But I thought you'd decided to wait until Inspector Price had completed his investigation into Smith's death?'

'That was my original plan. But three months have passed now and it is quite clear the good inspector is no closer to making an arrest.'

David's brow beetled forward. 'That isn't really what you mean, is it? What you mean is the good inspector still hasn't come up with sufficient evidence to arrest Marcus.'

'There is no evidence that Marcus was responsible for Smith's murder, and so far the police have failed to come up with a viable alternative suspect. Like myself, Marcus cannot wait forever. We have given Inspector Price his opportunity and now it is time to move forward.'

'You think Marcus is guilty, don't you?'

'What I think is immaterial. And I don't wish to discuss it any further.'

That was hardly a surprise to David. But the days of acquiescing to his father's wishes were in the past. 'I think you should be prepared for Marcus to be questioned over Laurence's death.'

Thwarted, Richard scowled. 'Do you have any specific reason to suspect Marcus had a hand in Laurence's death or are you merely speculating on the possibility?'

'Neither. I am simply pointing out that the police will

begin by looking at the obvious. If I were investigating Laurence's death, and learned that one of the guests at the wedding was not only a convicted killer but might reasonably have had grounds to feel ill will against the victim, I know where I would begin. Especially if the guest in question had already made plans to leave the country.'

*

'Then you can't think of anyone who bore Laurence a grudge?' DI Hall studied his widow's pale face as she spoke. Collinson had been right: the girl did look frail and shaken, but that was no reason not to proceed with a bit of gentle questioning. 'There's no one who might have wanted to harm him?'

'Apart from Marcus Drake, you mean?' Jennet lifted a hand towards DS Collinson, sitting beside Hall on the drawing room sofa. 'I've already explained to the sergeant that Inspector Price knows all about the friction between the two of them. Didn't he tell you?'

'Yes, he told me. But I usually find it pays to cast the net a little wider at the beginning of an investigation, if only to eliminate all the other possibilities before we jump to the obvious conclusion.' She let the thought settle and then asked, 'Were any close members of Laurence's family present at the wedding? Only I haven't heard anyone mention his parents, or any siblings.'

'Laurence didn't have any close family. His parents died several years ago and he was an only child. I think there was an aunt on his mother's side, but she was estranged from the family and not in touch with him.'

'Do you know where she lives?'

'I'm afraid I don't, and I don't think Laurence did. I believe she emigrated to Canada, but that was when he was a small child.' Jennet frowned. 'There are the Lancefields, of course. They are the closest thing to family Laurence had, but it's a very recent connection. He didn't know about them until…' Her voice faded to a whisper. 'Well, until Eva mentioned them to him.'

Had that been a problem? 'He had two homes, didn't he? One in Hertfordshire and one in Canary Wharf? Can I ask which of them you were planning to live in after the marriage?'

'Neither. At least, not as a permanent arrangement. We planned to divide our time between them.'

'And Liberation Park?'

A hint of pink suffused Jennet's pale cheeks. 'I was stepping back from the business side of things.'

'Completely stepping back? Or would you still have been involved in some respects?'

'I would have retained a share of ownership, but no longer acted as general manager.' Jennet's jaw stiffened, and she shot a questioning glance at DS Collinson. 'What does this have to do with Laurence's death?'

Collinson held her gaze with a faint smile. 'It helps the investigation if we can form a view of his life.' He bent forward and rested his forearms loosely on his knees. 'It must have been very difficult for the two of you, conducting a relationship on a long-distance basis. I know I would find it hard if my girlfriend was living hundreds of miles away from me.'

'We didn't find it difficult at all. We both had busy lives and no desire to live in each other's pockets. I had this place to run and Laurence had his work as an author and consultant. We were perfectly happy with the way things were.'

'Then why the decision to take a step back from Liberation Park?'

The colour in Jennet's cheeks deepened. 'Laurence wanted us to spend more time together. He wanted to travel, initially to research his family's history on St Felix and then more widely to study some of the cultural aspects of Caribbean history.'

'Like Obeah?'

DI Hall's question rendered Jennet momentarily speechless. She folded her hands primly in her lap. 'Laurence was an expert in his subject.'

'And is that how he made his living? From the study of witchcraft?'

'He had a private income from shares and annuities. His family left him very well provided for.'

It didn't quite answer the question, but the information was useful all the same. 'Did Laurence have any shares in Liberation Park?'

'No, it's very much a family business. To be honest, my mother wouldn't have appreciated his involvement. She's very protective of the place. She sees it as my inheritance.'

Ah, there was that word again – inheritance. Hall slipped her spectacles from her nose and pretended to examine them. 'Did Laurence make a will, Jennet?' She peered up at the girl with unfocused eyes. 'And before you ask, I'd like to know in case there was a third party who might have been disadvantaged financially by his marriage to you. Someone who might have been looking forward to inheriting his property and his income.'

'When we met, Laurence had a will in place which left a small bequest of family jewellery to his aunt, on the assumption she could be traced. The rest was bequeathed to charity. But after we became engaged he changed the will in my favour. The bequest to his aunt remained, and I would inherit the rest. If I predeceased him, my share would revert to charity.'

'So, after your marriage the will would be null and void and the entire estate would go to you?' Hall didn't wait for an answer. 'Thank you for your honesty. It's helpful to know I can eliminate that particular possibility.' She placed her glasses back on her nose. 'Is it true Laurence's family made their money from the sugar trade?'

'I believe so. I didn't ask too many questions about that. It wasn't a particularly wholesome way of making a fortune. But I can't take the moral high ground, given Liberation Park was also built on sugar money.' Jennet tilted her head to stare at Hall. 'I take it Inspector Price has explained *how* Laurence was connected to the Lancefield family? That sugar was at the heart of it?'

'Yes. And that was how they were both connected to Eva McWhinney, wasn't it? By way of their common ancestors on St Felix.' Hall smiled. 'Did you ever meet Eva?'

'No.' The question appeared to make Jennet uncomfortable. 'Is that relevant to Laurence's death?'

'Isn't her death the reason Marcus Drake bore him a grudge?'

'Perhaps. I certainly can't help wondering whether his connection to the Lancefields led to his death in the way it led to Eva's. I don't know how or why, exactly. But I trust Inspector Price to get to the truth.'

If the suggestion was meant to offend DI Hall, it fell on stony ground. Momentarily distracted by an unexpected train of thought, she turned her head away to stare across the drawing room. And she couldn't help wondering whether the penny had dropped yet for DCI Price: that Jennet Payne had also known exactly where Eva McWhinney was going to be the night she lost her life.

7

'Well, you certainly know how to give a girl a good time, I'll say that for you.' Kathryn turned her head and surveyed her surroundings. 'Saturday night at a motorway service area? I can't believe you've saved all you best moves until now.' The cafeteria was busy, bustling with a steady stream of southward-bound holidaymakers. 'I still don't see why we had to drive home tonight, given everything that's happened. It would have made a lot more sense to spend another night at Liberation Park and drive back in the morning. We could have offered our support to Jennet.'

Rather than leaving her to the tender mercies of DI Hall? 'I know it's turning out to be a long and tortuous journey. But I have to get back to Cornwall tonight.' Ennor knew Kathryn was disappointed, and that disappointing her was in danger of becoming a habit. 'Have you any idea how I feel about this, Kathryn? Laurence thought my presence at the wedding would keep him safe.' Just as Eva McWhinney had trusted that the detective's presence at Salvation Hall would do the same for her. His failure to protect those innocent members of the Lancefield family was a nightmare from which he would never wake. 'Laurence put his faith in me and I let him down.'

'You didn't let him down. You don't even know for certain he was murdered. Only that his death was suspicious.'

'You don't take taxine by accident and Laurence wasn't the suicidal type.' Ennor pulled back the cuff of his shirt and glanced at his watch. 'I think it's time we hit the road again.' He stood up and waited for Kathryn to follow suit. 'I know you won't like me asking this, but are there any yew trees at Salvation Hall?'

She rose to her feet and unhooked her shoulder bag from the back of her chair. 'You think Marcus prepared a toxic decoction at Salvation Hall and took it with him to the wedding?'

She made it sound ridiculous. 'That taxine must have come from somewhere.' He turned on his heel and began to make his way between the tables, heading for the exit to the car park. 'Why not Salvation Hall?'

'It could have come from anywhere.' She stepped up beside him and slipped her arm into his as they walked. 'Have you any idea how common yew is? Or that you park your car next to a yew hedge every time you come to Salvation Hall?'

'The hedges around the turning circle in front of the house?'

'Yes. Which means you could have harvested some of the leaves and prepared the decoction yourself.' She pulled on his arm. 'And you can't object to that suggestion – it's a possibility, isn't it? And in murder cases, isn't it all about means, motive and opportunity? You had access to the means every time you came to Salvation Hall and you had the opportunity because you were a guest at the wedding and spent several hours with Laurence on Thursday evening. Not to mention the twenty minutes you spent chatting to him at the wedding reception.'

'That's absurd. What motive could I have for murdering Laurence?'

'I don't know. I'm just trying to make a point. Anyway,

why are you asking about yew trees?' They had reached the cafeteria's exit and Kathryn blinked as the doors slid open, momentarily blinded by the unexpected glare of shimmering evening sunlight. 'I thought you were more worried about Becca?'

'I'm trying to consider all the possibilities.' He stepped through the door, pulling Kathryn gently with him as he strode out towards his car. 'Hall and Collinson aren't interested in Becca.' Although that might change when they picked up his message about the brochure Tom Parkinson had found in her kitchen. 'Right now, they're only looking at two suspects – Marcus and Jennet. If there are yew trees at Salvation Hall, they need to know.'

'They can't possibly consider Jennet a suspect.'

'Why not? She's probably just inherited all of Laurence's wealth and that's one hell of a motive.'

'Do you agree with them?'

'No. I'm still looking at Marcus and Becca. I can only think of three motives for Laurence's murder: inheriting his wealth; revenge against the Lancefield family in general; or revenge for letting Eva walk straight into the hands of a murderer. I can't see any point in Jennet murdering him for the money when she'd just married him and would benefit anyway. Becca might have done it to take revenge on the family.'

'But you're favouring Marcus, because you still believe he murdered Zak.'

'You still haven't proven to me that he didn't.'

'As I recall, that wasn't what you asked me to do. You asked me to help flush out Zak's killer, not to prove Marcus innocent of the crime.'

It was a fair cop. 'What is Laurence's death going to mean for the family?'

'Strictly speaking, not much. David was upset when I broke the news, which is understandable, though I wouldn't have called them particularly close. Not in the way David has grown close to Barbara. Laurence occasionally called Richard to say hello, but I'm not aware he was ever in touch with Marcus or Nancy. Or Barbara, for that matter. I think if anything, they're more likely to be upset by the general idea of the family still being at risk.'

They were close to the car now and Ennor pulled the key fob from his pocket. 'Changing the subject completely, I didn't ask you what was in the box you brought out of Liberation Park before we left.'

'Ezekiel Taylor's Bible. Jennet offered to loan it to me so I could study it.' Kathryn drew her hand from Ennor's arm and walked around the car to the passenger door. 'Changing the subject back again, you still haven't told me why we had to drive back to Penzance tonight.'

'I've agreed to talk to the family on DI Hall's behalf.'

'And it has to be tomorrow?'

'Marcus and Nancy are planning to fly out to St Felix any day now, and you've alerted the family to the news of Laurence's death. What's to stop them from bringing those flights forward?'

'You truly think they would do that?'

'Maybe they would and maybe they wouldn't.' Ennor opened the car's door with a weary smile. Either way, he wasn't prepared to take the risk.

*

Steph Hall nestled into the soft folds of the sofa's cushions and balanced the laptop precariously on her knees. Back home, showered and comfortable in her pyjamas, she felt a tiny thrill of rebellion as she clicked on the keyboard's keys. Work on a Sunday evening had been verboten for as long as she had been married, but Graham had taken the kids to his mother's for tea, so there was nobody there to stop her. With a fair wind, and his mother's predictable habit of serving up a double helping of dessert, she should have time to come up with at least a cursory view of the business affairs of Liberation Park; it would be enough to know if it was a viable business or whether something lurked in the balance sheet which might suggest a motive for murder.

She brought up a search engine and typed in "Liberation Park", then followed the link to the venue's glossy website. A scroll of rolling images filled the screen and she craned her neck forward to peer at them as they swept past her eyes: the imposing exterior with its impressive portico; the tiny, private chapel where couples tied the knot; the elegant dining room, its tables set with glittering cutlery and fine bone china; and – she cringed at the sight – the bridal suite.

It discomfited her to see a potential murder scene portrayed so publicly on the internet. Just hours earlier, that luxuriously furnished space had hosted quite a different rite of passage: it had accommodated a corpse, and the faint smell of death still lingered in Steph's perceptive nostrils. Pity the next couple planning to consummate their marriage in the bed where Laurence Payne met his untimely and unexpected end.

She ran her eyes across the crisply lettered menu at the top of the website's homepage and slid the cursor up to the tab for "news". A lengthy inventory of press mentions dropped slowly down the screen and she selected the first in the list: an article from the local newspaper dated almost seventeen years ago.

Hall put her fingers up to the screen and pinched at it to zoom into the print. 'The meticulous restoration undertaken by Rosemary and Alexander Taylor would be worthy of an award.' She spoke softly under her breath as she examined the grainy, black and white photograph presented: a picture of Jennet Payne's self-assured, elegant mother standing alongside a tall, handsome, silver-haired man with laughing eyes and a genial, almost whimsical smile. 'So, what went wrong in your marriage, Mrs Taylor?' Hall muttered the question with genuine curiosity. 'The ex-

Mr Taylor looks affable enough.'

There was no sign of Jennet in the picture. Hall did a quick mental calculation and decided the girl would only have been in her early twenties, maybe even younger. Away at university, perhaps? Or boarding school, if the family's budget had allowed for it. Somehow, at some point, she had wandered into the family business: was that before or after her parents had divorced?

Hall stroked a finger across the laptop's mousepad, scrolling the screen upwards to reveal a pair of additional pictures: the black and white photograph on the left showing a vast, decaying space lined with water-damaged plaster, its crumbling ceiling punctuated with fraying electricity cables; the colourful image on the right revealing the magnificent, antique-filled drawing room where she had first broken the news to Jennet that her husband's death would have to be investigated.

She whistled softly. Where the hell did the money come from to undertake that sort of restoration? And what about keeping the place afloat? Did hosting weddings really generate enough income to fund the maintenance? To pay the bar and restaurant staff, the cooks and the cleaners and the groundsmen? Was the ex-Mr Taylor still investing in the business, or had he taken his cheque book and his credit cards with him when he left?

And, if he *had* pulled the financial plug on his ex-wife and daughter's aspirations, had Jennet and her mother been secretly hoping Laurence would step in to fill the breach?

8

'My heart quite breaks for Jennet.' David spoke softly, his words burdened with regret. 'If only we had known, we could have stayed at Liberation Park to offer our support.'

'Why would Jennet need our support? She has her mother, and the hotel staff. And what about the dozens of family and friends who were guests at the wedding?' Marcus, at the other side of the breakfast table, was busy pouring his first coffee of the day. 'And let's not forget that Inspector Price and Kathryn were on hand when the news came through.'

And just as well that they were. David eyed his stepson with reproving eyes. 'I am well aware that Inspector Price was on hand. He already knows Laurence's death was not from natural causes and a police investigation is inevitable.'

'I hope you're not going to suggest one of us was responsible? Although I suppose it could have been Inspector Price. He never seems to be too far away when the murders occur. We only have his word for it that he's investigating.'

'Marcus, your flippancy is becoming tiresome. The inspector still hasn't closed the case on Zak Smith's death. It's inevitable he will look at us.' David lowered his voice. 'He is most certainly going to look at you.'

'He can look all he likes. I've never denied that I didn't like Laurence but I didn't kill him. And I'm getting very, very tired of everyone looking at me as if I was some sort of homicidal maniac.' Marcus hissed the words through tightened lips. 'Yes, I blamed him for Eva's death. But I didn't kill him because of it, any more than I murdered Smith in revenge for it. Anyway, it wouldn't say much for Inspector Price if one of us managed to commit the murder while he was keeping us under observation.'

Except that Inspector Price wasn't with them for every waking minute. 'Has it occurred to you that the police might stop you from returning to St Felix tomorrow?'

'They won't have to stop me. Because I've already decided to postpone my return.'

For a moment, David thought he had misheard. His brow folded into a frown. 'Your flight has already been booked. My father has changed his own plans, to fly out to the island in July, and he's expecting you to be there.'

'Then he'll have to be disappointed.' Marcus forced a smile. 'I'm not a fool, David. I know where this could lead. So, yesterday evening, after you broke the news of Laurence's death, I went over to Penzance to talk things through with Ian Mitchell. And his advice to me was to stay in this country until the police complete their investigations and charge someone with the murders.'

'My father thinks it would be better if you were to put some distance between yourself and the investigations.'

'That's because your father thinks I'm guilty of the crimes, whereas Ian believes me when I say I'm innocent. And he's made me realise I can't move on with my life until these crimes are solved. I can't prove I'm not the killer; the only thing I can do, in the absence of any evidence against me, is make it clear that I'm not running away.'

'Then what about Woodlands? And the foundation? Do you plan to just let those slide?'

'Of course not. The foundation is Nancy's to manage,

and I can deal with the estate's affairs remotely, with a little help from Honeysuckle.'

'You plan to manage things from Salvation Hall?'

'I plan to manage them from Hemlock Row.'

David sucked in a sharp breath. He leaned forward and rested his elbows on the table, folding his fingers under his chin. 'Eva's bequest to you is none of my concern, of course.' Though he had wanted many, many times since the reading of Eva's will to ask his stepson what he planned to do with his inheritance. 'But do you think that would be a wise move?'

'Yes, or I wouldn't consider it. I can't see Inspector Price will have an issue with it: he didn't object to me being bailed to live with you and my mother in Edinburgh last year while I waited for my case to come to trial. And I plan to offer him every assistance with his investigation.'

'Will you ever return to St Felix, Marcus?'

The young man's face softened and he stared down into his coffee. 'I don't know. I thought I would. In fact, before I heard the news of Laurence's death I was still hopeful I could make a go of it. But his murder changes everything.'

'My father will be heartbroken if he has to see out his final days there alone.'

'He won't be alone. The whole Woodlands estate is excited about his decision to return. They can't wait. And he'll have Nancy with him, and Honeysuckle; and you and Barbara will fly out to visit.' Marcus sighed. 'I know he wants me there, but it isn't for my benefit, is it? He might deny it, but he wants to revisit his youth through me. And I'm not sure I can do that for him anymore. I'm not saying I won't. Only that I'm no longer certain.'

David lifted his elbows from the table and cupped his face with his hands. 'Marcus, you will be alone in Edinburgh. Your mother would never forgive me for letting you walk away without someone in your life.'

'And even now she's gone, you're still putting her needs

before mine.'

'I didn't mean it like that.'

'It hardly matters what you mean. My mind is made up: I'm driving to Edinburgh tomorrow. I'll make myself useful while I'm there. I know there are still a few pieces of artwork to be packed up. If you give me a list, I'll start packing them. I can probably bring some of them back down with me in the car. Then you can decide which you'll keep here, and which will go to St Felix for use by the foundation.'

'And in the meantime we must just wait and wonder what you plan to do next?'

'In the meantime, I'd like you to be happy I have somewhere to go to clear my head; somewhere I can go to decide for myself just what *I* want to do with my life when this nightmare is finally over.'

*

DS Collinson turned the BMW off the main road and onto a narrow country lane. 'Liberation Park is quite remote, isn't it?' He pressed gently on the accelerator, guiding the car slowly between the tall, gently swaying grasses that lined the road. 'Remote enough for the council not to bother trimming the verges, anyway.'

'I wouldn't call four miles from the main road that remote.' Beside him, in the passenger seat, DI Hall was chewing thoughtfully on a thumbnail. 'Did you manage to corroborate DCI Price's story?'

'Yes. I fired off an email to DCI Grant last night and she called me first thing this morning. She backs up everything he told you about the Lancefield murders. She investigated the murder of Geraldine Morton, the girl mistaken for Eva McWhinney. And she's been in dialogue with DCI Greenway over Eva McWhinney's murder.'

'How did she take the news of Laurence Payne's

death?'

'I think her exact words were "bloody hell, here we go again.".' Collinson cast a sideways glance at Hall. 'She speaks very highly of DCI Price, by the way. She said he's one of the most instinctive officers she's ever worked with.'

'A woman died because he was foolish enough to invite Eva McWhinney to Salvation Hall.'

'But his initial thinking was correct, wasn't it? It drew the killer out into the open.'

'You could hardly say that the end justified the means. It wouldn't be my idea of instinctive.'

'I thought you saw him as an extra pair of hands?' Collinson caught her expression from the corner of his eye: the furrowed brow and the hint of cynicism around the lips. 'I don't suppose you've spoken to him this morning? He's been trying to reach you.' The sergeant cast another swift glance in Hall's direction and noted the guilty flush beginning to creep across her neck. 'He called me to ask if there was a reason you weren't returning his calls.'

She shuffled awkwardly in her seat. 'I did know he'd tried to call me yesterday evening. To be honest, I was so intrigued by the information I was digging up on Liberation Park that I lost track of time until it was too late to call him back.' She sniffed. 'What have I missed?'

'The Smith girl still hasn't turned up, but they searched her home yesterday and found a brochure for Liberation Park.'

'Are we going to have to consider that as an additional lead?'

'I would have thought so.' They were approaching a junction and the sergeant slowed the car to turn to the left. 'DCI Price has emailed me a couple of photographs, so we can ask the hotel staff if anyone recognises her.' Collinson took a hand from the steering wheel and slipped it into his jacket pocket, pulling out his phone and handing it to Hall. 'They're attached to the most recent email in the inbox.'

He waited until she had opened the attachment and then said, 'DCI Price has asked us to follow up on the brochure. The hotel should have a record of how and when she made the request, and when they responded to it.'

'Whose investigation is this?' Her words came out a little too sharply, and she turned her head away. 'Am I screwing this up?'

'Of course not.' Collinson tried to sound encouraging. 'It's not exactly a straightforward case, is it?' He flicked on the car's indicator, more through habit than necessity given the deserted nature of the road, and slowed to turn in through the grand, gilt-embellished gates of Liberation Park. 'But the girl was connected to nearly all the deaths that have hit the Lancefields so far, either directly or by association with her brother. At the very least, we'll have to eliminate it.' He trundled the car slowly down the gravel drive towards the house. 'What do you make of Becca Smith?'

'She looks Cornish.'

'Like a pixie?'

Hall jabbed him with her elbow. 'There's no point in trying to make me laugh. I know I'm off the pace this morning. But I'll pull it together before we get out of the car.' She took another look at the photographs. 'I meant she looks like one of those beach babes you see when you're on holiday: blonde, bronzed, and scruffy in a way that looks achingly cool.'

'You sound disappointed.'

'What, because she's tanned, hip and trendy and I'm an exhausted mother of two with milk-bottle legs and bad taste in jackets?'

'As if.' They had reached the end of the driveway and Collinson brought the car to a halt beside the gatehouse. 'Because we already have two leads to follow up: Jennet Payne and Marcus Drake. And a third one is probably one too many.'

'I don't know, Jim. There's something bothering me about Jennet, I won't deny that. She told me yesterday she planned to stop working at Liberation Park, but she didn't sound too happy about it. I'm wondering if Laurence was pressuring her to give up her interest in this place.'

'That's not a motive for murder though, is it? She could have just called off the wedding.'

'Unless she flipped. Let's face it, murder can result from an argument over a parking space if there's enough ego at play.' Hall unclipped her seat belt. 'Let's just say I'm not ready to discount her as a suspect. She could be a good actress. When I asked her about Eva McWhinney yesterday she turned a bit twitchy. I couldn't tell if it was jealousy. I guess that's another question for DCI Price: was there any funny business between Eva and Laurence?'

'You think he might have been playing away?'

'That. Or maybe just tempted. Maybe jealousy *is* a motive we could consider. It dawned on me last night, when I was talking to her, that she knew Eva was going to be at Canary Wharf with Laurence. And Price didn't seem to be aware of that.'

'A link between Jennet and whoever murdered Eva McWhinney?'

'I'm just saying it could be another line of enquiry. Maybe Jennet wanted Laurence – and his wealth – for herself, and didn't appreciate Eva bringing the Lancefields into the mix.' Hall frowned. 'She also seemed very invested in the idea of Marcus Drake being responsible. What if that was just to cover up her own motive?'

*

Ennor followed Kathryn into the library and sat down beside the desk, watching as she sank into the familiar mahogany and leather confines of the captain's chair. She looked tired, her chestnut hair pinned back into an untidy chignon and her usually pink cheeks greyed by the pallor of a long car journey and a late night. 'I don't think anyone saw me arrive. I parked my car halfway down the drive and walked the rest of the way.' He waited for her to respond but she offered him nothing more than a weak smile. 'You're not happy about me being here, are you?'

'I'm just tired from the journey. We didn't get back to Salvation Hall until well after one o'clock.' She clearly still hadn't forgiven him for refusing to spend another night at Liberation Park. 'The dismal atmosphere in the house doesn't help. Or the prospect of watching you question the family all over again because of another death.'

'Question the family, or question Marcus?'

She dismissed the question with a withering glance. 'Have you spoken to DI Hall this morning?'

'No, DS Collinson. It sounds as though Hall still has Jennet in her sights.' Price tugged on his ear. 'Collinson happened to let slip that Hall has just been promoted. This is her first case as a DI.' An unlucky break, if ever there was one: finding herself in the thick of the Lancefield family and its murders. 'I hope she realises what she's in for.'

'And I hope you're not making light of the situation.'

'I'm not. But I've suggested Marcus and Becca are the most likely suspects for her case and she's still haring off after the wrong person. You only had to look at Jennet to see how raw her grief was.' But that kind of instinct only came with practice and Hall hadn't had enough of that yet. Perhaps this case might even be the making of her. Price rested an elbow on the desk. 'Did you tell the family I was coming?'

'When you specifically asked me not to? Why would I?' Kathryn bridled. 'If you want to know where everyone is, Marcus and David are in the kitchen having breakfast and Nancy has gone down into the village with Barbara to pick up the Sunday papers, so your fears about them skipping out to St Felix before you could speak to them were unfounded. Richard is in the Dower House, but as he and Barbara weren't at the wedding I'm assuming you don't need to speak to them.'

She sounded jaded, her patience fraying around the edges, and he knew his decision to arrive at Salvation Hall unannounced to the family was just a further unwelcome test of her loyalties. 'I would like to speak to Richard, as it happens. He deserves to know what's going on. But I'm going to start with Marcus.'

'I'm sure he'll enjoy that.' Kathryn swayed gently in the captain's chair. 'What would you like me to do?'

'Be on hand with coffee and sympathy.'

'For you, or for Marcus?'

'That depends on the outcome of the conversation. I'm going to stress I'm only speaking to him informally, to save DI Hall a journey down to Cornwall.' There was a white cardboard box on the desk and Ennor tapped a finger against it. 'Is that the Liberation Park Bible?'

'Yes and no. It's the book that was discovered during the renovation of Liberation Park, but it's not a full Bible at all. It's a copy of an annotated version of the King James VI Bible that was used in the West Indies.' Her soft, hazel eyes suddenly flickered with interest. 'Some people refer to it as "The Slave Bible", but it's really just a collection of tracts.'

'You must be disappointed then?'

'Good heavens, no. I don't think Jennet realises what she has. It's quite a rare piece. There are only three other known copies in existence, and they're all in university libraries.'

'I don't suppose I should be surprised slaves weren't considered deserving of a full edition of the Bible.'

'It wasn't about being "deserving", and I don't believe the intention was ever for it to be given to slaves to use for themselves. After all, it was published in 1807 and the majority of slaves could neither read nor write. No, this was produced by a Christian society for use by missionaries and clergymen in teaching and worship, so it was probably for Ezekiel Taylor's own use. It's been suggested any passages referring to freedom from slavery were excluded from the edition, in order to keep slaves subdued and avoid inciting rebellion. But there is also a view those passages were excluded not because slaves would rebel, but because slave owners simply feared they would. That fear was seen as a barrier to encouraging Christian practices on plantations, and the Church wanted to overcome the barrier, so they produced this book' – she tapped on the cover with her finger – 'to persuade the slave owners that nothing would be taught or preached which might threaten their safety. It was a means of persuading them to permit slaves to attend church on Sundays and convert to Christianity.'

'And which view do you subscribe to?'

'The view that this conversation has nothing at all to do with why you're here, and you're just trying to curry favour by showing an interest in another dusty old document.' She rolled the chair backwards a little, away from the desk. 'I suppose you'd like me to let David and Marcus know you're here to speak to them.'

Ennor smiled at her warmly. 'I didn't realise I was so transparent.'

9

DS Parkinson leaned his elbows on the desk and stared down at his page of handwritten notes, his wife's admonitions still ringing in his ears. Maybe Ennor Price *was* a bad influence, and maybe he shouldn't have been working unpaid overtime on a Sunday, but he couldn't agree with her that the lack of an overtime budget meant the case was unimportant.

There had been more than a hint of jealousy in Claire's fury; an unfounded anger that he was choosing to prioritise the hunt for Becca Smith over spending the day with his wife and child. It would have been futile to remind her that policing was a vocation: that he was choosing to work because his job mattered to him. But the truth was, he would have been unlikely to make the sacrifice for anyone other than Becca.

He could still remember their first encounter in the grubby, untidy interior of Holly Cottage on the Salvation Hall estate. Back then he'd thought her nothing but a slattern: capable of working as a housekeeper if the Lancefields paid her a wage, but unwilling or unable to provide a clean and hygienic home for her family. But with the benefit of hindsight, he could understand her reluctance. Some women would respond to their partner's infidelity with an instinctive pride and the determination to keep up appearances; he suspected his own wife was among them. But Becca had never been the proactive sort, and Parkinson was of the opinion now that her slovenly ways were simply a sign of her sorrow. She had been just too defeated, too ground down by Philip McKeith's repeated acts of betrayal with Lucy Lancefield to find the strength to put on a show.

Or perhaps just too resentful to make the effort to woo him back.

There was no doubt in his mind that Becca was possessed of a vindictive streak. She had wished a thousand plagues on Marcus Drake and the Lancefield family in the last few months, and had shown no qualms about helping her murderous brother to stay on the run from the law. But would she go as far as murder herself? Was it possible she would travel up to Yorkshire to poison Laurence Payne without a moment's thought, if not for herself than at least for little Frankie's future?

He picked up a pen and began to slide it slowly down the page in front of him. There were only two facts he could be certain of at this stage: she didn't turn up for her planned night out, and her mobile phone had been unresponsive since some time on Saturday morning. He'd put in a request to her mobile phone provider to trace the last few calls she'd made and received, but the data was slow in coming through. His working hypothesis was that she travelled back to Truro after dropping off Frankie at her mother's, but the request for CCTV footage for the nearest camera to the station had only just been submitted, and even then it was a long shot. The best hope he had was to request and then check footage from Truro station, in the hope of catching a sight of her alighting from a train. But the request for that footage hadn't even been made yet and impatience was sitting heavily on his shoulder.

He dropped the pen on the desk and swivelled in his

chair, turning to his computer screen, and thought for a moment before tapping with brisk fingers at the keyboard. Within a few seconds he was staring at a train timetable, the weekday arrivals at Truro from Hayle. 'Arrivals at ten twenty-eight and eleven twenty-seven. That would narrow it down a bit.' He retrieved his pen and scribbled the times in his notebook. 'But what would she do after that?' He rested the end of the pen against his lips. 'Go back to the house, or change for another train?'

The question was destined to go unanswered. With a sharp burst of ringtone, the mobile phone on his desk skittered into life and he swept it up and pressed it to his ear. 'Tom Parkinson.'

The voice at the other end of the line was slow and deliberate. 'Sergeant Parkinson? It's Mandy Jessop. I'm calling in reply to your request for information: the last known location of Rebecca Smith's mobile phone.'

'Is this a formal interview, Inspector Price, or are you just being inquisitive?'

'Let's call it an informal chat.' Now wasn't the time for Price to explain to Marcus why he couldn't conduct a formal interview in the kitchen at Salvation Hall. He pulled his chair a little closer to the table and offered up a nonchalant smile. 'I offered to save my Yorkshire colleagues the trouble of an unnecessary trip to Cornwall. You're not under any obligation to speak to me, but I'd appreciate it if you would. And it would help the family in the long run. Whatever information we can gather about Laurence's last hours will help to bring the investigation to a speedy conclusion.'

'Then I'll do whatever I can to help you.' Marcus relaxed a little. 'Can we start by establishing that it wasn't me who killed him? I don't deny I didn't think very much of him, but murdering him wasn't on my agenda.'

'No one has suggested it was.' Price felt his cheeks warms slightly under the lie. 'At this stage we're just trying to form a picture of his last forty-eight hours.'

'Am I permitted to ask how he died?'

'I'm not at liberty to share that with you at the moment. Only that the death was suspicious and is to be investigated.' The inspector leaned back in his seat and folded his arms across his chest. 'Can we begin with the events of Thursday evening?'

'You already know what happened on Thursday evening. You were there yourself.'

'Humour me, Marcus. It's called procedure.'

Marcus frowned. 'Well, David, Nancy and I arrived at Liberation Park half an hour before you and Kathryn. After we checked in, I went up to my room to shower and change, and then I went back down to the bar to join David and Nancy for a pre-dinner drink. If you recall, we were already seated in the restaurant enjoying our first course when you came down to eat. We were at the table adjacent to yours, so I was in your field of vision for the rest of the meal. And then we returned to the bar, until you and Kathryn finished your desserts and came to join us.' Marcus paused. 'I think it was around nine thirty when Laurence joined us for a drink. All six of us shared the same table in the bar and Laurence was with us for – what would you say? A couple of hours?'

'That sounds about right. I don't remember him showing any signs of feeling unwell at that point, do you?'

'No.' Marcus shook his head. 'After he left, I had another drink with David. As I recall, you and Kathryn left the table and Nancy followed about five minutes later.'

'And you didn't see Laurence again that evening?'

'I didn't see Laurence again until the wedding ceremony. I have no idea where he was during the morning or early afternoon.' Marcus tilted his head. 'Didn't you think it was odd there was no best man or bridesmaids at the wedding?'

'Not particularly. It's not mandatory to have attendants for the bride and groom. Why do you think it odd?'

'It suggested to me that Laurence didn't have anyone to ask to be his best man. That he was the ultimate loner.'

If it was an attempt to deflect the line of questioning, Marcus could have saved himself the trouble. 'So, you didn't see Laurence at all between eleven thirty on Thursday evening and three o'clock on Friday afternoon. What did you do in the morning?'

'I had breakfast in the restaurant, which you already know, because you were sitting at the next table. After that, I went back to my room to read the morning paper, then I met up with David and Nancy for a walk around the hotel grounds. We had lunch in the bar, and then I went back up to my room to change for the wedding.' Marcus smiled. 'You can fill in the blanks after that, Inspector. You were at the same wedding, and I was in your sights for pretty much the whole time. I suppose there is a risk I slipped something into Laurence's food or drink when no one was looking, if I was quick enough. But I can promise you I didn't.'

'Who suggested anything had been slipped into his food or drink?'

'Laurence left the wedding party because he felt unwell, didn't he? I'm guessing whatever made him feel unwell was the thing that led to his death.'

'Are you still planning to fly out to St Felix tomorrow, Marcus?'

'Why? Were you thinking of trying to stop me?' Marcus seemed amused by the suggestion. 'As it happens, I'm planning to postpone my return. It seems to me that if I fly away to the Caribbean you will consider it a suggestion of guilt. So, I've decided to stay in the UK while the investigation is ongoing. That way I can be available for further questioning, either by yourself or the detectives investigating Laurence's death.' His lips curled with a wry smile. 'Or should I say, "the detectives *officially* investigating Laurence's death"?' I take it you have no objection to my travelling to Edinburgh tomorrow?'

'Edinburgh?'

'Yes, I'm planning to stay at Hemlock Row. The house hasn't been rented out yet, and as I'd be the beneficiary of any rents paid on it, I might as well stay there myself. It's not as if I'd be depriving anyone but myself of the income.' Marcus folded his arms and turned his head away. 'Do your worst, Inspector Price. Pull out a notebook and scribble down everything I've said. Take me in again for questioning. Insist on a formal interview. Keep me under surveillance in Edinburgh. It's all the same to me. You will have my full cooperation.' He turned back to fix the policeman with a defiant gaze. 'Do you worst, because there is nothing to find.' He jutted out his chin and lowered his voice to a whisper. 'There is nothing to find, because I have nothing to hide.'

*

Riley Gibb was a slim, well-spoken blonde; a little on the young side, in DI Hall's opinion, to be managing a place like Liberation Park, and a little on the defensive side when it came to answering a reasonable question.

'To be honest, Riley, I would have preferred to ask Mrs Payne directly. But I think she's had enough distress in the last thirty-six hours and I thought you might consider it a kindness to relieve her of the burden.' Hall watched the girl's face as she spoke and saw the wide, green eyes flicker with a hint of hesitation. 'Of course, if you don't feel qualified to reply…'

The girl, her ego suitably pricked, shook her head. 'It isn't that I don't feel qualified. I've been the manager here for two years now.' She pursed her glossed lips and appeared to be weighing up how much to reveal. 'Of course, I'm just the *manager*, not the general manager, so I don't have access to the business accounts. That's all dealt with by Rosemary and Jennet. But I do have sight of the bank statements, because I help with the reconciliation of income against expenditure.'

They were sitting in a small, tastefully furnished office to the rear of the hotel's reception desk, and the policewoman turned her eyes around the room. 'I can imagine the outlay on a place like this can be quite eye-watering. Not just the day-to-day cleaning and maintenance, but the whole keeping-up-appearances thing. Does it have to redecorated regularly?'

Riley blinked, thrown slightly off guard by the turn of Hall's questioning. 'It's only been done once since I started working here, and only the public and reception rooms. I think it used to be decorated annually – someone told me they used to close the hotel up for a month in the winter so it could be done. But I think the decorator put up his prices or something, so Rosemary decided to take a different approach. We open for weddings the whole year round now. And conferences, of course, although we don't do as many of those as we used to. So many businesses make use of virtual meeting rooms these days. There just doesn't seem to be the money about to pay for face-to-face meetings, especially when they have to cover the cost of rooms and meals as well as the function rooms.'

'But the hotel does break even, over all? I mean, there isn't any question of financial difficulty?' Hall tried to make the question sound casual. 'My cousin's just got engaged and she's got her heart set on a fancy wedding. I'm sure you're on her list of possible venues.'

'Oh, that's lovely. And you can reassure your cousin that there's no question of us going under. But…' Riley fidgeted. 'Well, I can't deny things get a bit tight now and again. It's the same for most hospitality businesses, especially those at the upper end. When people have to make cutbacks it's always the luxuries they cut back on, isn't it?' The manager seemed to have shed her initial discomfort at answering Hall's questions. 'It doesn't help, of course, when costs are rising and interest rates are going up. Given our operating margins have been squeezed lately, I think we do very well to keep the ship afloat.'

'I suppose you must be kept quite busy at the moment, with summer being the main wedding season?'

'Yes, we are. At least…' The girl hesitated again, almost erring on the side of caution before relenting. 'I'm afraid we have suffered several quite significant cancellations over the last couple of weeks. Three weddings, all cancelled without much in the way of notice – certainly not enough time for us to be able to book in alternative functions. One of them was for three hundred guests and the couple had reserved every available room for the weekend.' Disappointment tugged at the corner of her mouth. 'They lost their deposit but I suppose that was a small price to pay against the total bill.' She looked down and examined her fingers. 'I'm afraid it left us with a loss because there had been an error on our side. We'd already paid in advance for the marquee hire and the deposit we retained didn't anywhere near cover it: the deposit was only a little over five and a half thousand pounds, so we lost about four thousand pounds overall. Rosemary was furious but Jennet said it couldn't be helped and we should just learn the lesson for next time.'

DI Hall put up a hand. 'I'm sorry, did you say the couple had paid a deposit of five and a half thousand pounds? However much were they paying for the wedding?'

'Well, the deposit is ten percent, so just a little over fifty-five thousand.' Riley made it sound like an everyday occurrence. 'That included the rooms and dinner for the guests, of course, as well as the additional yurts?'

'Yurts?'

'Yes. We couldn't accommodate all of the guests who wanted to stay overnight, so we suggested that as an option. They were luxury ones, of course.'

'Oh, of course.' Hall bit down on her tongue; fifty-five thousand quid and half the family sleeping in tents? 'Tell me, Riley, did Laurence – Mr Payne – make any sort of investment in the business?'

The young woman visibly recoiled and her voice sank to a whisper. 'Oh, I couldn't really say. That wasn't any of my business.'

'He was very wealthy though, wasn't he? I can't imagine he would have minded injecting some cash into the place when it meant so much to Jennet.'

'Oh, he wouldn't have minded, but Rosemary wouldn't…' Riley froze, and put a hand up to her mouth. 'I shouldn't be talking about this.'

Hall wrinkled her nose. 'It's just between you and me, Riley. It won't go any further.' She tapped the girl gently on the arm. 'What wouldn't Rosemary do?'

'Well, she did suggest Laurence might help them out with a short-term loan, and he didn't discount the idea. But he wanted to secure his investment.' Riley leaned forward towards the detective. 'He didn't just offer a small amount to tide the business over, either. He offered to buy a twenty percent stake in Liberation Park. It would have put the business back on its feet again, if only Rosemary would have agreed to it.'

'I thought you said she wanted him to invest?'

'I said she wanted a loan.' Riley lowered her voice to a conspiratorial whisper. 'But she wasn't prepared to give him a share of the business in return for it.'

10

Kathryn looked up, her attention drawn away from her studies by the unexpected squeak of hinges. The library door was already ajar, and she peered over her reading glasses at the incomer. 'Barbara?'

The woman had paused in the gap between door and frame, her kind eyes hesitant but hopeful. 'I hope I'm not disturbing you. Do you have five minutes to talk?'

'I always have time to talk to you.' Kathryn rolled the captain's chair gently backwards, away from the desk. 'I can't settle to any meaningful work this morning. I'm supposed to be refining a catalogue of artefacts for Nancy to use at the foundation, but I'm just too unsettled.'

'Is Inspector Price still in the kitchen with Marcus?'

'He's still in the kitchen, but I think he's speaking to David now. I don't know where Marcus is. Did you want him?'

'No, I wanted you.' Barbara sat down on the chair beside the desk. She was holding a small newspaper in her hand and she held it up for Kathryn to see. 'We don't normally take this one, it's the local rag. But Nancy spotted the front page and thought we should buy a copy. Did you know about this?'

Kathryn took the paper from Barbara's hand and placed it down on the desk, reading the headline aloud.

'Local woman missing since Thursday.' The black and white image of Becca Smith, emblazoned across the page below the headline, was not a flattering one. Clipped from a large photograph, it showed the girl at her worst: patently drunk, her head rested on the shoulder of an invisible companion, and her eyes closed as if in a stupor. 'How on earth did they get hold of this?'

'Then you *did* know. I thought you must.' Barbara placed a hand on Kathryn's arm. 'Richard will be so disappointed you didn't tell him. Why on earth didn't you say something?'

'Because I was asked to keep it to myself.' The balancing act expected of her, the need to weigh up her loyalty to the family against her loyalty to Ennor, was becoming an impossible task. Kathryn had always known that sooner or later she would have to make a choice. Now, without realising it, it would seem she had already done so. 'I can't tell you why, because it would jeopardise the police investigation into Becca's disappearance. You do understand that, Barbara? That it's a police matter?'

'*I* understand that, but I'm not sure Richard will. Frankie is his goddaughter, and now he's seen this he's worried sick about her.' Barbara frowned. 'And for what it's worth, although he probably won't admit it, he's worried about Becca too.'

Of course he was. Kathryn turned her attention back to the newspaper, skimming her eyes down the page. 'Does it say how they got hold of the story?'

'Her mother approached the newspaper to make an appeal because she didn't think the police were doing enough to find her.'

Well, Ennor and Tom would just love that. 'Where is Frankie now?'

'I assume she's still with Becca's mother. I suppose we should be thankful they didn't go the whole hog and put a photograph of the child on the front page too.' Barbara's frown deepened. 'I suppose they think Becca is involved in

Laurence's death.'

'It depends who you mean by "they". The detectives in Yorkshire don't think she has anything to do with it. They think it's far too much of a coincidence for a girl missing in Cornwall to be connected to the death of a man she didn't know over four hundred miles away.'

'But Inspector Price doesn't agree with them.'

'Ennor doesn't know what to think. But he lives by the rule "reject nothing until a crime is explained". He's keeping an open mind. I should say anything further but now that whole of Cornwall knows thanks to this' – Kathryn prodded the newspaper with a censorious finger – 'I suppose I can tell you that Sergeant Parkinson is doing everything he can to find her. They have no overtime budget but he's working today because he's as worried about her as Richard must be.'

Barbara regarded Kathryn with an expectant gaze. 'Do you think she's responsible for Laurence's death, Kathryn?'

'No, I don't. But not because I have any regard for her, or because I think she wouldn't go so far in her attempts to hurt the family. I just think she's too disorganised to come up with such an elaborate plan. And even if she wasn't, she's too lazy to travel all the way to Yorkshire to execute it.'

'Then it has to be one of us, doesn't it?' Barbara made the pronouncement quietly. 'I suppose I'm going to be next.'

'Next?'

'Well, I'm the last one, aren't I? Dennis, Eva, now Laurence – all distant cousins to Richard and David, and all murdered. Now there's just me.'

'Those murders weren't committed by the same hand. Dennis was murdered by Jason and Jason is in prison. Eva was murdered by Zak and he's dead. Laurence can't have been murdered by either of them, can he? And what about Stella's death? She wasn't a Lancefield cousin, she was David's wife.'

'She was also an innocent bystander, not a deliberate target, just like Geraldine Morton. The other deaths occurred because Richard wanted to extend the family. And I can't subscribe to the notion of a mysterious family curse wreaking vengeance on the Lancefields for all their odious sins of the past. Dennis didn't die because his ancestors bought and sold slaves, Eva didn't die because her ancestor experimented on slaves and Laurence didn't die because his ancestors sold their slaves out to a cruel and wicked master.' Barbara shook her head. 'I don't know why I didn't see it before. I'm the last Lancefield cousin standing. How do I know the killer isn't coming for me next?'

*

'I'm assuming Marcus didn't offer you any refreshment, Inspector Price, so I've brewed some coffee.' David Lancefield waved a hand towards the freshly brewed cafetiere on the kitchen table. 'It's Sumatra Mandheling. I hope that's not too strong for your taste.'

The stronger the better, as far as Price was concerned. He gave a nod of appreciation. 'I do appreciate your willingness to speak to me this morning, by the way. And before we go any further, David, can I just say I'm sorry for your loss.' He checked himself. 'I'm sorry, I should have said "before we go any further, *Mr Lancefield*." It was a long drive back yesterday evening and the line between attending Laurence's wedding as a guest and visiting Salvation Hall on police business has become a little blurred. I hope you'll make allowances.'

'No apology necessary, I'm sure.' David's faint smile was reassuring. 'I've already been challenged by Kathryn on my failure to use your given name at the wedding. But we seem so frequently to find ourselves in the roles of murder investigator and witness that I'm not sure I can change the habit.' His eyes narrowed a little. 'Which brings us back to the reason for our present meeting. I take it you would like to know if I witnessed anything in Yorkshire which might help to identify Laurence's killer?'

'I'd like to know if you saw anything unusual.'

'Apart from your own presence there as a guest? Oh, I'm not so foolish as to think Laurence invited you simply as Kathryn's escort.'

'Do you think he would have felt it necessary to invite me if Marcus hadn't been on the guest list?'

'A fair question, Inspector.' David appeared to consider it as he lifted the cafetiere from the table and set about pouring a cup for Price. 'I have wondered why he invited Marcus to the wedding at all, and asked myself if we – my father and I – went too far in our efforts to encourage warmer relations between them. But I've also wondered about the marked lack of guests on Laurence's side. I almost felt our little family group were there to demonstrate he had some family to speak of.' He pushed the coffee cup towards Price. 'He was very disappointed, you know, that my father didn't feel up to making the trip.'

'I'm sure.' Price stared at the coffee. 'How were things on the journey home? I suppose Marcus must have breathed a sigh of relief to be leaving Liberation Park. He clearly didn't enjoy being at the wedding.'

'No. And again, I hold myself responsible for encouraging him to accept the invitation. On the way home he let slip just how much the situation had pained him: he told me he considered it insensitive of Laurence to invite him to witness his "happy ever after" with Jennet, when Marcus had lost his own "happy ever after" with Eva.'

'And, to make it worse, Richard had offered Laurence and Jennet a honeymoon on the Woodlands estate, where Marcus would cross paths with them?'

David nodded. 'Oh, I think Marcus could have been relied upon to give them a wide berth. The estate covers many acres and the cottage was far removed from the main plantation house. Of course, that won't be an issue now.'

'Because Laurence didn't live to enjoy his honeymoon.'

'That, and the fact that Marcus has decided not to return to St Felix at the moment. Did he tell you?'

'Yes, he did.'

'And you have no issue with him travelling to Edinburgh?'

'I can't see it being a problem.' Better, in Price's view, for Marcus to be in Edinburgh than St Felix, under the circumstances. At least DCI Grant could keep an eye on him. 'I've asked if he would be good enough to wait until Tuesday before he travels, in case DI Hall decides to come down to Cornwall to interview the family, and he's agreed. In fact, he seems quite keen to assist.'

'I see.' David's brow creased. 'I suppose you will also be speaking to Nancy this morning?'

'If she will agree to it. Is there something in particular I need to ask her?'

A flicker of uncertainty sparked in David's eyes. And then he quietly said, 'I've always felt a very deep affection for Nancy. She has always felt like a part of our own extended family. Of course, my dear Stella didn't agree with me on that point. She and Nancy were always crossing metaphorical swords. They almost took pleasure in riling each other.' He seemed to be choosing his words with care. 'But since Nancy and Marcus returned from St Felix to attend the wedding, I've noticed a growing antagonism between them. I always considered them friends, but she has become quite brittle towards him. I think she enjoys baiting him, almost in the way she used to bait Stella.'

'About something in particular?'

'Zak Smith's murder.'

The answer caught Price off guard. 'Smith's murder? What does she know?'

'I'm not sure she actually *knows* anything. But she was goading Marcus about it yesterday, in the car on the way home. The two of them quite got on my nerves with their bickering. The journey home to Penwithen was seven and a half hours of squabbling, punctuated by long stretches of miserable silence. I took a turn at driving between Birmingham and Bristol. That took my mind off things a little.' David rubbed at his temple with his fingers. 'Of course, witnessing all of these crimes has changed her. It's changed all of us.'

'Does Nancy think Marcus murdered Smith?'

'Don't you, Inspector?' David's eyes glinted with a mild bemusement. 'Who else could it possibly have been?' He didn't wait for an answer. 'I don't want to believe it of him, of course. But I can see he had a motive. More than one motive, in fact – Smith murdered both his mother and the object of his affections. Poor Stella would have been distraught. She wouldn't have wanted Marcus to risk his liberty a second time on her account. But we both know, don't we, that despite his calm exterior he can be hot-headed when he's provoked, though thankfully it takes a lot to provoke him.'

'From what you tell me, Nancy seems to have the knack.'

'Indeed she does.' David's eyes widened as bemusement made way for curiosity. 'And what of Nancy, Inspector Price? Will she be permitted to return to St Felix tomorrow, or is she also on DI Hall's radar?'

*

'DS Collinson? It's Tom Parkinson in Penzance.' The sergeant sat upright in his chair as the call was answered. 'I've been trying to reach DI Hall but she isn't picking up her calls. I don't suppose you know where I can find her?'

'She's with Jennet Payne at the moment. Can I help?'

'You most certainly can.' Parkinson relaxed a little, relieved at the prospect of sharing what he'd discovered. It wasn't just that DI Hall wasn't picking up; he couldn't get through to Ennor Price either, and the information Mandy Jessop had just provided regarding Becca Smith's mobile phone was burning a hole in his notebook. 'Did you make any headway with the brochure request?'

'I did. I spoke to the hotel's bookings administrator this morning, and she confirmed the brochure was ordered by email on Monday of last week. I have a copy of the request for you, I'll send it over.

'And it was ordered by Becca herself?'

'The email address given was a Hotmail address for a Becca Smith. She wanted the brochure sending as soon as possible; she made out her fiancé wanted to go abroad to get married, and she wanted to come up with an impressive alternative to persuade him to stay in this country so that more of her family could attend.'

'So they sent it out to her straight away?'

'The same day. It went by first class post.'

'Did she give a telephone number in the email, as well as an address?'

'Yes, a mobile number. I've already tried to call it. It just rings out as number unobtainable. It's either a false number or else the SIM has been disconnected.'

'Can you give me the number? Does it end five-seven-two?'

'No. six-seven-three.'

'I don't know about a false number, but I can tell you it's not Becca's regular number.' Parkinson wasn't sure whether that was a relief or a disappointment. 'What about the photographs I sent you? Have they been circulated to the hotel staff?'

'They have, and no one recognises her. I've shown them to Jennet Payne and Rosemary Taylor too. They have no recollection of seeing Becca, or anyone resembling her, at Liberation Park.' Collinson clicked his teeth. 'I know we can't explain the brochure request. But I still can't see how your missing girl has anything to do with Laurence Payne's death.'

'It's tempting to ask if you'd stake twenty quid on that statement, but I don't think it would be fair to take your money.' Parkinson gave Collinson a moment to think about it, and then said, 'I've been following up on the last calls made to and from Becca's regular mobile. Nineteen calls were made to her phone between the last known sighting of her on Thursday and the phone going inactive on Saturday morning. Six of the calls were made on Thursday evening by friends here in Cornwall trying to locate her when she didn't turn up for a night out. Seven were made by her mother on Friday evening with another three on Saturday morning; and three were made by me, also on Saturday morning. All of the calls went unanswered, all of them diverted to voicemail, and all of them pinged on a mast in East Yorkshire, not fifteen miles away from Liberation Park.'

The silence from the other end of the line was deafening. And then Collinson said, 'Run that by me again?'

'We have evidence to show Becca's phone was active in the East Yorkshire area on Thursday evening, Friday evening and Saturday morning. We're as certain as we can be she was in the vicinity of Liberation Park. As to whether she had anything to do with Laurence Payne's death – well, I think that's probably for you and DI Hall to work out.'

11

The heat in the orchid house was stifling.

Marcus closed the door behind him and hovered beside the shabby Lloyd Loom chair in the corner. Beneath the seat, Samson was dozing in his basket, his small body rising and falling with laboured, irregular breath. 'Isn't it too hot for him in here?'

'Who? Samson?' Richard Lancefield spoke without looking up, his gaze still firmly fixed on the contents of a small, shallow drawer beneath the potting bench. 'He has the sense to go outside, if it pleases him.' The old man dropped a hand into the drawer and rummaged around with gnarled fingers. 'I have no idea what possessed me to hang on to all these unnecessary items.' He pulled out a pair of rusting scissors and dropped them into a small wicker basket beside his feet. 'Sentimentality, probably. I brought those scissors from St Felix.' He tipped his head towards the young man without looking at him. 'Are you going to tell me why you're here?'

Marcus hesitated and then sat down, placing his feet with care so as not to disturb the sleeping animal. 'I wanted to talk to you about my plans for the next few days.'

'Has Inspector Price forbidden you from flying back to

St Felix?'

'No. But he's agreed it would be acceptable for me to delay my flight and spend some time in Edinburgh.'

Richard turned his head to look squarely at Marcus. 'At Hemlock Row?'

'Yes. Do you mind?'

Richard grunted, and turned his attention back to the drawer. 'I'm planning to leave for Woodlands myself in six weeks. I had hoped you would be there to receive me.'

'And I had every intention of being there. But you must see that Laurence's death changes things. I know the police will be looking at me, and I don't want them to think I'm running away. I'd rather stay here until they find his killer.'

The old man withdrew his hand from the drawer and bent to pull a small wooden stool from under the bench. 'You didn't feel the same when Zak Smith died.' He sat down on the stool and rested his hands on his knees. 'They hadn't found his killer, but you were happy to leave for St Felix.'

'I know. But I can see now it was a mistake. I should have stayed here.' Marcus frowned. 'Did you think I was running away?'

'What I think isn't of any consequence.'

'Then you have no objection to my staying at Hemlock Row?'

'Why should I? The house doesn't belong to me. It's held in trust for Eva's charities, and the income is your inheritance. She wanted you to have it. There is no tenant in place yet and I can see no reason for the trustees to refuse you the right to live there for a while, in lieu of any rent. After all, we still hold the keys.' The old man shrugged. 'I don't think it would do to spend too much time there, of course. Spending time with one's memories can be a blessing in a time of crisis, but it wouldn't do to become maudlin. Eva has gone, and she will not be coming back.'

'I know that. It isn't about the memories.'

'Then why Hemlock Row?'

'Because I need to get away from Penwithen and I don't know where else to go.'

Richard smiled to himself. 'Marcus, you are a young man of considerable means. We pay you a competitive salary to manage the Woodlands estate and you have the rental income from Eva's other properties that was bequeathed to you.'

'I haven't touched a penny of the bequest. I daren't.'

'Because you don't wish to profit from her death?'

'Nothing as noble as that. I simply can't convince myself that DCI Price won't knock on my door one day and tell me I have to hand it all back. They call it proceeds of crime, don't they?'

'But you had no hand in Eva's death.'

'I had no hand in Lucy's death either, but it didn't stop the police from trying to build a case against me. You don't have to be guilty of a crime to serve time for it, do you? There is such a thing as a miscarriage of justice.' Why had he ever thought that the old man would understand? 'Then there's the matter of Laurence's death. Inspector Price has questioned me again this morning and I get the impression he's lining me up for the role of serial killer.'

'Did he tell you that Becca Smith has gone missing?'

The news caught Marcus by surprise. 'No, he didn't. When did this happen?'

'On Thursday, the day you all travelled up to Yorkshire for the wedding.' Richard stood up and pushed the stool back under the bench. 'The story has been reported today in the local newspaper. Nancy brought a copy home with her from the village. I can't help wondering whether there is a connection between Becca's disappearance and Laurence's death.'

'Becca? No, I can't see that.'

'Perhaps we don't know her as well as we think. I didn't think her foolish enough to assist that brother of hers to stay on the run, but I was wrong.' Richard reached into the potting-bench drawer and pulled out a small ball of twine. 'It would be ungrateful of her to murder a member of the family when I've provided her with so much support, but I have long since learned some people are simply lacking in conscience. It would be a relief to be proven wrong. I sincerely hope she will turn up after some foolish, thoughtless jaunt; not only for myself but for Frankie's wellbeing. But I fear that is unlikely to be the case.'

'So, where do you think she is?'

'On the run, like her brother.' Richard dropped the ball of twine into the basket. 'It will add to Inspector Price's woes, of course.' He pulled a small, metal tin from the drawer and took off the lid. 'Empty. What rubbish I have accumulated over the years. I cannot leave all this detritus here for Barbara to deal with.' He turned to look over his shoulder at Marcus. 'Have you informed Nancy that you plan to delay your return to St Felix?'

'No, I wanted to speak to you first. Will she still fly out tomorrow?'

'Unless Inspector Price thinks it unwise. Or unless she decides to stay here a little longer and wait until you're ready to join her.'

'I think that's very unlikely. We don't have a great deal to do with each other these days. I don't think Nancy will lose any sleep if she has to return to St Felix without me.'

*

'It changes everything, doesn't it?' Jim Collinson wasn't sure just what reaction he was expecting from Steph Hall, but it wasn't indifference. 'DS Parkinson has firm evidence Becca Smith was in the area from Thursday evening to Saturday morning, and when you couple that with the hotel brochure he found in her kitchen, it points to her being a viable suspect.' He waited for Hall to fasten her seatbelt before starting the car's engine. 'Surely we have to follow it up?'

'We already are following it up. We've circulated the photographs of her to the hotel's staff, and nobody recognises her. We've also shown them to Jennet Payne and Rosemary Taylor and drawn a blank.' The inspector pushed out her lips. 'And there's no way, even if she was in the area, that she could have administered the taxine to Laurence, is there?'

'Can we be certain of that?' Collinson put the car into gear and pressed slowly on the accelerator. 'She could have obtained the materials to make taxine here at Liberation Park.' The BMW moved forward at a snail's pace and as it rolled beyond the gatehouse he pointed through the windscreen towards the hotel's grounds. 'See those fancy trees? They're topiary chess men. The ones you can see from here are the queen, the bishop and the rook. The head gardener gave me a tour of them while you were talking to Jennet. He reckons those things are over two hundred years old. They were planted by the Huntsford family, the original owners of Liberation Park, and sculpted into topiary shapes when Ezekiel Taylor took over the property at the beginning of the nineteenth century.'

'And that matters to us because…?'

'They're not just trees.' The car began to pick up speed. 'They're yew trees.' Collinson gave Hall a moment to think about it. 'So, assuming Becca Smith knows what a yew tree looks like – and given her late partner was the head gardener at the Lancefield's estate, it's probable that she does – she could have obtained the murder instrument here, on site.'

Hall growled softly. 'Do we know yet why the hotel sent her a brochure?'

'She requested it last week, by email. They sent it out the same day.'

'That could just be coincidence. How do we know it wasn't a genuine enquiry?'

Trust Steph to clutch at straws. 'She doesn't have a fiancé. And even if she did, she's an unemployed hospital cleaner. Not exactly Liberation Park's usual type of clientele.'

'Then maybe she was just being nosy. If she's heard about Liberation Park in connection with the Lancefields, she might have just wanted to see the place for herself.'

'She could have done that by looking at their website.' Collinson cast a sideways glance at Hall. 'Is there a reason you don't want to keep an open mind on this one? Because it sounds to me as though she was in the area, she had a grudge against the Lancefields and she had access to the means to make taxine.'

'Jennet Payne and Rosemary Taylor were also in the area, also had access to taxine and also had a possible motive for wanting Laurence dead.'

'Which was?'

'The hotel is teetering on the brink of financial disaster. Laurence was prepared to buy into the business but Rosemary refused; she was happy for him to make a loan, but she wasn't willing to give him a share of the business in return for it. She expected him to just cough up the money because he was marrying her daughter. But he wasn't on the same page.' Hall turned to look at Collinson. 'Isn't it more likely Laurence was murdered because he wouldn't give in and cough up the money? What if Jennet agreed with her mother and murdered him so she could keep Liberation Park afloat?'

'I thought she was planning to step back from the business?' They were approaching the gates which led from Liberation Park to the winding country road beyond, and Collinson slowed the car. 'Steph, why are you so obsessed with the idea of Jennet being involved in her husband's death?' He turned the car left onto the lane. 'It's beginning to sound personal.'

'It's not personal. But you know how this goes: most murders are committed by someone close to the victim.

Rosemary wanted Laurence's cash for the business and Jennet...? Well, I still can't help wondering whether she didn't want to leave the business. I don't know which of them poisoned him. Maybe they were in on it together.'

'DS Parkinson is arranging for access to CCTV footage for Becca Smith's local train station, to see if she set off for Yorkshire on Thursday. He's suggested we might check the footage for Paragon Station to see if she arrived in Hull on Thursday evening. He thinks we'd be looking at a three-hour window between seven and ten in the evening.'

Hall closed her eyes. 'Jim, will you let it go? There is nothing concrete so far to suggest this murder has anything to do with either the Lancefield family or Price and Parkinson's missing girl. Price has already suggested Marcus Drake might have been responsible for the murder, but he hasn't got back to us yet with the results of his conversations with the family, and he's already changing tack and focusing on Becca Smith. I thought he would be an asset, but he's all over the place and I don't want our team wasting time on pointless searches when we have our own investigation to deal with. First thing tomorrow I want Liberation Park's accounts taking apart, and I want Rosemary Taylor and Jennet Payne interviewed on a more formal basis.' Hall paused to draw in a breath, opening her eyes and turning them to Collinson. 'If you want to make a concession to DS Parkinson in return for their help in questioning the Lancefields, have someone chase the CCTV footage for Paragon Station but send it down to Penzance. Let them trawl through it.' She rolled her eyes. 'Is that your mobile phone ringing?'

'Yep.' Collinson pulled the phone from his jacket pocket and handed it to her.

She pressed at the keypad with her thumb. 'DS Collinson's phone, DI Hall speaking.' She lowered her head, listening. 'And where was it found?' She turned incredulous eyes to Collinson as she waited for the answer.

'And it was Jennet Payne who found it?' She nodded to herself. 'Thanks for letting us know.' The call ended, she handed the phone back to Collinson. 'That was Terry Bradley. We need to turn the car around and go back to Liberation Park. Jennet Payne has found a mobile phone on the path behind the gatehouse.' Hall covered her face with her hands. 'She reckons it belonged to Becca Smith.'

*

'I do apologise for any inconvenience, Inspector Price. I had to pop into Penzance. There were things I needed to pick up before I fly back to St Felix tomorrow.' Nancy turned her back and set about filling the kettle. 'I wasn't sure if you'd still be here when I returned.' She dropped the kettle onto its stand and tapped at the switch, and then turned on her heel to offer him an artificial smile. 'But as you are, I assume it's fairly important that you speak to me? Is it about Laurence? Or is it about Becca?'

Price met the smile with good humour. 'Kathryn told me over lunch that Becca's disappearance had been reported in the local paper. We'd been trying to keep the matter private out of respect for the family. We thought they'd already endured enough negative press coverage thanks to Zak's escapades.' At least now he knew that respect wasn't at the top of Sadie Smith's priorities, any more than patience was to be found among her virtues. 'I wanted to speak to you about Laurence, but if you have any information to volunteer about Becca I'd be glad to hear it.'

Nancy stepped forward to sit at the kitchen table, bringing with her a subtle fragrance of jasmine and a vacuous gaze. 'I can't help when it comes to Becca, I'm afraid. I can only say Richard was very disappointed to learn he hadn't been notified.'

'Then you'll be pleased to hear that I've apologised to

him, and he fully understood why we'd been trying to keep the story under wraps.' Not that Price needed to justify his actions to Nancy. 'Were you surprised to be invited to Laurence's wedding?'

'Not particularly. I think he extended the invitation to all of us as a courtesy to Richard, though Richard himself didn't feel up to making the journey. Marcus and I were summoned back from St Felix to accompany David, and Barbara agreed to stay here to keep Richard company.' Nancy placed her elbows on the table and folded her slim, manicured fingers under her chin. 'Did you know Laurence and I were distantly related, Inspector Price? We shared a common ancestor on St Felix.'

'Kathryn did mention it.' She'd also mentioned the connection was so distant that under normal circumstances it would barely warrant a mention, but Price had long since concluded that nothing relating to the Lancefields could ever be remotely described as "normal". He was well aware that Nancy had gone to great lengths to dig up the evidence, trawling though endless piles of dusty old documents in the hope of finding at least some shred of evidence to prove she was distantly related to the family she served. 'Was Laurence aware of the connection?'

Nancy arched her neck. 'We did discuss it. I think he was mildly embarrassed that it proved his line of the family was descended from an illegitimate Creole.'

'George Payne.'

'My goodness, Inspector, have you been studying the Lancefield's family history?'

'Only those parts I think might be relevant to my investigations.' Price smiled, and gave her a moment to think about it. 'His line might have been illegitimate to begin with but, if I understand correctly, his father William adopted George's child, making the line legitimate. Which is how Laurence came to inherit that particular line's wealth.' He watched her face as he spoke, and saw the soft line of her jaw begin to stiffen. 'I suppose it must be frustrating to know your own line wasn't recognised in quite the same way.'

'Must it?' Her dark eyes were suddenly guarded. 'I suppose that would depend on how much value you place on material wealth. Speaking for myself, I've always been grateful for the comfortable life I have enjoyed. I may be too distantly related to Richard to inherit Salvation Hall, but I was lucky enough to live here while working as his secretary. And now I'm lucky enough to be living once more on the Woodlands estate.' She tilted her head. 'Who could live in the Caribbean and not feel blessed?'

Price could hazard a guess. 'Do you think Marcus feels blessed to live in the Caribbean?'

'I very much doubt Marcus feels blessed in any aspect of his life. He's never been the same since he murdered Philip McKeith. You saw for yourself at the wedding just how low his mood was, and how disagreeable he could be.'

'Yes, but I attributed it to the fact I was present. It was clearly making him uncomfortable.'

'Being at Laurence's wedding was making him uncomfortable. I suppose the burning question is how uncomfortable?' A wry smile tugged at Nancy's lips. 'Do you think his antipathy towards Laurence might have led him to murder again? Or perhaps that's the question you've come to ask *me*?'

'I've come to ask if you saw anything suspicious while you were staying at Liberation Park. Anything that might shed a light on Laurence's death. Marcus's feelings towards Laurence don't come under that category, because we were all well aware of them. He didn't exactly make an effort to hide them. So, can you remember anything else that might be relevant?'

'I'm afraid not.'

'Can you think of any reason why someone might have wanted him dead?'

'Apart from Marcus? Well, Laurence was a very wealthy man, but the only person likely to benefit financially from his death would be Jennet. And I very much doubt she would murder her husband on their wedding night.' Nancy looked Price directly in the eye. 'I suppose there is always the possibility of revenge against the family.' She arched an eyebrow. 'Which, whether you like it or not, rather brings us back to the question of Becca Smith's disappearance.'

12

Kathryn pushed her hands into the pockets of her raincoat and quickened her step. 'We'll be lucky to get there before that cloud breaks.' She lifted her eyes to the cloud in question: a vast, dark swirl of cumulonimbus that threatened to drench the lane before them. 'I can't believe we didn't bring an umbrella.'

'I'm sure we'll be none the worse for a drop of rain, will we, Samson?' David Lancefield, walking beside her, addressed his words to the terrier trotting at his heel. 'We're almost at the end of the lane and we only have to skirt the churchyard and cross the road. The Lancefield Arms will still be there, whatever time we arrive. And I'm sure Amber will look after us, wet or dry.' There was a hint of resignation in his voice. 'Do you think she'll have any news of Becca?'

'I doubt it. I'm sure she would have notified Ennor or Tom if she'd heard anything.' Amber, at least, could be relied upon to do the right thing. 'But you didn't invite me along just to talk about Becca, did you?'

'No.' He bent his arm and offered it to Kathryn. 'I thought I felt a drop of rain then, perhaps we should pick up our pace.' His smile warmed as she slipped her arm through his. 'I wanted to talk to you about Laurence. About what might have happened to him. And I'd like your advice on a matter that's been troubling me. I think' – he stumbled over the words – 'I think we must all stop deluding ourselves and accept Marcus is responsible.'

'Oh, David, do you truly believe that?'

'As I explained to Inspector Price, it breaks my heart to think of it. But I can see no other possibility. I don't believe for one minute that Becca would be involved, however deep her hatred for the family.'

'But if you've already shared your views with Ennor, what can I do to help?'

'We need to persuade Marcus to confess.'

'To confess?' They had reached the end of the lane and Kathryn followed David's lead as he steered her gently to the right, around the edge of the churchyard. 'How do you propose to do that, if Marcus denies he had anything to do with it?'

'He must be made to see what damage this is doing to the family. As long as he refuses to admit his guilt, suspicion will continue to alight on the rest of us. Just as it did when he murdered Philip.' David cast a glance into the churchyard as he spoke, and slowed his pace. 'It's only a matter of months since I brought Laurence to visit St Felicity's. We walked together in the churchyard and I showed him Lucy's resting place, and Stella's. Now Laurence himself is dead. How many more will die before this matter is resolved?' David frowned. 'I have suggested to my father that Marcus must be made to confess, as he confessed to Philip's murder, but my father does not agree with me.'

'Because he doesn't believe Marcus is guilty?'

'Good heavens, no. Because he has decided to return to St Felix himself, and it suits his own ends to have Marcus safely returned there to support him.' David turned to look at Kathryn as he spoke. 'You give my father far too much credit for integrity, Kathryn. He engineered a confession from Marcus when Philip died, because he didn't want the investigation to drag on and impact the family. For what it's worth, I don't believe Marcus had anything to do with Eva's murder. But I do believe he murdered Zak Smith, and that he may have been responsible for Laurence's death. I don't know yet exactly how Laurence died; Inspector Price has not shared that piece of information with me. But I suspect he has shared it with you. And though I wouldn't ask you to break his confidence, I would ask you to tell me whether you believe it feasible: could Marcus have been responsible for Laurence's death? Could he have committed some act, while we were staying at Liberation Park, that would lead to Laurence dying on Friday evening?'

'Before I answer your question, I want you to know I don't believe Marcus to be guilty. But' – she found the words hard to express – 'Yes, he could have committed the act which led to Laurence's death.' David stopped, and she felt his arm suddenly stiffen. 'Before you say anything, I want to add this: any of us could have committed that act. You, Nancy, myself or Ennor. Even Jennet or Rosemary. In fact, just about anyone present in the hotel in the forty-eight hours before he died could have been responsible.' Had she said enough to reassure him? Would it be safe for her to say more? 'If I tell you how Laurence died, will you promise not to share the information with anyone until Ennor has made it public?'

'My dear Kathryn, please don't burden yourself with the responsibility. I can work it out for myself. It can only have been a slow-acting poison.' David set off walking again, his pace slow and steady. 'Was it something that could be readily obtained by anyone?'

'It was taxine.' She fell into step beside him. 'They don't know yet in exactly what form it was administered, only that it was most likely added to his food or drink up to forty-eight hours before he died.' She pulled gently on David's arm. 'Do you think Marcus would even know what taxine was, or how to produce it?'

'I think he's intelligent enough to procure the

information if he was looking for a slow-acting poison that could be prepared from a natural and readily available source.' They had reached the kerb and David stopped, turning his head to check for traffic before stepping out into the road, drawing Kathryn and Samson in his wake. 'But I very much doubt the same could be said of Becca.'

*

'I hadn't planned to come into the office today, but interviewing Nancy just about finished me off.' Price slipped off his jacket and draped it over the back of his chair before sitting. 'Have you been here all day?'

'Yes. Much to Claire's dissatisfaction.' DS Parkinson closed the office door behind him and leaned against the wall. 'I told her it was only for the morning, but things started to move so thick and fast I didn't dare go home in case it all kicked off.'

'And has it all kicked off?'

'No. But it's certainly moved on since we last spoke. They've found Becca's mobile phone at Liberation Park.'

Price whistled through his teeth. 'It's definitely Becca's?'

'The screensaver was a bit of a giveaway. DS Collinson set up a brief video call to show me – it's a photo of Becca with Philip and Frankie. I've seen that phone myself. It's definitely hers.'

'Well, that muddies the water, doesn't it?' Price rested his elbows on the arms of his chair. 'They've had no confirmed sightings of her?'

'No, but they've only asked around at Liberation Park. They haven't done a broader search. Collinson said he was going to follow up on any sightings at the nearest mainline station, but that wouldn't be until tomorrow. He said Hall didn't seem that keen. She was still focusing on Jennet Payne, but I guess that might have changed now the phone has turned up.'

'They know calls to her phone were pinging from a mast near Liberation Park?' Of course they did. 'If the phone is there, and it was registering calls on Saturday morning, where the hell is Becca now?' Price tapped an impatient finger on the desk. 'Have they examined the phone?'

'It's locked with a PIN.' Parkinson screwed up his face. 'Hall's bagged it up for forensic examination pending it being unlocked, but it's already been handled by Jennet Payne and she handed it to one of their uniformed team.'

'Who just took hold of it without thinking first that it might be crucial evidence?' Price shook his head. 'I should have stayed at Liberation Park, shouldn't I?' It was easy to say that with hindsight. He lifted his hand. 'Let's get back to basics. One' – he began to count through his fingers – 'Laurence is dead. Two – Becca is missing. Three – a brochure for Liberation Park has been found in Becca's house, supposedly requested by her. Four – Becca's phone has registered calls in the vicinity of the hotel. Five – the phone has been found in the grounds, close to where Laurence's body was discovered. It sounds like a no-brainer.' So, why did he feel so uncomfortable? 'It's too obvious, Tom. We must be missing something.' An obvious something. A something too painful to consider. 'Have they managed to trace the original request for the brochure found at Becca's house?'

'Yes, it came in as an email request.'

'From Becca's regular email account?'

'No. From a Hotmail account.'

'So anyone could have created it to masquerade as Becca.' Including Becca herself, if only she had been devious enough to think of it. Price folded his hands behind his head and rocked back in his chair. 'I won't believe she went to Yorkshire until I see evidence of her boarding a train or hiring a car at this end, and evidence that she got off the train or parked up at the other. Solving

Laurence's murder might be DI Hall's investigation but tracking down Becca is ours. She isn't just a missing person now, she's a missing person at high risk of harm.'

'You think something's happened to her?

'Don't you? For pity's sake, Tom, you know Becca better than most people. Just think about it.' Price lowered his hands and counted through his fingers a second time. 'One – she'd probably never even heard of Liberation Park. Why would she request a brochure for a place she'd never heard of? Two – she might have known yew trees are poisonous, but I doubt she'd have the knowledge to make a decoction. Three – we have no firm evidence to show she travelled to Yorkshire. Four – her phone has turned up at Liberation Park but no one at the hotel admits to having seen her. Five – and most importantly of all – she would never walk away from Frankie.'

Parkinson stepped forward and sat down beside the desk. 'I never thought I'd say this, but I hope you're wrong. 'I'd rather she was alive and guilty than innocent and dead.' He raised troubled eyes to Price. 'What's the plan?'

'I'll put in a call to DI Hall and talk it through with her. We need hard evidence that confirms Becca's movements on Thursday, including evidence putting her in the vicinity of Liberation Park. I'll settle for CCTV footage of her boarding or alighting a train, or a confirmed sighting of her arriving by car or taxi. If we can get that, then we go back to Liberation Park to look for her.'

'And if we can't?'

'Then we'll have to cast the net wider down here. We can talk to Sadie Smith again, but I don't think she's keeping anything from us. It might be worth talking to her brothers, to see if Becca confided in one of them. Robin is the most likely. And we'll need a public appeal. Thanks to Sadie, the story already has some visibility. I might not like the way she went about it, but I can't deny it might produce a lead or two, if someone comes forward with a confirmed sighting.' Price paused to draw a breath. 'Have you heard from Becca's bank yet?'

'Yes. Because it's Sunday, and they're running some sort of technical housekeeping procedures, they can't let me have anything until tomorrow. But they've promised me a breakdown of debit and credit card transactions by ten o'clock tomorrow morning.'

'And the car hire firms?'

'Of the ones I checked with, three have confirmed they have no record of a Becca Smith hiring from them in the last seven days. I'm still waiting for the other four to confirm. Those operating at a national level have confirmed they have no record of a booking at any branch. If we draw a blank I guess we'll have to extend the search to other small operators in – what? A twenty-mile radius?'

'Make it fifty.' Price felt a sudden prickling of the hairs across the back of his neck. 'We're not leaving any stone unturned. Finding Becca is going to be the key to this investigation. It's my belief that if we can find Becca, we're going to be one step closer to the killer.'

*

'When Riley told me you were in the gatehouse, I thought she must have been mistaken.' Rosemary Taylor stepped forward and sat down on the edge of the bed, so close to Jennet that their knees were almost touching. 'Now the police have finished in here, we need to start preparing it for next weekend.'

Jennet turned red-rimmed, disbelieving eyes to her mother. 'Please don't tell me you expect next weekend's booking to go ahead. My husband died in this room. Before long it's going to be in all the newspapers. Can you imagine the headlines? "Wealthy groom dies on wedding night. Body found in bridal suite." How many bookings do you think we'll retain after that?'

'Darling, you're upset.' Rosemary took Jennet's hand in hers. 'People are really not quite as sensitive as you think. And even if they were, self-interest will always prevail. The couple who've booked for next weekend have their own happiness to think of, never mind the dozens of guests who have already made arrangements to travel. They won't get another booking for months, possibly for the rest of the year. It's the height of the season. And in any case, as long as we don't cancel from our end, they would have to forfeit their deposit if they backed out.' She squeezed Jennet's hand. 'I will admit that putting them in here for their wedding night might be pushing things a bit too far. We could claim there's a problem with the electrics or the plumbing, and move them to the Regal Suite on the top floor of the main house. The room is far more impressive than this one, it's just a matter of them sacrificing the extra privacy. If they raise an objection we can always offer a discount.'

Jennet drew back her hand with a hiss of disgust. 'Have you any comprehension of the situation we're in? This isn't just about the business. They think we're suspects.'

'Suspects?' Rosemary waved away the suggest with a flick of her fingers. 'How on earth could we be suspects? You told me yourself the phone you found belonged to that girl – what's her name? The girl who held a grudge against the Lancefields?'

'Becca Smith.'

'That's right, Becca Smith.' Rosemary nodded. 'Surely the discovery of her phone close to the gatehouse is a clear indication she was involved. Perhaps she and that Marcus Drake were working together. Perhaps he arranged for her to come up to Liberation Park and commit the murder while he attended the wedding.'

'And just how did she manage to administer taxine to Laurence while she was here? She wasn't masquerading as a guest at the wedding, she would have been noticed. And she wasn't working in the kitchens or on the bar, we had a full roster of permanent staff and no temps brought in for the event.'

'Well, I don't know.' Rosemary shrugged, a nonchalant hunch of the shoulders that suggested she didn't particularly care. 'Perhaps she simply came here to pass the stuff to Marcus so he could administer it to Laurence. It's a far more plausible explanation than looking at you or I as suspects. Marcus hated Laurence, and that girl hated the Lancefield family as a whole. What motive could we possibly have that would stack up against that?'

'Money.'

The word brought an angry blush to Rosemary Taylor's cheek. 'And just what do you mean by that?'

'DI Hall thinks that we've been struggling to keep Liberation Park afloat. She asked me if Laurence was planning to invest in the business.'

'DI Hall is just fishing in the dark. You only have to look at the woman to know she's out of her depth. Anyway, I thought she came back to talk to you about the mobile phone?'

'She did. But she went to great pains to tell me that the finding of a mobile phone is circumstantial and doesn't mean she won't be keeping all other lines of enquiry open. Including the possibility that Laurence's death was somehow connected to the business.' Jennet pressed her lips together in a forlorn attempt to stem a tear. 'As things stand, I will inherit everything Laurence had to leave: the house in Hertfordshire, the apartment in London, and his portfolio of investments. At current valuation, that's probably in the region of seventeen million.'

Her mother's face paled. 'Did you say seventeen million?'

'It wouldn't matter to me if it were seventeen billion. I would give every penny of it up if only Laurence were here today.' Jennet's face contorted. 'Why do you have to be so cold about everything? Why do you only care about the money?'

'Darling, that simply isn't true. I admit I have concerns about the business, and sometimes that makes me sound a little materialistic.'

'A little?' Jennet coughed out a laugh. 'Laurence's death is the answer to your prayers, isn't it?'

'Jennet, that's not fair.'

'No. What's not fair is that I've lost Laurence in the cruellest way possible. And all you can think about is what it means for Liberation Park.' She pulled a clean cotton handkerchief from the pocket of her dress and dabbed at her eyes. 'DI Hall is going to investigate how Becca's phone ended up outside the gatehouse, and she's going to talk to DCI Price about it. That doesn't mean she's finished with us.'

'But in the meantime, you agree next week's booking should go ahead?'

'You can do what the hell you like about next week's booking, because I won't be here to see it.' Jennet stood up and pushed the handkerchief back into her pocket. 'If DI Hall has no objections, I'll be leaving for Hertfordshire as soon as possible.'

13

Kathryn took a good, long look at Marcus Drake. He looked tired and slightly bemused; older than the handsome young man she had first encountered barely nine months ago, and more withdrawn. 'How can I help you?'

'I sought you out because wanted to ask your advice.' They were sitting on the small damask sofa in the middle of the library and he scanned her face with hopeful eyes as he spoke. 'I'm thinking of resigning from my role at Woodlands.'

The declaration took Kathryn by surprise. 'I'm sorry to hear that. I thought you were happy on St Felix?'

'I was. But I'm going up to Edinburgh as soon as Inspector Price thinks it's appropriate, to spend some time at Hemlock Row. I may stay up there indefinitely. I think it's time for a fresh start.'

'Forgive me, Marcus, but won't you be lonely?'

'You don't think it's already lonely, living with a family that thinks I'm a serial killer?' He gave a soft snort of self-deprecation. 'I know David wants me to confess to killing Laurence, but I'm not going to admit to something I didn't do, just so that family can move on. I confessed to killing Philip because I killed him. It's a simple as that. I'm sorry I took a man's life, more sorry than you could possibly know, and I'm not proud of it. But once was enough for me.' He leaned towards her. 'Why do they think it was me, Kathryn? You're close to Inspector Price. You must have some insight into his thought processes?'

Could she honestly answer that? 'Well, trite though it sounds, you have form.' She took off her reading glasses, letting them dangle at the end of their chain. 'You've already committed a murder and confessed to it, so you have the ability to take a life. You had a motive to murder Zak: he admitted to murdering your mother and the woman you loved. The jury is still out when it comes to your motive for killing Laurence.' She folded her hands neatly into her lap. 'Then there was the mobile phone found under your bed. The one that showed calls between yourself and Zak.'

'You mean the phone that showed calls between that number and Zak. It doesn't prove I made the calls. The only fingerprints found on that phone belonged to the housekeeper who found it, Nancy and David.'

'So, how do you explain the phone being under your bed in the first place?'

'Someone must have put it there. It might even have been Zak himself. We know he died in the potting shed but we don't know what he did immediately before that. The doors at Salvation Hall are never locked during the day. How do we know he didn't let himself in and plant the phone in my room?'

'How would he know it was your room?'

'He only had to look around him; there was aftershave and a razor on the dressing table, so it was obviously a man's room. And the clothes in the wardrobe would hardly have been David's or Richard's choice.'

'They dusted your room for fingerprints, Marcus. There was no evidence of Zak's prints anywhere. Just yours and the housekeeper's.'

'Then he must have worn gloves.' Marcus frowned. 'Do you think I offered him money to murder Eva?'

'You've already asked me that question and my answer hasn't changed: no, I don't. Any more than I think you murdered Laurence. But I do think you know more about this whole affair than you're revealing.'

'Would you like to elaborate on that?'

'I don't think I can, at this stage. But it feels to me as though you're hiding something, something that weighs heavily on your shoulders. And if I'm right, I can't help thinking now would be the time to share what you know with someone you can trust. If you can't speak to Ennor, then perhaps you could share it with me?'

The young man turned his head away. 'Who do you think murdered Laurence?'

'I don't know. But I know Becca's disappearance has complicated things.'

'You think she might have been responsible.'

'It's a theory, albeit a weak one.' Kathryn hesitated, and then asked, 'I don't suppose you've had any communication with Becca? You got on quite well with her once upon a time. I remember how kind you were to her after Philip's body was found.'

'You seem to forget that was before she discovered I'd killed him.' Marcus turned towards her. 'You don't seriously think I've been colluding with Becca in some ridiculous campaign of revenge against the family? What would be the point in that?' He shook his head. 'Is there any wonder I want to get away from the Lancefields? Admitting to Philip's murder doesn't give them the right to nominate me as the family scapegoat.'

'Is that the only reason you've decided not to return to St Felix? Or is there something else?' Kathryn noted a flicker of hesitation in the clear, blue eyes. 'I was wondering, perhaps, if you simply weren't happy there?'

'Well, since you insist on dragging it out of me, it's Nancy. Ever since Richard sent her back to Woodlands for good she seems hell bent on making my life a misery. It's been bad enough, trying to come to terms with Eva's death, without Nancy constantly criticising and undermining me.'

So that was it? 'She's taken Richard's decision very badly, but I think things will improve when he flies out to join you both. She's missing him, and she's missing her role as his secretary. And she's taking it out on you.'

'If only I could share your confidence.' Marcus looked deflated. 'To be honest, Kathryn, I'm just beginning to realise I don't have to put up with it. With any of it. Eva left me a legacy: a legacy I've been afraid to draw on until now. But it's the one thing that guarantees I don't have to go back to living in Richard's pocket. I'm tired of pretending we're all one big, happy family just to keep up appearances and make the old man happy. I'm tired of looking over my shoulder, and I'm tired of having to plead my own innocence.' He stretched out a hand towards her. 'You're the one person in this household that believes me. The one person who has been willing to fight my corner. But even you can't seem to understand just what my loyalty to the Lancefields is costing me. And if I can't get through to you, then I think it must be time to move on.'

*

Ennor Price never tired of the view from his study window. And that night he needed the comfort of that view in a way he'd never needed it before. He let his eyes wander down over chimneys and rooftops and the canopies of gently waving palm trees to rest on the foam-flecked, rippling waters of Penzance harbour, anchoring him to the safe and certain familiarity of his surroundings.

Barely nine months had passed since he'd stared out of that tall, arched window and contemplated the murder of Lucy Lancefield. Little had he known it would lead to his friendship with Kathryn, let alone that he would be called upon to investigate murder after murder after murder. He'd never expected to become an expert in the most heinous of crimes, if expert was what he had become. But then, he supposed, it was all a part of life's rich pattern.

Wasn't it?

He could think of a few more elaborate phrases to describe the direction of his life since they had buried Richard Lancefield's granddaughter. But none of them could convey the madness, the frustration, the sorrow or the heartache. None of them could describe the gut-wrenching sense of ineptitude that plagued him as each unexpected tragedy unfolded.

He drew his eyes away from the window and lifted the glass of chilled Cornish ale from his desk to take a long, slow drink. The latest of those misfortunes rested heavily on his mind. Barely thirty-six hours ago he had dismissed Becca Smith's disappearance as a distraction, an isolated and unimportant event that was getting in the way of a murder investigation. And yet again, time had proven him wrong. As the hours had passed, so his concern for Becca had grown.

I'd rather she was guilty and alive than innocent and dead.

Tom Parkinson's words were still ringing in his ears. And in the next few minutes he'd be speaking to DI Hall, asking her to work with him to locate the missing girl, confessing – he could hardly believe he was thinking this – that he had no idea now whether Becca was a victim or a suspect, but that it could only be in the best interests of both their investigations to find her.

He stared down at the mobile phone resting silently on his desk. It was three minutes to six, just three minutes to go until their call. Three more minutes of peaceful, solitary reflection.

He turned his eyes to the right, and the once-plain wall that now documented the thought processes of the last nine months. A diagram of the grounds at Salvation Hall; a print of Millais' painting of Ophelia, to remind him of

Lucy Lancefield; a copy of the Lancefield's family tree created for him by Kathryn, so he could understand how each of the distant cousins was related to Richard and David; a map of the Leeward Islands, the source of all the Lancefield fortunes; photographs of Lucy and Eva McWhinney, pinned side by side to the wall, their resemblance so strong they might have been sisters; and a modest, coloured postcard bearing the image that haunted him the most: David Martin's study of Lady Elizabeth Murray and her cousin Dido Belle; the print that had been a gift from Nancy to Lucy in the days before her death.

Somewhere in those images, he thought, is the answer to end all answers. If only I could fathom…

His hopeful reverie was shattered by a sharp, persistent vibration, and his mobile phone suddenly shuffled sideways across the desk. Price heaved out a sigh and jabbed at the screen with a finger. 'DI Hall? You're three minutes early.'

'Well, you know how it is, DCI Price. Us northern girls are keen. We just want to get on with the job.' She sounded curiously upbeat. 'I take it Sergeant Parkinson has kept you in the picture while you've been at Salvation Hall? Only we're drowning in suspects up here now, I was hoping you might be able to take one or two of them off our hands.'

'I'll do what I can, but I'm not making any promises.' Price sipped on his ale. 'I've spoken to David Lancefield, Marcus Drake and Nancy Woodlands this afternoon, but I haven't turned up anything significant that would help to identify Laurence's killer. For what it's worth, David and Nancy both think Marcus was responsible, but neither of them can offer any hard evidence. In both cases it's based on their assumption he was also responsible for murdering Zak Smith.'

'For which there is also a lack of hard evidence.'

'Correct.' Price put down his glass. 'I've asked Nancy and Marcus to remain at Salvation Hall for a few days, to give you the opportunity to talk to them if you want it. Both have agreed, but Marcus is planning to travel up to Edinburgh later this week so you might want to make an early decision. Always assuming you think there is a benefit in speaking to him.'

'Are you saying Marcus is no longer your number one suspect for my murder case?' Hall laughed softly. 'Is he your number one suspect for Becca Smith's disappearance?'

'No. But her disappearance has made the family nervous.' Price folded his arms on the desk. 'How did you come across the phone?'

'Jennet Payne found it behind the gatehouse. She'd gone for a walk to clear her head, and claims she saw it just lying on the path. We have no reason at this stage not to believe her. Though it doesn't make any sense, does it? The phone is here, but there's no sign of Becca.'

'Then we have to take steps to bring sense into the equation. I think we make the assumption she travelled by train to East Yorkshire, look for evidence of that, and if we find it, we request a thorough search of Liberation Park'

'When will we get that evidence?'

'I'm hoping by tomorrow evening at the latest.' Price lifted his head as he spoke, and slowly ran his eyes once more across the wall, taking in the maps, the family tree, the photographs, the prints… 'and Ophelia lying peacefully in her watery grave.' He whispered the words under his breath. And then a familiar, unmistakeable prickling sensation made its way across the back of his neck. 'DI Hall, I'm going to have to call you back. I can't explain right now, but there's something I have to do. Something I have to see for myself.'

Something, he thought as he abruptly ended the call, that couldn't possibly wait until the morning.

*

'It's odd, isn't it?' Nancy leaned against the arm of a plush, velvet-covered armchair and folded her arms to steady herself. 'Just as you begin to move into Holly Cottage, Becca goes missing.'

'There's nothing odd about it at all, Nancy. It's not even a coincidence. Why do you always try to make mischief out of nothing?' Barbara bent down to a large cardboard box and pulled out a small, gilt-framed oil painting. 'David insisted I bring this over from the main house, but I don't know where to hang it. I thought it might go over the fireplace, but I can't decide if it's too small.' She lifted the picture up and held it against the chimney breast. 'Would it work?'

Nancy leaned back a little to consider the placement. 'No, it's too small.' She tilted her head. 'Is that *The Redemption*?'

'Of course it's *The Redemption*. What other sailing ship would I be hanging in my living room?' The older woman lowered her arms with a frown. 'What if I just stand it on the mantelpiece?' She rested the painting gently on the ledge and stepped back to look at it. 'Yes, that could work. A pair of candlesticks on one side, and a jug of flowers on the other.' She turned her head to look over her shoulder at Nancy. 'Have you just come here to plague me, or are you going to make yourself useful? If you dig into that crate behind the sofa you'll find a kettle and a box of mugs. You know where the kitchen is. I'm sure you came over to Holly Cottage often enough when Becca lived here.'

Nancy smiled. 'That's what I love about you, Barbara. I never have to wonder what you're thinking. You're so exquisitely direct and to the point.' She slid off the chair's arm and wandered over to the sofa. 'Is this furniture new, or have you had it reupholstered?'

'It's been reupholstered. I think they've done a marvellous job. Velvet isn't always easy to work with.'

'It will certainly bring a feeling of comfort. It was

nothing more than a hovel when Becca lived here. She showed no respect for the place.' Nancy reached into the crate behind the sofa and pulled out the kettle. 'Did Inspector Price come and speak to you today? About Laurence and what might have happened to him?'

'No, why should he? I wasn't at the wedding.'

'But you might have had an opinion.' Nancy rested the kettle on the edge of the crate. 'What do you think happened to him?'

'I have no idea. I try not to bother myself with things that don't concern me.' Barbara had moved away from the fireplace and was busy pulling a framed photograph from a large, plastic bag. 'I didn't ask you about the spinet, Nancy. Was your mother pleased when it arrived in St Felix? I hope she's enjoyed playing it.'

'You're changing the subject, Barbara.'

'Of course I am.' Barbara pulled on the stand at the back of the frame and positioned the picture at a jaunty angle on top of a nearby bookcase. 'And now I'm going to change it again. You haven't told me yet, how you feel about being at Woodlands.'

'Truthfully? It feels odd to be back there permanently. I'm not used to it after so many years in England. Were it not for the fact that Richard plans to return to St Felix, I would ask if I might come back to Salvation Hall.'

'Then you must be pleased DCI Price has asked you to delay your flight back.'

'For the opportunity to spend a little more time here, I am pleased. But I cannot see why the police may want to speak to me again. I've already told them everything I know.' She shook her head, jiggling long, glossy curls. 'I am sorry Laurence is dead. I didn't have much of a relationship with him, but I do think he is a loss to the family. He knew so much about Obeah, and about the history of the St Aldate's plantation. I was quite looking forward to him visiting St Felix with Jennet. I was going to take them over to St Aldate's to meet the family who live there now.' Nancy pushed out her lip. 'Do you realise, Barbara, that you are the only remaining cousin of all the distant cousins Richard and David discovered?'

'Of course I do. Though I don't see why you would feel the need to point it out to me.'

'I was thinking how unsupported the family will be if Marcus is eventually found guilty of Zak's murder. There will only be yourself and David. And much as I would wish Richard would live forever, we must be practical – he may not have many years left. And those he has, he plans to spend resting on St Felix. Of course, if Richard were to recognise me as a member of the family…'

'Nancy, you need to give him time.'

'You said you would speak to him on my behalf.'

'I said I'd speak to him when the time was right. I thought you understood that.' And now was not the time to let Nancy know she had already tried and that Richard, when approached, had refused to even discuss the matter.

Barbara felt a sudden, unbidden pang of compassion for the girl. She was infuriating, headstrong, and the few weeks she had already spent back on St Felix seemed to have sharpened her edges and fuelled her sense of entitlement.

But she was still Richard's only surviving granddaughter. She was the natural heir to the Lancefield fortunes, and nothing more than an old man's prejudices and obstinacy stood in the way of her being openly recognised and inheriting what was rightfully hers.

14

Richard Lancefield beamed at Kathryn across the supper table. 'It is quite a pleasure to have your company this evening. I had assumed you would be consoling Inspector Price. He must be quite overwrought.'

That was one word for it. 'The trouble with Ennor is he's his own worst enemy. The more the pressure mounts up, the more difficult he finds it to let go and unwind. He was like a coiled spring when he left Salvation Hall this afternoon.' And the coil would likely be even tighter after a free and frank discussion with DI Hall. 'Anyway, it's been a long time since you and I were able to just sit and enjoy a meal and a glass of wine. How on earth did you manage to come up with paella?'

Richard chuckled. 'The same way I always arrange my catering these days. I phoned down to The Lancefield Arms and asked Amber to send me something from the kitchen.' He waved his fork towards the other end of the table. 'She's sent lemon posset and a cheese tray for dessert. It's remarkable how quickly she's got the hang of my palate. A wise head on young shoulders. Very much like yourself.'

'I don't feel I've been able to offer up much in the way

of wisdom lately. Now that everything has been sent back to St Felix there doesn't seem much left for me to help with.' In truth, there hadn't been much she had been *asked* to help with. Not since Ennor had taken to watching the family like a hawk, waiting for whichever of them murdered Zak to slip up.

The old man seemed to read her thoughts. 'I know this has been a difficult time for you: your loyalties have been tested, and I don't judge you for it. I've watched your blossoming relationship with DCI Price with great pleasure.' He put down his fork and patted her hand with his gnarled fingers. 'You may not have realised it but you were a lonely soul when you arrived at Salvation Hall, and now you have a family in us and a fierce ally and friend in the inspector. I would never, I hope, ask you to compromise your own sense of justice and fair play by pledging allegiance to us, regardless of the outcome. Loyalty is to be valued, but not if it is blind to the consequences; it must be wisely given.' He drew back his fingers and tapped on the table. 'Which is why I have sought your company and your wisdom this evening. Not to ask for blind loyalty, but the benefit of your wisdom.' He chuckled again. 'You are still my Minerva.'

Kathryn put down her fork and picked up her wine glass with a slight sense of unease. 'Is this about Marcus?'

'No, it's about Becca. Inspector Price has apologised for not telling me she had disappeared. But I had the sense he would not have done so, had the local newspaper not got hold of the story. For some reason he chose to keep the information from us.'

'If you're wondering why he made that choice, then I'm afraid I can't be much help. Only to say he didn't think it would be fair to Becca's family to broadcast the news, when they've already been through so much.'

'So, it wasn't because he considers her a suspect for Laurence's murder?' Richard scratched thoughtfully at his chin. 'Speaking for myself, I find it very hard to believe

Becca would have murdered Laurence after everything I've done for her. Despite her disloyalty I have given her every possible support because I don't want my goddaughter to grow up in the shadow of her mother's criminal record. But perhaps I have to accept that my support is not enough. And I have to draw the line at murder.' Richard bowed his head. 'It broke my heart to accept that Philip must have murdered Lucy, not just because he was my friend and counsellor, but because of the impact it might have on little Francesca in the years to come.'

'But how can I be of help? I'm not quite sure what advice you are asking for.'

'If there is a possibility that Becca murdered Laurence, then Inspector Price is the man to investigate the crime. I wondered whether I should speak to him directly about it. Whether he would welcome the question, or consider it an interference?'

Kathryn frowned, and blew out a breath. 'I can't confirm for you whether Becca is a suspect. That would have to come from the police.' She couldn't fight a growing sense of disappointment. 'I suppose you would welcome Becca as a suspect if it drew suspicion away from the family?' She was trying to tread carefully, but the path was littered with minefields. 'You are bearing in mind that her brother's murderer still hasn't been identified? I don't think you could reasonably expect her to be suspected of murdering Zak and leaving his body in your potting shed. That crime still has to be solved.'

'That crime is already solved. It is only the lack of evidence which prevents the good inspector from bringing it to the door the perpetrator.' Richard licked his lips. 'Which brings me to the matter of Marcus. I take it you've heard of his plans to spend some time in Edinburgh? I wondered if, in your opinion, he was running away from something? The police have failed to find anything concrete to confirm he was responsible for killing Smith, so I am struggling to see what he might be running from? I have already provided him with a safe harbour and a new life in St Felix. What more could he possibly want?'

Apart from the knowledge that he was believed and the freedom to choose for himself? 'Is it really a new life, with Nancy standing in the wings, watching over him?' Kathryn reached out for the bottle of Chablis on the table and began to fill her glass. 'Is it possible Marcus might be finding her difficult to handle?'

'I viewed that as part of his rehabilitation.' Richard's smile was a wry one. 'But I can see she needs me there to keep her in check. It may be that giving her the privilege of serving as my secretary at Salvation Hall has damaged her sense of propriety. She has developed ambitions far beyond her place, and seems inclined to forget that Marcus is a member of the family.'

'Just as she, herself, is a member of your family.' Kathryn's pulse began to quicken. 'For pity's sake, Richard, has the time not come to recognise her? Has it truly never occurred to you that the way to family harmony might be to accept publicly she is your granddaughter, and give her the position and the respect she deserves?'

*

The heavy oak door at the front of Salvation Hall was already open when Price arrived, and David Lancefield was leaning against the doorframe, his face a study of faint bewilderment. 'I was over at Holly Cottage when you called. Marcus said you asked for me and not for Kathryn. Does that mean there has been news of Becca Smith?'

'No, but I need your help, Mr Lancefield – David.' Price had parked his car beside the yew hedge and he waved his key fob towards it to lock it. 'I'd like your permission to walk down to the lake. And I'd like you to come with me, if you would.'

If David was further confused by the request he was

too polite to say so. 'Let's take Samson with us.' He whistled over his shoulder for the terrier and the creature was out of the door in a moment, trotting gleefully along the front of the house before disappearing through the archway in the adjacent wall. 'It would appear he already knows where we're going.' David let the door swing shut behind him as he stepped forward to follow in Samson's wake. 'May I ask what brings you here so late in the evening?'

'Of course.' Price knew the answer would sound bizarre. 'If it's not inconvenient, I would like your permission to stand beside the lake for a while.'

'Stand beside it?'

'Yes.' How the hell was he supposed to explain it? 'Do you believe in intuition?'

'Well, I wouldn't say I was a superstitious man, by any stretch of the imagination. But I think I understand that sometimes we are guided by our instincts and not by conscious reasoning.'

'Conscious reasoning is a significant part of my work as a detective. But sometimes it simply isn't enough.' Price ducked his head as he followed David through the archway and into the garden. To his left, the terrace where Stella Drake Lancefield lost her life was illuminated in the fading light by the table lamps in the dining room beyond. To the right, the rolling lawns and flowerbeds leading down to the vast ornamental lake were glowing under the diminishing late-May sunlight. He narrowed his eyes to a squint. The surface of the water's edge was green with swathes of leaves, round and waxy saucers floating freely on their fleshy stems. He turned his head quizzically in David's direction. 'When do the waterlilies flower?'

'From June to September, usually. Though you might spot one or two early bloomers. You will have to look closely. They will be closed up now, the flowers always close in the evening.' David's brow creased as they began to walk slowly across the grass. 'Your visit has nothing to do with horticulture, of course. Just what is it you hope to see?'

'I don't know. I only know that if I stop trying to force all the available facts into a pattern to suit my purpose, there is a slim – and probably desperate – chance that my brain will take all the bits and make sense of them for me.'

'The penny will drop of its own accord?'

'Something like that. I don't think I'm the only old-school detective who thinks it helps to sit by the side of a crime scene and wait for the answer to come.' Price was at the water's edge now and he began to walk slowly to the right, staring down into the murky depths as he went. 'This is where Lucy's body was found, isn't it?'

'I didn't see for myself, Inspector. You might recall I was in Edinburgh when my daughter was murdered.'

'Forgive me. I was thinking again of the facts.' Price turned to look over his shoulder at David. 'Do you believe Philip McKeith was responsible for her death?'

'Is it necessary for me to answer that? Am I never to be allowed to put the past to rest?'

'Can you put the past to rest when Zak Smith's killer is walking free? When that same killer might also have murdered Laurence Payne?' Price paused, and then added, 'When that killer might also have murdered Lucy?'

'Might also have…?' David's jaw clenched. 'I will give you the benefit of the doubt, Inspector Price, because I believe you have the interests of justice at heart. But if you are trying to suggest now that Marcus murdered my daughter…'

'I didn't mean…' Price stopped, and stared hard across the lake. 'Can you see something in the water? At the far side.'

David lifted a hand to shield his eyes from the low glare of the sun. 'It's just the light on the water.'

'No, it isn't.' Price quickened his step and paced along the water's edge. 'It's where we recovered Philip's body, and there's something floating there.' His pulse was beginning to race. This is what he'd come for: for his intuition to lead him. He'd wanted the answer to come. But he hadn't wanted history to repeat itself. And if this answer was what he feared, it could be the biggest regret of his life.

It took him barely fifteen seconds to reach the spot. He stared down into the water, his heart pounding and his mouth dry, and then he threw up a hand behind him. 'Stay where you are.' He bent his head to take a closer look, and felt his stomach churn with a gnawing, desperate ache as he took in the bloated face, the muddied broderie anglaise trim of her blouse, the strands of algae threaded through the blonde wisps of hair that eddied like a halo around her head. For the second time in his life he was looking down at John Everett Millais' painting: Ophelia submitting peacefully to her watery grave.

Only this time Lucy Amelia Lancefield wasn't cast in the starring role. And there had been nothing either peaceful or submissive about this particular Ophelia's muddy, ignominious end.

15

Tom Parkinson stared down at the sheet of paper on his desk with tired, misty eyes. 'We finally fished her out at about one o'clock.' The phone's receiver, resting in the crook of his neck, began to slip and he put up a hand to stop it. 'We're due to see the pathologist at two this afternoon, but the initial view was strangulation. The scarf used as a ligature was still around her neck.'

'So, she was dead before she went into the water?' At the end of the line, Jim Collinson sounded subdued. 'It's not the outcome any of us expected, is it?'

And not the outcome any of them, particularly Tom Parkinson, had wanted. He was still struggling to comprehend how intuition had led Ennor Price to discover the body, given how low an opinion his senior officer had of the girl compared with his own mostly patient forbearance with her temper, her hostility and her tantrums. The triumph of an older man's experience over hope, perhaps. 'She didn't deserve it, Jim. She was a belligerent, venomous little baggage, but she didn't deserve what was done to her.'

'It sounds like it matters to you.'

And that was the truth. It did matter to him. 'They always tell you not to get involved, don't they? That you can't do your job if it gets personal. But how the hell are you supposed to do the job if it *doesn't* get personal? There's a three-year-old kiddie without a mother or father this morning. I've got a toddler myself.' It was beyond his comprehension how anyone could murder a young woman and deprive a child of their only surviving parent. And cruel in the extreme to sink her body in the spot where the man she had loved had met his death. 'Anyway, from your perspective it eliminates her from the investigation into Laurence Payne's death. That should clear the way for you a bit.'

'Should it?' Collinson snuffled a laugh. 'Steph doesn't think so. She was on the phone to me last night within minutes of your guvnor sharing the news. We've called off the search for Becca, because it's pretty obvious she never came up to Liberation Park. But there's still the matter of the hotel brochure and the mobile phone. Steph has a new theory: that the motive for Becca's murder was to keep her out of sight so we would go on looking for her, and never for the real killer. It was a crafty bit of misdirection that's come unstuck. Which means it must have been carried out by someone down in your neck of the woods: most likely, Marcus Drake.' The sergeant paused, then said 'I might as well give you an early heads up… we'll be coming down to Cornwall to question him.'

'Has Price been told?'

'I don't know. Anyway, we're going back to Liberation Park this morning to break the news to Jennet Payne. Steph wants to question her again about where and how she found Becca's mobile phone.'

'Were there any fingerprints on it?'

'Only Jennet's, and those of one of our officers. It must have been wiped clean before it was placed on the path.' Collinson sniffed. 'What's happening at your end today?'

'Price is at Salvation Hall already. It was difficult to do much last night. We managed to recover the body under arc lights, but we had to settle for taping off the outbuildings in readiness for a search today. The pathologist thinks Becca died on Thursday but wasn't put into the water until one or possibly two days later. She'll be confirming that this afternoon. In the meantime, we'll be looking for evidence of where the body might have been stored.' Again. 'We're also going down into the lake. There was a piece of cord tied around Becca's wrist when we pulled her out. We think it was tied to something intended to weight the body down, but it didn't hold.'

'I take it you've already considered the obvious question?'

'Why the body didn't go straight into the water?' Parkinson felt his jaw clench. 'Because the bastard who killed her didn't have time to do it before driving up to Yorkshire for a wedding.' He swallowed hard. 'Forget I said that, Jim. Only I've been watching that girl's life unravel ever since Marcus Drake murdered her partner.'

'Don't worry about it. The number of murders you've dealt with over the past few months would challenge anybody. I take it you're going to be questioning the family today?'

'Price is doing that. I'm going over to Hayle to break the news to Becca's mother. We still need a formal identification on the body. I'm hoping a family friend will help with that if her mother doesn't want to do it.'

'Well, I don't envy you that one. But I'll leave you to get on with it. One of us will be in touch later this morning about the trip to Cornwall. In the meantime, you know where to find us.'

Parkinson closed his eyes as Collinson ended the call, but it didn't bring him any comfort. Truth be told, the scene that had greeted him at Salvation Hall the night before had been imprinted so deeply on his soul he didn't think the image would ever leave him in peace again. He couldn't blank out the sight of Price, ashen-faced, pacing restlessly up and down beside the lake; the police diver, already waist-deep in water, his hands gently steadying the body, holding it safe until the arrival of the pathologist; and Becca herself, her once-pretty face bloated and discoloured; her badly bleached hair stained green with pondweed and algae; her long, white broderie anglaise blouse still ballooned with the water that had inflated it. It was a brutal way to be dismissed from the list of suspects lined up to answer for Laurence Payne's murder.

And he would never be able to forgive himself if he and Price couldn't bring her killer to justice.

*

'I think you should have something to eat.' Barbara turned a solicitous eye to David. 'It's not going to be an easy day and you're already suffering from lack of sleep.'

David waved the suggestion away with a weary hand. 'I can't think about food. I'm still trying to process what happened yesterday evening. That poor girl...' His voice trailed away. 'I wanted to climb into the lake and pull her out, but Inspector Price held me back. He said she had to be recovered by the experts, to ensure no damage was done to the crime scene.' His mouth twisted, anguished by the thought. 'He meant Becca, Barbara. *She* was the crime scene. No longer a human being, but a *crime scene*.'

His cousin gave a reassuring murmur. 'Could you tell what had happened to her?'

'No. But she was wearing a white blouse and denim jeans, the clothing mentioned in yesterday morning's newspaper coverage; the clothes she was supposedly wearing when she went missing on Thursday.'

They were seated side by side at the table in the conservatory, and Barbara pulled her chair a little closer to David's, close enough to lay a hand gently on his arm. 'It's given you a nasty shock. Do you think it might be better to rest in your room, rather than sitting here?' She tilted her head towards the vast expanse of glass in front of them.

Beyond the window, in the garden, uniformed and plain-clothed police officers were drifting back and forth. 'It won't do you any good to watch the proceedings. If Inspector Price finds anything, I'm sure he'll come straight to the house and tell us.'

'But I want to watch. I want to be involved in the search for her killer, and if watching is the only way I can do that, then I will watch.' He clamped his lips inwards. 'We treated her very badly, Barbara. We expected too much of her, and my father cast her out without stopping to think of the consequences.'

'You don't need to remind me. Richard cast her out because she tried to warn him Jason was a danger to the family. How do you think that makes me feel? Jason was my nephew.' At least that was always how she'd thought of him. 'Did you notice how Nancy and Marcus reacted when Inspector Price broke the news? They both looked dumbstruck, but that's no guarantee of an easy conscience, is it? And it wouldn't be the first body Marcus had consigned to the lake.' It was a difficult truth, but it had to be said. 'Hopefully, Inspector Price will make some headway with his investigation now. He has to bring all of this madness to an end. Whatever the cost to the family.'

'You're thinking of what will happen if it were Marcus.'

'I'm thinking of what *will* happen when the killer is named.' They would have to be prepared. 'Have Marcus and Nancy always been so openly at odds with each other?'

'I wouldn't have said so. Of course they were both in Lucy's shadow when she was alive. My daughter was a force of nature, she quite took after her mother rather than me. You know, she planned to turn Salvation Hall into a hotel, just as Jennet and her mother have done with Liberation Park. The parallel is quite remarkable.' David turned to look at Barbara. 'Lucy wanted to rebrand this place to bury the family's heritage. Marcus was completely on board with the idea, and he already had a background in hospitality and business development. I can't imagine Nancy would have liked it, but she had come to terms with it. In any case, she had no influence over the decision. It was my father who put his foot down.'

'Did you think it a good idea?'

'Not particularly. I'll admit I wanted to bury the heritage, but I would have been quite happy to do that by disposing of the estates altogether.'

'And now?'

'I'm still trying to make my peace with it. I've given my father my word I'll take care of everything after he's gone, but I was expecting to rely very heavily on Marcus. If he is proven to be the killer, I'm not sure how I will cope. I know you and Kathryn will support me here in England, but I hoped he would handle things out in St Felix. To be my "man on the ground", as it were.' David frowned. 'Where is Marcus, by the way?'

'He's in the drawing room, waiting for Inspector Price. I think Nancy has gone to the Dower House to speak to Richard.'

'And Kathryn?'

'Probably on her way from Penzance as we speak. I was going to ask her to help me finish hanging the curtains in Holly Cottage today, but that will have to wait until the police have completed their search. I don't know what they expect to find there. I've been in and out of the place every day for the last week, and I haven't seen anything out of the ordinary.' Barbara wrinkled her nose. 'We'll have to find something in the main house to occupy us in the meantime. Perhaps I'll use the time to finish clearing out Lucy's suite.' There was something she wanted to ask, but it wasn't the easiest of questions. 'Did Lucy get on well with Nancy, David?'

'Oh, yes, I think so. I never heard of any unpleasantness between them. Why on earth should there be?' He took a moment to think about it. 'There was the incident of the print, of course. A little frisson of discord when Nancy gave Lucy a framed print to hang on the wall in her suite. It wasn't to Lucy's taste at all, and I think she may have been a little ungracious at the time. But it soon smoothed over.' David leaned towards his cousin. 'If you want to know more about the print, have a word with Kathryn. She showed quite an interest in it herself, when she arrived at Salvation Hall.'

*

'There are times, Inspector Price, when I wonder whether I should just confess to all the unsolved murders, even though I'm not guilty of them. I've never been to prison, thanks to the skills of Richard's legal team, but right now the idea of a structured day, copious amounts of solitude, and the guaranteed certainty of a mundane, uneventful existence look positively appealing.'

It was a scenario that might soon become a reality for Marcus, whether he confessed to the murders or not, and Price couldn't help wondering if the young man was tempting fate. 'If it's mundanity you're after, I have some pretty mundane questions for you.' They were sitting at the darker end of the long, narrow drawing room at Salvation Hall and the policeman cast a surreptitious glance around him. The grandeur of the room was breathtaking: his eye didn't need to travel as far as the vast bay window at the other end for him to know that sunlight – unimpeded by the presence of drapes or shutters – would be casting its rays through the glass, warming the centuries-old mahogany floorboards and glinting against the ornate frames of the family portraits that adorned the walls. Was the rarified atmosphere of the Lancefield family's estates finally getting to Marcus Drake? There was only one way to find out. 'When did you last see Becca Smith?'

Marcus shrugged. 'It would be months ago, before I

left for St Felix the first time. After Richard dismissed her from Salvation Hall, she took a part-time job at a café in Penzance. I called in one day for a coffee and she was there, behind the counter.'

'Did you speak?'

'No. She took one look at me and bolted into the kitchen. Another woman came out to serve me.'

That was hardly a surprise. 'Has she made any attempt to contact you over the last few months?'

'No. Why would she?'

'She made no attempt to contact you after Zak's death?'

'No. I know Richard's lawyer got in touch with her to offer her legal assistance, and I believe Richard himself met with her to discuss the situation. But no one else in the family was involved, as far as I know.'

Price ran his tongue around his teeth. 'You do realise this turn of events immediately eliminates her from the enquiry into Laurence's death?'

'Of course I do.'

'And that it narrows the field somewhat?'

'Yes. Probably to myself, David and Nancy.'

And possibly further than that. Price pulled a notebook and pen from the pocket of his jacket and flipped the notebook open. 'Can you tell me what time the three of you left Salvation Hall on Thursday?'

'Just after one o'clock. I thought we were leaving it a bit late but David had some estate business to attend to in Newlyn before we could leave, and Nancy had an errand to do in Penzance.'

'And you were here at Salvation Hall?'

'Yes. After breakfast I moved into the conservatory to read the morning papers, and then I spent an hour or so with Richard in the Dower House discussing the Woodlands estate. After that I walked down into the village to pick up some provisions for the journey. I took Samson with me. I'm sure he'll be happy to provide me with an alibi, if you ask him.'

Price forced a smile. 'I'll have a word with him later.' He scribbled a few words in the notebook and then asked, 'What time did you get back from Liberation Park on Saturday?'

'I think it was around seven thirty. We made good time, considering it was the weekend.' Marcus frowned. 'And no doubt you will want to know what I did when we got back. Well,' he scratched at his ear, 'Barbara had kindly prepared a light supper, so we all ate together in the kitchen. At least, Nancy, Barbara and I ate together. David had gone over to the Dower House. We didn't learn until after supper that Kathryn had called to share the news about Laurence.' The young man's face took on a puzzled look. 'Was Becca already dead by then, Inspector Price?'

'I'm afraid I can't answer that question yet.' Not least because he wouldn't have the answer for another couple of hours. 'And after supper, what did you do then?'

'David came back to the main house and broke the news of Laurence's death. We were all shocked, obviously. Nancy and Barbara stayed in the kitchen, talking, and David asked me to go with him to the library, which I did.' A cloud crossed Marcus's face. 'Only when we were alone did I discover he wanted to grill me about my latest incarnation of "serial killer".'

'He accused you of murdering Laurence?'

'He might as well have done. He asked me to do the decent thing and confess. Which is quite a challenge when you're innocent.' Marcus blinked, and looked suddenly much younger than his years. 'And now I suppose you've come to do the same, Inspector Price.'

Price sighed, and leaned back against the sofa's cushions. 'If you didn't murder Zak, Laurence and Becca, who did?'

'I really couldn't say.' The vulnerable expression, so fleetingly settled on Marcus's face, made way for an indifferent, almost vacuous gaze. 'Was Becca's body weighted down, Inspector Price?'

'Why do you ask? Do you think that's relevant to how and why she died?'

'When I killed Philip McKeith in the heat of the moment, I put his body in the lake to hide it. I never denied the fact. And I weighted it down with a set of iron manacles, to make sure there was no way in hell the body would float up to the surface. If I had murdered Becca, don't you think I would have done the same this time?'

'Possibly, if there had been something available to weight it down with. But all the manacles and chains and other abominable paraphernalia that was available to you then have been sent back to St Felix.' Price lowered his voice. 'And I don't recall you weighting Lucy's body down with anything when you put it into the water. Was that because she was a woman, and you couldn't bring yourself to do it?'

16

'I've already booked my tickets.' DI Hall sank back into her office chair. 'And before you ask, I don't need to go home and pack. I brought an overnight bag with me.'

Jim Collinson met the news with a visible shrug, though he wasn't sure it was quite enough to mask his disappointment. 'You're the boss.' It hadn't taken long for her to forget they were a team, but it would be pointless to ask why she hadn't discussed it with him first. 'I mentioned to Tom Parkinson that we'd be travelling down to Cornwall, but I didn't realise it was going to be as soon as today.' Or that she'd decided to make the journey without him. He studied her face and thought he saw a hint of sudden hesitation. 'What time's your train?'

'I'm on the twelve twenty-eight: change at Sheffield and arrive in Penzance around ten to nine. It's a tight change, but with a fair wind I'll make it.' She answered with uncertain eyes, her confidence ebbing slightly with the realisation her news had not been welcome. 'Look, Jim, I thought we needed to move fast, so I just went ahead on the assumption I'd be travelling alone. And I need you to hold the fort up here.'

'Does DCI Price know you'll be arriving today?'

'No. I have tried to call, but he's not picking up.' She

rested her arms on the desk. 'You do understand that I've got to take control of this? We've already agreed that Becca's phone turning up at Liberation Park could be an attempt at misdirection, and so far it's worked, hasn't it? We've taken the brochure that was found in her kitchen, added it to the mobile phone, and jumped to the wrong conclusion.' She tapped her fingers on the desk. 'Hasn't the similarity struck you yet?'

'Similarity to what?'

'What happened with Philip McKeith.' Hall turned back to look at the sergeant. 'It was assumed McKeith murdered Lucy Lancefield because he disappeared. Everyone thought he'd gone on the run. According to Price, Becca even received text messages from his mobile phone, as if he was still alive. But he turned up dead, didn't he? His body had been deposited in that bloody lake at Salvation Hall, just like Becca's body. It's almost the same piece of misdirection.' She leaned forward and looked into Collinson's face. 'Marcus Drake was responsible for that piece of misdirection.'

He couldn't deny she had a point and yet still he wasn't convinced. Would Drake be foolish enough to set the same trail? 'This all hinges on who had the opportunity to plant Becca's phone up here, doesn't it? Three of them travelled to the wedding. How do we know it wasn't one of the other two?'

'David Lancefield or Nancy Woodlands?' Hall frowned. 'What motive would either of them have to murder Laurence Payne?'

'Isn't that something we should be trying to find out?' The words were out before Collinson could stop them. He saw a flash of indignation in Hall's deep, brown eyes, and his heart sank. 'I just meant...'

'I know what you meant.' The indignation made way for a weary kind of resignation, and she let out a deep sigh. 'We both knew this wasn't going to be easy. But it wasn't my fault you were passed over for the promotion.' She slipped her glasses off her nose, holding them down in front of her so that she could examine the lenses. 'I know you've got the ability to run this case just as well as I have. And I know you'll have your own ideas about how we should go about it. But neither of us can ignore the fact that I'm the senior officer now, and it's up to me how we play it.' She leaned sideways to pull a tissue from the pocket of her trousers. 'I'm making the assumption at this stage that Marcus Drake is the most likely suspect for Laurence Payne's murder. I'm making that assumption on the basis he's already confessed to one murder and that he admitted to setting a false trail by sinking the victim's body in the lake at Salvation Hall. In addition, we know there was bad blood between Marcus and Laurence; information that was provided by Jennet Payne and backed up by DCI Price. In some respects, whether he murdered Becca Smith is neither here nor there.'

'But the investigation into Becca's death is a current one, and it's on Price's patch. Don't you think we should wait to see what happens as a result of the interviews he's doing at Salvation Hall today?'

'No, I don't. It's more than likely Marcus murdered Smith, and Price has failed to bring that home. How do we know he'll run a successful investigation into Becca's murder? We can't just sit on our hands and hope he can make a case.'

'Then surely we need to work with him. We need to collaborate, not just wade in unannounced as if his investigation is inconsequential.'

Hall raised her glasses to her face and breathed heavily on the lenses. 'And is that what I'm doing?' She rubbed vigorously at the glass with the tissue, her eyes focused on the job in hand. 'Wading in?'

'Yesterday you were convinced Jennet Payne had a hand in her husband's death.'

'That was before Becca Smith's body was found.' Hall balanced the glasses back on her nose. 'I'd appreciate a lift to the station, Jim. And then I'd like you to go over to Liberation Park as we'd planned, to break the news about Becca Smith and see if you can get any more information on the finding of her phone. While you're there, you can let Jennet know we're turning our attention back to the Lancefield family.'

*

Kathryn rolled the captain's chair a little closer to the desk and rubbed at her eyes with a weary fist. She was tired that morning: tired from being up until the early hours; tired of the drama; tired of the killing. She had arrived at Salvation Hall quietly and slunk into the library almost unnoticed by everyone except Samson. The terrier, perhaps sensing her discomfort and her need for a supportive companion, had followed her silently into the library and now lay curled up beside her feet, his soft, warm body pressing gently and reassuringly against her ankle.

It occurred to her now that of all the killings, the murder of Becca Smith had been the one which had affected her the most. All of the others had left her numb, as if she were standing outside of the drama. She had never met Lucy or Philip, never met Dennis Speed or Geraldine Morton: they were little more than names to her; players in a performance for which she hadn't even been in the audience. Stella, Eva and Laurence she had barely known, and Zak Smith she had seen but never engaged with. But Becca?

There had been a time, when Becca was the housekeeper at Salvation Hall and Nancy away in St Felix, that Kathryn had been required to keep the girl in line. The arrangement had not been an easy one. But the girl had been real, in every sense of the word: noisy, petulant and unafraid to speak her mind, she had worn her passion for the late Philip McKeith on her sleeve, and her unabated resentment of the Lancefields like a twisted badge of honour.

And now, in one final, unintended act of revenge, she had turned the full glare of the spotlight directly back onto the family. She had delivered the truth from beyond the grave: the murderer lay within the Lancefield's household. Someone Kathryn had lived and worked shoulder to shoulder with over the last nine months had lured a man to the potting shed to strike him with such ferocity that his skull was shattered; someone she had trusted must have administered poison to a man on the night of his wedding, leaving his newly wedded wife a widow; someone she might have defended had strangled Becca and dumped her body in the lake, leaving her fatherless child an orphan.

Whoever it was, she had dined with them, laughed with them, commiserated with them, possibly even protected them. She had maintained her loyalty to the family, the killer amongst them, while Ennor had gone diligently in pursuit of the truth. After Zak's murder, when she refused to believe Marcus was guilty, Ennor had challenged her to show him the real killer. And she had failed to rise to the challenge. And now she was beginning to see why: showing him the killer would mean pointing the finger at a friend. No, more than that; it would mean admitting to herself that someone she deemed a friend was capable of such unspeakable acts of violence.

The thought touched a nerve and she shivered, lifting her eyes to the wall above the desk. The collage of framed photographs had initially been Kathryn's own idea: a pictorial reminder of the work she was doing for Richard, a way to focus her mind on building more than a historical family tree. She had become part of Richard's mission to build a flesh-and-blood family to support his son in the wake of his daughter's death. But how many of those newly discovered cousins had lost their lives in the process? Only in the last few days had Richard proudly added a newly acquired photograph of Laurence and

Jennet to the collection. And only in the last few days had Laurence died.

Kathryn stared at the photograph. Four days ago, she and Ennor had driven to Liberation Park to join in Laurence and Jennet's wedding celebrations. David, Nancy and Marcus had joined them. And between the moment of their arrival and the eve of the wedding, one of them must have administered a decoction of taxine to the groom. But when, and how, could it have happened? Even more to the point, *why* had it happened? David had no reason to dislike Laurence that Kathryn could think of and Nancy barely knew him. If anything, Nancy's tenuous family connection to Laurence should have made her his defender. Only Marcus had the anger, the bitterness, the motive to do away with the man he blamed for ruining his own chances of happiness. How could Kathryn ever hope to prove to Ennor that Marcus wasn't the killer, when she couldn't deny that he alone had the motive for the killing?

Or was she looking at the problem from completely the wrong way up?

She let out a sigh and rested her elbows on the desk, lowering her chin onto her upturned hands and cupping her face with her fingers. Every death had been considered in its own right, but the geographical spread of the unsolved murders had led to a fragmented, disjointed police investigation. Zak Smith had first attempted to murder Eva in Edinburgh, leading DCI Grant to investigate. He had eventually murdered her in London, bringing DCI Greenway into the equation. And now Laurence had been murdered in Yorkshire, and DI Hall was looking for his killer. And every one of those investigations had been muddied by the occurrence of yet another murder in Cornwall. No, not just in Cornwall, but in Penwithen.

Not just in Penwithen, but at Salvation Hall itself.

Stella had died on the terrace, instead of Eva. Zak had died in the potting shed. And now Becca's lifeless body had been pulled from the lake. Ennor had always believed the answer to the killings lay at Salvation Hall, that it lay within the Lancefield family itself.

But what if the answer didn't lie at Salvation Hall? What if the answer *was* Salvation Hall?

*

'Is it necessary for us to have this conversation in the drawing room, Inspector Price? After all, if it's only another informal chat we could just as easily use the kitchen.' Nancy was clearly ill at ease in the tall, wing-backed chair beside the fireplace. Rather than sitting back in its depth, she was perched on the very edge of the cushion, her long tanned legs neatly folded to the right, her hands resting primly in her lap. 'It's not as if there is very much I can tell you anyway, if this is about Becca. I was as shocked as the rest of the family when her body was discovered.' A sudden flicker of mischief lit Nancy's eyes. 'Especially as you seemed to know just where the body would be found.'

Price, sitting opposite on the sofa, took the jibe in his stride. 'It's called gut feeling, Nancy. When you've been a detective as long as I have your instinct will lead you.' He hesitated, and then added, 'But you don't always know what you're going to find. I didn't expect it to be Becca's body. I just felt that being close to the lake might help my thought processes.'

'Then you must be very gratified with the results.' Nancy moved her hands a little and began to fiddle with the thick, gold chain around her wrist. 'What would you like to ask me?'

'I've been told you went into Penzance on Thursday morning, before setting off for Liberation Park. I'd like to know where you went.'

Her dark eyes registered surprise. 'Good heavens,

you're making me sound like a suspect for Becca's murder.'

'You are a suspect, Nancy. Everyone in the household is a suspect until they've been eliminated.'

'I see.' She stopped fiddling with the bracelet and settled her hands back into her lap. 'Well, I left Salvation Hall after breakfast and drove straight to Penzance, where I parked in the harbour-side car park. I walked up to Chapel Street to Richard's tailor, to drop off a pair of trousers that needed an alteration. And I called in at the florist on my way back to the car to buy flowers for the Dower House.'

'And can you remember what time you parked, and how long you were there?'

'Not exactly. But I may have the receipt from the car park, if it helps you at all. I tend to just drop them into the door pocket.' She frowned. 'Tell me, Inspector, what motive do you think I could possibly have for murdering Becca? She and I had no relationship to speak of.'

'Not recently, perhaps. But surely you were quite close at one time, when Becca worked here at Salvation Hall?'

'I wouldn't call us close. As she was the housekeeper and I was Richard's secretary our paths crossed as a matter of routine. We had to find a way of working together or life would have been intolerable.'

'Are you sorry she's dead?'

'As a fellow human being, of course I'm sorry she's dead. But if you're asking whether I have any particular personal reason for mourning her passing, then no, of course not. She was lazy as a housekeeper, nagging as a partner to Philip, rude to Lucy and repeatedly insolent to Richard, despite all the financial help he bestowed upon her. She encouraged her brother to throw rocks at the Lancefields and protected him when he went on the run. If she had turned him in, Eva might still be alive. And so might Zak himself, if you think about it.'

'But not Laurence.' Price watched Nancy's face as he

spoke. 'Zak wasn't responsible for Laurence's death.'

'But Becca might have been.'

'I don't see how. You must realise Becca's death immediately eliminates her as a suspect?'

'Does it? How do we know she didn't murder Laurence and come back here to commit suicide in remorse for her actions? Throwing herself in the lake and waiting to drown is just the sort of melodramatic gesture she would make.'

And so it might have been, had Becca actually drowned. 'Do you think she would have abandoned Frankie?'

'Perhaps she didn't see it as an abandonment. Becca knew Richard would always take the best possible care of Philip's child. In fact, Frankie might thrive now Becca isn't there to drag her down and hold her back.'

It was a damning indictment. Price straightened his back and rolled his neck around to relieve a growing tension. Questioning a spirit like Nancy was never an easy task, but in the past he'd always risen to the challenge, perhaps even enjoyed the experience of playful, good-natured banter. But there was nothing playful or good-natured about this particular exchange.

Nancy had changed. There was no question that girl was still beautiful on the outside – the long limbs, glowing skin and glossy curls were as beguiling now as the very first day Price had set eyes on her. But what he'd once believed to be a mischievous streak was showing signs of malevolence. 'The last time we spoke, I asked you to postpone your return to St Felix until DI Hall had decided whether or not she wanted to question you about Laurence's death. I can advise you now that she does.'

The impact of his words was immediate. Nancy's eyes flashed and she jutted out her chin. 'And just how long is that going to take? I had hoped to be back at Woodlands by the end of the week at the latest.'

'It will take as long as it takes, Nancy. And when I have a definitive cause and time of death for Becca, I will also be back to question you again.' He stood up and turned on his heel to make for the door, and then hesitated, looking back over his shoulder at the smouldering girl. 'I wouldn't think of packing for St Felix just yet. If you try to leave Salvation Hall before both of those interviews have been conducted, I'll arrest you for attempting to pervert the course of justice.'

17

Amber Kimbrall looked up at the policeman through tear-sodden lashes. 'You will catch him, won't you, Sergeant Parkinson?' She was finding it difficult to speak, her lips twitching uncontrollably with a gut-wrenching mixture of grief and disgust and fury. 'Whoever did that to Becs, you will make them pay for what they've done?' Her face was smeared with mascara and she put up a hand to brush away the salty tears. 'Oh, for pity's sake.' She frowned at the dirty streaks across the back of her hand as she spoke. 'It's a good job no one can see me.'

'What the hell does it matter if anybody sees you?' Parkinson placed a comforting arm loosely around her shoulders as he pulled a crisp, white handkerchief from his pocket. 'You've done some very brave things in the past few months, but that was without doubt the bravest of them all.' He shook out the handkerchief and handed it to her. 'Now wipe that snot off your chin and I'll treat you to a coffee in the most exclusive café in Truro.'

'I didn't know there was an exclusive café in Truro.' She dabbed at her face, wiping away the telltale signs of distress. 'Is it far?'

'It's not far at all.' He began to gently steer her along the corridor. 'We just go through those swing doors at the end and turn left. There's a vending machine just a few yards along.'

Amber snuffled a laugh. 'I thought you said an exclusive café?'

'Well, it's sort of exclusive, isn't it? How many people do you think get to visit a police mortuary?' He gave her shoulders a squeeze. 'We don't let any old riffraff in here, you know.' He pushed on the left-hand door, holding it firm until she was safely on the other side. 'You have to have the right connections and qualifications to be admitted.'

She began to walk slowly to the left, sniffing into the handkerchief as she went. 'Let me guess – you have to know a policeman, and you have to be able to identify the deceased?'

'Correct on both points.' The walk to the vending machine was a short one and Parkinson pointed to a small Formica-topped table against the wall. 'Take a seat over there and I'll put the order in.' He fished in his pocket and pulled out a handful of coins. 'Flat white, cappuccino or latte?'

'I'll go for the latte, please. Does it come with a gin and tonic chaser?'

'Unfortunately not, but I'll see what I can do about that when we get back to The Lancefield Arms.' The sergeant rattled a succession of coins into the machine and jabbed at the selection panel with his fingers. It had taken some courage for the warm-hearted landlady to identify her late friend's body, not least since Becca's remains had spent at least twenty-four hours in the water. The mortuary team had done their best to make the task as comfortable as possible, but it had still been a sobering experience. A vending-machine latte was hardly a reward for the effort, but he needed a coffee himself to steady his nerves. 'You do know how much we appreciate what you've done today?'

'Well, I could hardly leave it to Sadie, could I? She was

almost hysterical when you broke the news to her. She's already had to identify Zak's body in the last few months, dealing with Becca's death is likely to tip her over the edge.' She nodded as Parkinson placed a plastic cup on the table in front of her. 'I haven't had chance to ask you yet: how do you know Becs died before she was put into the water?'

'Ah, that's down to the wonders of science.' He rattled a few more coins into the vending machine and selected a flat white. 'Dr Frinton, the pathologist, examined Becca's body when we took it out of the water and she was able to confirm just by looking that Becca didn't drown.' He didn't want to reveal too much. 'We won't get the exact timings of what happened to her until we're given the full post mortem results this afternoon.' The vending machine clicked and spat out another plastic cup full of hot, steaming liquid. 'This flat white looks exactly the same as your latte.'

'It probably is the same.' Amber pushed a stool towards him as he made his way to the table. 'I was a bit surprised DCI Price didn't break the news to Sadie.'

'He wanted to. But I asked him to let me do it.' Parkinson sat down at the table and sipped on his coffee. 'When Sadie reported Becca missing, I took the whole thing with a pinch of salt. I should have taken it more seriously. And I should have been more patient with Becca when she was alive.' He screwed up his face. 'Anyway, I've got a girl of my own about the same age as Frankie. I can't stop wondering what would happen to her if anything happened to me and Claire.'

'You know your trouble, Sergeant Parkinson? You're just too human to be a police officer.' Amber traced a thoughtful finger around the top of her coffee cup. 'It has to be somebody at Salvation Hall, doesn't it?' She didn't wait for him to answer. 'I'm surprised they didn't make any attempt to weight the body down, like when Philip was murdered.'

'How do you know they didn't?' It would be easy to tell her what he knew, but not pragmatic. 'When a body is put into the water, it tends to sink because there's no air in the lungs. But as it begins to decompose, the bacteria produce gases that inflate the gut and the chest. That makes the body rise up again, and why she was floating on the surface.' He lifted a hand to demonstrate the point. 'And that might happen even if the body was weighted, if the weight wasn't enough to keep it anchored.'

It was hardly the most scientific explanation, but it seemed to satisfy her curiosity. 'I suppose now there'll have to be an inquest, like there was when Zak died.' Her face drew solemn again. 'You know, I can't stop thinking about the text she sent on Thursday morning.' Amber's face began to crumple again. 'Why didn't I just agree to meet her for lunch, Sergeant Parkinson? If I'd agreed to meet her for lunch, she might have told me where she was going, who she was meeting... because that's the key to it, isn't it? We need to find out how she came to be at Salvation Hall in the first place, when she was supposed to be going out with friends in Truro?' A silent sob escaped the girl's lips and she put Parkinson's mascara-stained handkerchief up to her mouth. 'I can't stop thinking that maybe there was something she wanted to tell me, or something she wanted to ask me. And if only I'd said yes, if only I had taken the time to listen to her, she might still be here with us today.'

*

Richard Lancefield halted inside the lychgate and glanced around him to take stock. The churchyard at St Felicity's was peaceful and the musky, cloying fragrance of a generous floral tribute on a nearby grave filled his nostrils and momentarily lifted his spirits. A twice-weekly walk to visit the graves of those he had loved and lost had become a fixture in the old man's calendar, but today's visit was not one of routine.

He bent slowly to unclip the lead from Samson's collar and the terrier was off, curly tail wagging, his canine instincts drawing him directly to Lucy's grave. Richard watched as the dog snuffled his way around the blue-black marble slab that marked the spot, searching for a suitable resting place before settling down beside a delicate, marble angel: the addition to Lucy's tomb placed in remembrance of Emma Needham.

He walked slowly over to Lucy's grave and turned his eyes down to the marble slab. 'I'll be leaving for St Felix soon, my dear, but I'll come and say goodbye before I go.' He rested his shooting stick on the soft, grassy path beside the grave. 'I hope you know you're still missed, my pet. I have Kathryn and Nancy, and dear Barbara is proving to be the best of friends to all of us. But they are not you.' No one could replace her. 'At least I know you will not be alone. Your father will be here, and Barbara and Kathryn. They, I'm sure, will come and chat with you, and bring you all the news from St Felix.' He felt an unbidden tear begin to sting at the back of his eye. 'And now you must forgive me, because there is someone else I must speak to.'

He pulled up the shooting stick and turned towards the most sheltered corner of the churchyard, picking his way carefully between gravestones and molehills until he reached the spot where a fine horse-chestnut tree spread its branches protectively over a simple, granite headstone. For once in his life he was lost for words, suddenly overwhelmed by silent grief for a friendship lost and a memory betrayed. And then he opened up the shooting stick and drove its feet into the soft, grassy ground beside the grave so he could sit. 'Well, Philip, I hardly know where to begin.' He hung his head, casting his mind back to the previous summer, remembering his young friend in happier days. Philip had been strong and fit, kind-hearted and endlessly patient with an old man's foibles and fancies.

But he had been foolish in love: carelessly bringing a child into the world with a woman he didn't want to marry, and then letting his passion for Lucy get the better of him. Perhaps if he'd been more faithful to Becca, things might have been different.

But what was done, was done.

'I do miss our chats, my old friend. I miss those coffees in the potting shed, and all our talk of orchid growing and which specimens might win us the cup in the annual show.' Richard sighed. 'Barbara has agreed to take over the orchid house when I return to St Felix, but she is quite the novice. It will be a learning curve for her.' He was beginning to ramble, and he knew it. 'Of course, there will be orchid growing on a daily basis once I have settled myself back at Woodlands. You know, it is one of my deepest regrets that I didn't take you out to St Felix, at least just the once. I think you would have thrived there. Like the orchids do.' As he had hoped Marcus would.

Richard cast another glance around him. The churchyard was empty and no one could hear him. And yet still the words were sticking in his throat. 'Philip, I have terrible news about Becca. She's gone, my boy. We found her body in the lake, just as we found Lucy's and yours. She was strangled with a scarf, just as Lucy was strangled with a scarf. And I don't know…' He pursed his thin lips inwards to stem a sob. 'I've often wondered about the night you lost your life. Whether Marcus was telling the truth when he told me he found you leaning over Lucy's body. He believed you'd murdered her, but I always thought you too gentle a soul to take a life. You loved our girl like you loved all of God's living creatures.' He bowed his head. 'But so many more have lost their lives since that night. Has all that misery and sorrow unfolded because I did wrong by you?'

He could hardly bear to think about it, let alone talk about it. He had never wanted to believe Philip was a killer. But the alternatives to that theory were almost too much for him to bear. 'Has all of this unfolded because of my error of judgement? Stella, Eva, Laurence, even Zak and Becca; have they all died because I couldn't... because I *wouldn't* see the truth?'

*

'No journey is ever wasted if it results in a coffee and a kind word.' Jim Collinson had arrived at Liberation Park to discover Jennet and Rosemary were not at home. But his disappointment at their absence had been short-lived; Riley Gibb had risen to the occasion and offered him a compensatory Americano with a pastry on the side. 'I suppose I should have called ahead to check they were here.'

'I think it was a spur-of-the-moment thing. Rosemary thought Jennet needed taking out of herself.' They were in the small manager's office to the rear of the hotel's reception desk, and Riley seemed curiously keen to speak to him. 'Has there been another development in the investigation into Mr Payne's death?' She checked herself, and put a hand up to her cheek. 'Heavens, I must sound like a gossip. Only, the staff are beginning to feel anxious about the situation.' Her shoulders sank a little. 'I'm afraid Rosemary isn't keeping us in the picture about how the investigation will impact the hotel.'

'Mrs Taylor hasn't given you an update then?' Collinson eyed the cinnamon swirl in front of him with a mild regret; what he'd assumed was an act of kindness was beginning to look like a bribe for information. But if the girl was worried for her job then she could hardly be blamed for that. 'There's a limit to the information I can share with you . But I can tell you I've come to advise Jennet that DI Hall is travelling down to Cornwall today to talk to some of the wedding guests about their time at Liberation Park.'

'I see.' Riley frowned. 'Does that mean Liberation Park can go on operating? We have a wedding booked in for next weekend and at this point I don't know whether it can go ahead. The couple are meant to be attending a rehearsal here tomorrow but when I asked Rosemary this morning if it could go ahead, she told me she was waiting for the police to say it would be okay.'

'Did she? It's my understanding the hotel can resume its normal operations providing everyone remains available to assist with the ongoing enquiry.' And that had been confirmed to Rosemary Taylor, though it wasn't in Collinson's remit to find out why she hadn't shared that information with her staff. 'Tell me, Riley, is Liberation Park a happy place to work? I mean, do you all get on well, the management and staff?'

The girl looked away, thinking. And then she turned back to him with a shrug. 'We've all had our share of ups and downs. Most of the staff don't have much to do with the senior management, only their immediate line manager. Obviously I have more to do with Jennet and Rosemary than most, and I've always found them good to work for. Of course, I didn't join the team until after Mr Taylor had left the business. He and Rosemary were already divorced by the time I arrived.'

'That must have been tough for them, divorcing after building a successful business together. Is Mr Taylor still a shareholder in the business?'

'Oh yes. The property belongs to him really, because he inherited it from a distant cousin. He's a sleeping partner now. I don't believe he draws any kind of income from the business, but he does have to be consulted on certain matters.'

'DI Hall tells me Mrs Taylor had asked Laurence Payne to invest in the business. Would Mr Taylor have been consulted about that?'

Riley's cheeks flushed pink. 'I wouldn't know anything about that, I'm afraid.'

'Did Mr Taylor like Laurence? I don't recall anyone saying he was here for the wedding.'

'I'm not sure the two of them have ever met. Mr Taylor lives in New Zealand now. He married again and has a second family. I believe Jennet speaks to him quite regularly by video call, though I have heard' – Riley lowered her voice – 'that he and Rosemary don't speak unless it's absolutely necessary. I don't think it was an amicable divorce.'

'What about Mrs Taylor? Did she like Laurence? Was she happy about the marriage?'

'She did seem to be happy at first. But I don't think she was happy about Jennet leaving Liberation Park. I think she hoped Jennet would go on dividing her time between Hertfordshire and Yorkshire. I think she's come to rely on Jennet quite heavily in the last few years.' Riley's frown deepened. 'She wasn't very keen on Mr Payne's interest in the occult. I have heard her once or twice make some quite scathing remarks about that.'

'But she wasn't too concerned his family made their fortune from the sugar trade?'

'Did they? I didn't know that.' Riley sounded puzzled. 'I can't imagine it would have worried her though. Lots of people have made their money from manufacturing, haven't they?'

Collinson suppressed a smile. 'Yes, I suppose they have.' Now wasn't the time to give Riley a history lesson. 'Laurence's death has left Jennet a very wealthy woman. Certainly wealthy enough to make a substantial investment in Liberation Park now. Do you think she'll stay on here? Only, my colleague DI Hall got the impression she wasn't too keen to leave the business after her marriage.'

'And she was probably right. I know Jennet feels a very strong connection to the place, and both her parents look upon it as her inheritance.' Riley sighed. 'I think it was a very difficult decision for her, to leave her role as general manager. But in the end she had to make a choice.'

'And she chose her husband over Liberation Park.'

'Good heavens, no. It wasn't like that.' Riley gave a knowing smile. 'That wasn't how she saw the choice at all.'

18

David sank back into the drawing room armchair with an air of quiet resignation. 'I'll do my very best to help you, Inspector, but I'm not sure I'll have anything particularly useful to say.' He looked tired but resolute, his face drawn but his eyes focused firmly on the detective. 'You must be heartily sick of the sight of Salvation Hall by now, let alone the requirement to keep interrogating its occupants.'

'I'm afraid it's an occupational hazard: to keep asking the same questions of the same people over and over again, in the hope of receiving a different answer.' Though not always having to ask them in respect of quite so many different victims. 'Can we start with Thursday morning? I've been told you went into Newlyn.'

'That's correct. It was inconvenient, given we had such a long journey ahead of us, but it was something I needed to deal with in person. We own a number of commercial properties over there and a tenant had breached the terms of his lease. I'd hoped to deal with it by phone but the agent wanted me to meet the tenant face to face. I think he thought my physical presence would add weight to the situation.'

'And did it?'

'Yes, but not in the way he planned. Technically there

was a breach because the tenant had sublet part of the property in contradiction of his lease. The agent wanted to terminate the agreement, but I have a great deal of sympathy with these small business owners – trading conditions are difficult at the moment and he needed to increase his cash flow. He knew the agent would be heavy-handed about it, if word got back, but there was no need for all the animosity. It just needed a friendly conversation. I've asked the agent to amend the lease to give the tenant permission to sublet on condition we can vet any future potential lessee.' David cleared his throat. 'Not that you needed all of that explanation. If you need an alibi for the time of Becca's death, the agent will be able to speak for me. I'll make sure his details are sent through.'

'I'm sure that won't be necessary.' The circumstances of the conversation were grave, but still Price felt the need to quell a smile. David might fit the profile of "means, opportunity and capability" when it came to murdering Becca Smith and Laurence Payne, but in his heart he could suspect the man of neither crime. 'Do you have any idea what Marcus and Nancy were doing that morning?'

'I believe Nancy went into Penzance. I don't know about Marcus. I think he walked the dog at some point, other than that I'm afraid I can't help.'

'But you noticed nothing untoward in the way either of them was behaving?'

'Nothing more than their usual bickering. As I mentioned yesterday, they do rather seem to be out of sorts with each other at the moment. I can't help wondering if spending so much time together on St Felix is causing friction. Kathryn has probably shared with you that Nancy has been tasked to set up an educational foundation on behalf of the family, and Marcus is managing several aspects of our estate. Their roles should be clearly defined, though I have asked Marcus to assist Nancy if he can. I think she rather resents the inference she needs his help.'

'You can't think of any other reason for her to feel resentful?'

'Nothing obvious.'

'Were they bickering in the car on Thursday, on the journey to Liberation Park?'

David considered the question. 'I can't say that they were. We all took a turn at driving; I seem to recall Nancy napping in the back of the car at one point. Marcus and I had a long conversation about affairs at Woodlands. There was general chatter about the forthcoming wedding.' He lowered his voice. 'Am I to deduce that something happened to Becca on Thursday?'

'I won't have the full post mortem results until this afternoon.' It didn't quite answer the question, but Price wasn't prepared to say more. 'I can confirm that it was murder, as we suspected, and not suicide.' He cast his mind back to the moment they discovered Becca's body. 'When we found her, I asked you to go back to the house and gather everyone together. Can you remember what happened?'

'I followed your instructions to the letter, Chief Inspector. I called everyone into the library and told them there had been an accident in the grounds. And I asked them all to stay in the house until you joined us. Barbara kindly volunteered to make coffee for everyone while I popped over to break the news to my father.'

'Did you tell him it was Becca?'

The question brought a blush to David's cheek. 'I know you asked me not to let anyone know, but under the circumstances... whatever your opinion of my father, he is very solicitous of everyone who forms part of the extended Lancefield household. And while Becca was no longer in our employ, Frankie is still his godchild. Anyway, I explained the need for confidentiality and he fully understood.'

It was hardly a surprise to Price. And given the shock that registered on every face in the room when he confirmed the news of Becca's death, he could only imagine Richard had been good to his word. 'You do realise we can no longer consider Becca to be a suspect for Laurence's death?'

'And that the field of suspects is narrowing? Poor Jennet must be quite beside herself, not knowing what happened to him. I had wondered whether I should go up to Liberation Park to pay my respects to her, and perhaps try to speak to Detective Inspector Hall. That was before Becca's death, of course. But given that DI Hall is already on her way to Penwithen…'

'I'm sorry?' Price caught his breath. 'She's on her way to Salvation Hall?'

'I assumed you would know. Amber called about an hour ago to tell me that DI Hall had made an overnight booking at The Lancefield Arms.'

*

'I didn't mean to disturb you.' Marcus halted in the doorway, his hand still on the door knob. 'I was looking for Kathryn.'

Nancy looked up from the book she was studying and observed him coolly through long dark lashes. 'Then I'm sorry to disappoint you.' She was reclining in the captain's chair, her long legs stretched out under the desk. 'Kathryn has gone to find Barbara, so I'm taking the opportunity to study this while the library is free.' She tilted her head towards the slim, hard-backed book she was holding. The book was open, and its cover rested carefully on the edge of the desk. 'I'm told Jennet found it when they were restoring Liberation Park, and believes it to be the Bible from the original owner's estate in the Caribbean. I've never seen anything quite like it before. I'm thinking of asking Jennet if she would donate it to the St Felix Foundation, in memory of Laurence.'

As if Jennet wouldn't have anything more important on her mind than bequeathing a dusty old book to a museum. Marcus swallowed down the thought and let the door swing shut behind him. He stepped over to the desk and sat down on the empty chair beside it. 'May I see?' He held out a hand for the book. 'I'm beginning to realise I haven't taken anywhere near enough interest in the work you're doing to set up the foundation.'

Their eyes locked and the dark, suspicious glint in Nancy's gaze was unmistakeable. But she smiled with her lips and closed the book gently, holding it out for him to take. 'It's not a full Bible, of course. It's an extract; a collection of tracts that were deemed suitable for sharing with the slaves who worked on the plantations. Kathryn thinks it was designed to persuade plantation owners it would be safe to permit the slaves to attend church.'

Marcus took the book from her and opened the cover. 'And what does Nancy think?'

'We have nothing at all like this at Woodlands, and such a thing has never been brought to my attention before. But Christian worship was never an issue on the estate because the Lancefields were relatively liberal masters. Everything I've read suggests they encouraged Christian conversion from a very early date. Certainly the Woodlands family Bible – the Bible in which we have recorded many generations of births, marriages and deaths – is a full edition. Nothing has been removed, and it was available to anyone on the estate who wished to read it.'

'Were they actually able to read it?' Marcus leafed slowly through the fragile pages. 'I thought slaves were uneducated?'

'Did you?' Nancy's glossed lips pursed. 'Then it shows how little you know about the subject.'

'Which is why I'm determined to learn more about it.' He snapped the book shut and handed it back to her. 'I've been toying with the idea of resigning from my post at Woodlands, but perhaps that would be taking the easy way out. Perhaps I should return to St Felix, and take a keener interest in the foundation.'

Nancy placed the book down on the desk and swivelled the captain's chair a little so that she was facing him. 'I thought I heard David mention you were thinking of moving to Hemlock Row.'

'Not moving there, Nancy. Just planning to spend some time there to clear my head. And I might still do that once Inspector Price has nailed Becca's murderer.'

She licked her lips. 'Won't that be a little difficult, if he names you?'

'In order to do that, he would have to come up with sufficient evidence to build a case. And what evidence does he have?'

The question hung between them and then Nancy snorted, a quiet cough of disbelief. 'Marcus, are you confessing to me?'

'I don't know, Nancy. Am I?' He settled back into the chair. 'You seem quite keen to cast me in the role of murderer. What evidence do *you* have?'

'It's not for me to come up with the evidence to prove you did it. I only know it would have been easy for you. You say you took the dog for a walk, but how do we know you didn't go to meet Becca?'

'Ah, well, that's the thing, isn't it? You don't know.' Marcus frowned. 'When he questioned you, did Inspector Price ask you when you last saw or heard from Becca?'

'Yes. I told him I hadn't seen her since she left Salvation Hall.'

'And was that true?'

'Of course. Are you suggesting I might have lied?' Nancy, suddenly riled, placed her hands on the chair's arms and arched her neck. 'They know you committed the murders, Marcus. Why don't you just admit it?'

'If I committed all the murders, then that makes me a serial killer.' His tone was almost teasing. 'Aren't you afraid to be alone with me, if I'm a serial killer?'

'Of course not. You have no motive for wanting me dead.'

'And yet you think I had a motive for murdering Zak and Laurence and Becca?'

'Of course. You murdered Zak and Laurence for revenge.'

'And Becca?'

'I can only conclude she had some piece of information she planned to share with the police.'

'So, you don't subscribe to the view I might have murdered her to plant a false trail. To make it look as though she murdered Laurence?'

Nancy hesitated. 'You are trying to confuse me. I don't know what you want me to say.'

'When I killed Philip, I put his body in the lake in the hope no one would find him, and everyone would think he'd gone on the run because he'd murdered Lucy. It was to plant a false trail.' Marcus bent his head forward and stared into her face. 'But you, of all people, know it wasn't my idea to do that.'

Nancy's shoulders stiffened and she shrank back from him. 'We said we would never speak of it, Marcus. We promised each other we would never discuss it. Not just with the family or the police, but with each other. You gave me your word that if I helped you, it would never be mentioned again. Not even between the two of us. Just like it never happened.'

'I know that's what we agreed.' He lowered his voice to a whisper. 'But that was before you made the mistake of trying to frame me for another murder.'

*

Lucy Lancefield's suite still felt like a shrine.

The self-contained apartment had been kept locked and

mostly unattended, and a faintly musty smell had replaced the lingering fragrance of her delicate floral perfume. Kathryn shivered as she closed the door and turned to survey the scene. The vast Liberty sofa, the polished glass console tables, the grand marble fireplace against the innermost wall: all were still in place. But the mantel had been cleared of its collection of family photographs with their elegant silver frames, and several of the walls bore the telltale shadows of pictures no longer hanging. 'When did you last come in here?'

Barbara stepped over to the fireplace. 'Last Wednesday.' She ran a finger across the mantel and examined it for dust. 'I'll ask Mrs Peel to come in and give it a thorough clean. I'm trying to persuade David to get rid of all the furniture. The room will never go back into use, but redecorating and refurnishing might go some way towards exorcising the ghosts.' She turned to look at Kathryn. 'Now, where's this print?'

'It's over here, in the corner.' Kathryn pointed, and made her way towards it. 'Nancy gave it to Lucy as a gift, not long before she died.' She lifted it from the wall and handed it to Barbara.

'Oh, it's Dido Belle and her cousin, Elizabeth.' Barbara gazed at the image with a smile of recognition. 'I saw the original once, at an exhibition in London. It quite took my breath away.' She hesitated, the implications beginning to dawn. 'And Nancy gave this to Lucy as a gift? Oh the silly, silly girl.'

There was no question that Barbara understood the significance. 'You know, don't you? About Nancy's connection to Richard?' Kathryn sighed, more from frustration than disappointment. 'I've been at my wits' end trying to respect his wishes and keep that secret under wraps.'

'It wasn't Richard who told me. It was Nancy herself.'

'Then she knows?' Kathryn sighed. 'And all this time Richard has been asking me not to tell a soul.'

'I wouldn't blame Richard; Nancy didn't learn the truth from him. She heard it from her grandmother. Angel shared the information with both Nancy and Honeysuckle just before she died.' Barbara carried the picture over to the window and angled it into the light to take a better look. 'I wheedled it out of her when she became so obsessed with confirming a connection between herself and Laurence Payne. I couldn't understand why it was so important to her. She admitted to me then she was Richard's natural granddaughter, but she wasn't supposed to know. And she asked me to speak to him about acknowledging her.'

'And did you?'

'Yes, but he flatly refused to discuss it.' Barbara sighed. 'I love Richard to pieces, but he's a cantankerous old so-and-so when he digs his heels in. He's obviously very fond of the girl and she's almost part of the family anyway: why not just acknowledge her? What difference would it make?'

A great deal for Nancy, but there wasn't only Nancy to think of. 'I don't believe either David or Marcus know the truth. I only know because I found evidence of it amongst the family's papers. There was a deed of gift to the man Nancy believed was her grandfather, requiring him to raise Nancy's mother as his own child in return for financial compensation.' It was a moment of realisation Kathryn would never forget. 'I've also been trying to persuade Richard to acknowledge her and to tell David the truth, but he won't budge. For a while, I was afraid it was some kind of prejudice, but now I'm not so sure.'

'Well, I think it's high time David was told. He obviously knows this gift to Lucy caused some unpleasantness.' Barbara looked down again at the picture. 'Was Dido valued by her family?'

'Of course she was. You can see it in her clothing, her expression, her touch on her cousin's arm: the very fact she is in the painting. She was much-loved. You know' – Kathryn took a step backwards and perched on the arm of the sofa – 'Ennor sees that picture in his sleep. He noticed it the first time he examined Lucy's room, and it's always troubled him.'

'Does anyone know why the giving of this picture as a gift would cause unpleasantness?'

'No. None of us can know for sure.' Perhaps none of them really wanted to know. 'Shall we hang it back on the wall for now? I know that it was one of Lucy's personal possessions, but it feels like part of the landscape.' Kathryn watched Barbara's face as she considered the suggestion. 'It weighs heavily, doesn't it, knowing about Nancy's lineage and not being able to share the information without betraying a confidence?'

'I should think it weighs very heavily for you, not being able to share the information with Ennor.' Barbara turned to the wall and lowered the picture onto its hook. 'I'm not sure I would have your strength of loyalty.'

Any more than Kathryn could be sure of herself. She blinked, and then turned her eyes across the room. 'You said there were some items still to be removed. Can I be of any help with that?' She wasn't sure changing the subject was the answer, but for now it was all she could do. She could feel Barbara's gaze upon her: the shrewd, perceptive, kindly eyes probing for clues, wondering whether either of them had the courage to say the things no one wanted to say; whether either of them would be brave enough to raise an alarm that would either end or prolong the family's misery. 'You said you'd taken most of Lucy's things to the charity shops in Penzance. What else is there to go?'

'There are some boxes in the dressing room. The one on the left is full of valuable first editions. David said they were collected by Lucy's mother and left as part of her inheritance so I was going to consign those to the attic. The other box of books could go. And there are some handbags in the wardrobe we need to dispose of. And then there's the box of stuff I brought from Hemlock Row.'

'You left it in here?'

'What else was I going to do with it? Eva left all of the contents of the house to David, but he couldn't bring himself to deal with her personal bits and pieces. With his blessing, I divided her jewellery between her friends from the hospital, and most of the rest was donated to charity. But there were things from her childhood – diaries, photograph albums, that sort of thing – which needed to be dealt with. Things of no material value, all intensely personal and yet of no interest to anyone else. It feels intrusive to look at them, and unfeeling just to throw them away. I'm going to take them over to Holly Cottage this afternoon, just in case I've missed anything important. And then, perhaps they can just go up into the attic too?'

19

Parkinson pulled the Mazda onto the shoreline at Marazion and turned off the engine. The camber of the parking space was uneven, tilting the front of the car upwards, and a beam of blazing sunlight shot directly through the windscreen. Price flinched and reached up to pull down the sun visor above the passenger seat, but it gave little in the way of relief, and he opened the door a fraction in the hope of finding a breeze. 'It's Monday, for pity's sake.' The place was crowded, the car park overflowing. 'What the hell are all these people doing here on a Monday?'

'Enjoying their retirement? Pulling a sicky? Avoiding the housework?' Parkinson tried to make light of the situation but his heart wasn't in the endeavour. 'At least we managed to get a parking space, even if it isn't ideal.' He turned to look at the inspector. 'It's too hot for coffee. Do you want a cold drink?'

'It's never too hot for coffee. And I'll take a Mars bar with it.' He turned away as Parkinson exited the car, casting his eyes west towards the sea of humanity that was thronging the car park and clogging up the queue at the coffee cart. His mind was still in the mortuary, the printed copy of Dr Frinton's preliminary report into Becca Smith's death lying idly in his lap, and he unfocused his eyes, resting his head against the seat's headrest.

The pathologist had confirmed the cause of death, and it had come as no surprise to Price to learn Becca was strangled with a scarf. The length of pale green cheesecloth had still been knotted tightly around the girl's neck when they found her. She had died on Thursday and her body put into the water on Saturday; their suspicions had been confirmed, though thanks to the deterioration of the body, further tests would be required to confirm she'd entered her watery grave in the evening.

As to where the body had lain between Thursday and Saturday, the good Dr Frinton had suggested a dry and relatively cool environment. They had searched for traces of Becca in the potting shed and the storeroom, and found none. The alternative possibility – finding traces of the potting shed or storeroom on Becca herself – were almost non-existent, thanks to the body being left in the water. The search would have to be widened to the gardens and the grounds. Parkinson's money was on the back gate to the estate, secluded enough for a corpse to be hidden in the surrounding undergrowth, and utilised so infrequently that the body might lie there for days without risk of discovery, and Price could think of no argument against the theory.

He opened his eyes and stared out of the door's window. Somehow, Parkinson had made his way to the front of the queue and was busy tucking what Price hoped was a Mars bar into the pocket of his jacket. It had come as a relief to the sergeant to learn Becca had died on Thursday, and not after her mother had raised the alarm. And it had come as a surprise to the inspector to realise just how angry his protégé was that the girl had died at all. He'd become so accustomed to Parkinson being the mellow, unruffled half of their partnership that he'd quite lost sight of the toll Becca's death had taken on the young man. It had become too personal for both of them. Maybe so personal it was a risk to the investigation.

He turned in his seat and reached over to pull his jacket from the back of the car, slipping a hand into the inside pocket to retrieve his mobile phone. A swipe of his thumb across the screen revealed four missed calls and a simple text from Kathryn: please call me. He was about to comply when the driver's door opened and Parkinson slid awkwardly into his seat. 'Coffee, as requested. I pulled rank and pushed my way to the front of the queue.'

Price took a paper cup from the cardboard tray in Parkinson's hand. 'I bet that went down well.'

'Like the proverbial lead balloon. But after that hour in the mortuary, I'm well past caring.' Parkinson pulled the Mars bar from his jacket pocket and handed it to Price. 'It's started to melt.'

'Like you, I'm well past caring.' Price, coffee still in hand, tore skilfully at the wrapper with his teeth and sighed with satisfaction as the paper ripped. He squeezed the bottom of the wrapper until the chocolate appeared through the tear. 'Have you any idea how many years of practice it's taken for me to perfect that manoeuvre?'

'More worryingly, how many Mars bars?' Parkinson levered the lid from his cup and placed it on the dashboard. 'Do you think the divers will find anything this afternoon?'

'I don't know. We can only hope. Whatever the killer used to try to weight the body down must still be down there. I guess it depends how big it is, and how obvious that it doesn't belong at the bottom of the lake. Dr Frinton is assuming something heavy enough to keep the body anchored, but not tied securely enough to the body to hold it in place once the chest cavity had begun to inflate.'

'Was the killer just half-hearted about it? Or did panic set in?'

'In a hurry, probably. Or maybe working in the dark. If their hands were wet it might have been difficult to knot the rope tightly enough.' Price could hardly bear to think about it. 'Whichever of them did it, it took a strong stomach.' He sipped on his coffee and felt the flush of heat make its way into his cheeks. 'I suppose there is a slim possibility it wasn't a solo act; that two of them acted together.'

'Marcus and Nancy?' Parkinson whistled through his teeth at the suggestion. 'Where did that idea come from?'

'I don't know. It doesn't even make any sense, in a way, because the two of them aren't getting on so well these days.' Unless that was *why* they weren't getting on. 'Unlike David Lancefield, I never thought of them as friends, but I thought they had an amiable relationship. It was pretty clear today that they don't.' Price turned to look at Parkinson. 'Nancy's alibi for Thursday morning is interesting. She claims to have gone into Penzance, to Richard's tailor in Chapel Street and then to the florist round the corner. Can you follow up on that?'

'Of course. Do you know where she parked?'

'On the Wharfe Road car park. It's pay on exit, so the cameras will have captured her numberplate when she arrived and left.'

'I'll get on to that when I get back to the station.' Parkinson ran his tongue around his teeth. 'Have you decided what to do about DI Hall yet?'

'There isn't much we can do, except show her some professional courtesy. Would you be willing to pick her up from the railway station?'

'Is she staying at The Zoological?'

'No, at The Lancefield Arms. As close to the family as she can get.'

*

'I wanted to speak to you about Marcus.' Nancy closed the door of the orchid house behind her and leaned against the frame. 'Did you know he was planning to spend some time in Edinburgh?'

'Of course I knew.' Richard answered without looking at her. He retrieved a small orchid from the potting bench and examined its roots through the clear, plastic plant pot. 'The change of scene will do him good. He'll return to St Felix when he's ready.'

'Do you think he will have the opportunity?'

'Of course he will. There is no concrete evidence to suggest he has done anything wrong.'

'So, your plan is that we just continue to live with a killer in the family?'

Richard pursed his lips inwards and turned his head hawkishly to look at her. 'Do you have any evidence to substantiate that accusation?'

'Zak's phone was found under Marcus's bed. How could it have got there if Marcus didn't put it there?'

'Obviously because someone else put it there. You cannot hang a man on circumstantial evidence, Nancy. Even you should know that by now.' Richard lowered the orchid pot to the bench and tipped it on its side. 'I think this specimen could do with repotting. The roots are beginning to rot.' He tapped the pot to loosen the bark within. 'I can't help thinking your time would be better spent if you were to concentrate on those things that concern you. How is your work on the foundation progressing? Do you have a documented plan to share with me yet?'

Nancy pouted. 'Almost. It needs some refinement.'

'Then please give it some. You would do well to remember you are employed by the estate and that the foundation is not a game. It is a serious venture to bring improvements to both the Woodlands estate and the island of St Felix. The whole island will be watching to see what you can deliver, and what you deliver will reflect on the family. Perhaps you could spend some time tomorrow refining your plan, given there is nothing else you can usefully do until Inspector Price gives you the green light to return home.'

'It will be difficult without all the relevant paperwork. I didn't bring it with me because I didn't expect to be at Salvation Hall for so long.'

'Then call Honeysuckle and have her email it over to you. You are not a fool, Nancy. I want to see what you've been doing over the last few weeks. The estate has a reputation to uphold. Have you had any help from Marcus?'

The girl's eyes darkened. 'He has tried to make suggestions but he doesn't really understand the island or the estate.'

'Then help him to understand. Marcus is a part of the family, and I expect the family to work together.' Richard reached up to the shelf above the potting bench, in search of a clean pot. 'I hope you are helping him to acclimatise. Or have you set out your stall to make things difficult for him?'

'Of course not. That would be unkind.' She bristled at the suggestion. 'But he's only at Woodlands because you want him to be. It's quite obvious his heart isn't in it.'

'Perhaps that is because he does not feel welcome.' The old man lowered the orchid's roots into the new pot. 'Your role is to support David and Marcus. You seem to be losing sight of that.'

An uneasy silence settled in the space between them. And then Nancy said, 'I've often wondered why you gave the running of the estate to Marcus, and not to me.'

'And why, pray, would I entrust the running of the estate to you?'

She braced herself and tilted back her head. 'Familia Super Omnia.'

The uneasy silence was suddenly brittle. Richard growled softly under his breath and turned forbidding eyes to look at her. 'My advice to you, Nancy, is to stop there and not say any more.'

'But why? Why should I be silent? I love the family and I love the estate. They are a part of me and I am a part of them.'

'Do not go any further.'

'But...'

The old man banged his fist on the potting bench. 'I know what you are planning to say. I know where this is leading. And I caution you against it. I know you have become party to a secret you were never meant to hear. And I will not have it spoken of. It is not just my wish that you remain silent. It is your mother's wish.'

'My grandmother wanted me to know.'

'She may have wanted you to know. She did not want you to bandy the fact about as if it were a piece of idle gossip. Your mother does not want what she perceives to be her shame publicly acknowledged. Do you think I haven't discussed it with her? Why else do you think she has counselled you against it?'

'Am I not entitled to make my own decisions?'

'Without question. But if you choose to ride roughshod over those who love you in pursuit of your own agenda, you must be prepared to live with the consequences.' Richard closed his eyes. 'Do not play games with me, Nancy. It will not end well for you.' He turned again to look at her, softening his tone. 'Why do you think I'm coming to end my days in St Felix? To be with you and your mother before it is too late.'

'But am I never to be acknowledged? What about my birthright?'

'What birthright? Your mother claims no birthright from me, so there is nothing to pass to you.' He growled under his breath. 'For pity's sake, Nancy, please just let this drop. If you don't, and you persist with this nonsense, for all it will hurt your mother and besmirch your grandmother's memory, I promise you now, I will wash my hands of you.'

*

Jim Collinson was in no doubt that his decision to return to Liberation Park had been the right one. Sitting with Jennet Payne and her mother in the drawing room, he was also under no illusion that his presence wasn't welcome. At least where Rosemary Taylor was concerned.

'I'm sorry we weren't here when you called earlier, Sergeant Collinson.' And even more sorry that he'd taken the trouble to return and try again, if the icy edge in her voice was anything to go by. 'It's been a very difficult few days and I thought Jennet should have a break, so I took her up to Filey for lunch. We have a friend there who runs a small bistro. The food is excellent and it gave us an opportunity to take a walk along the seafront afterwards, to blow away the cobwebs.'

Collinson bent forward and rested his forearms on his knees. 'I like Filey. It doesn't pretend to have any airs and graces.' He turned his eyes right to look at Jennet. She didn't look invigorated by the experience, and it occurred to him now just how tense the relationship between mother and daughter appeared to be. 'Did you enjoy the trip out?'

'I enjoyed the food immensely.'

Only the food? 'I wanted to ask if the news had reached you yet. Becca Smith's body has been found at the Lancefield family's home.'

'Does that mean she couldn't have been responsible for Laurence's death?'

'We think it's highly unlikely.' Collinson was watching both women carefully as he spoke. Jennet looked unmistakeably bewildered, but Rosemary? He could see the cogs turning behind the shrewd, confident eyes. 'We think her phone was brought to Liberation Park to plant a false trail.'

'You're suggesting that Laurence's killer wanted us to think Becca was responsible for his death.'

'That's certainly DI Hall's working assumption.' Even if it wasn't his own. 'She thinks that whoever brought the phone to Liberation Park also ordered the brochure found in Becca's home, in an attempt to point the finger at her.' He gave them a moment to think about it. 'DS Parkinson, down in Cornwall, has already confirmed for us that the email address used to request the brochure wasn't Becca's regular email address. We think the address was created on purpose, to make it look as though the request came from Becca. We're following up with the email service provided to see when that account was opened, and we'll be following up on the IP address the brochure request came from, to see if we can get closer to the source.'

Rosemary turned to her daughter and took hold of her hand. 'You see, darling? The police are almost certain one of the Lancefields murdered poor Laurence and used that girl as a scapegoat. And while I know it doesn't make things any easier it must give you some reassurance that justice will be served and things will soon get back to normal.'

Jennet stared down at her hand, trapped between Rosemary's fingers, and then very slowly, very deliberately, she drew it away. 'Will DI Hall be coming back to see me tomorrow?'

'DI Hall has gone to Cornwall to interview those members of the Lancefield family who came to the wedding.' Collinson sniffed, and tried to look reassuring. 'Is there something I can help you with, in her absence?'

'Perhaps.' Jennet tilted her head. 'I had planned to travel to Hertfordshire, but not without DI Hall's agreement. Do you share her assumption that one of the Lancefields murdered Laurence?'

The directness of her question brought a blush to the sergeant's cheeks. 'It's my role to support DI Hall with her investigation, not to form assumptions of my own.'

A flicker of understanding lit the young woman's eyes. 'Then I'll put the question another way. Does DI Hall still consider my mother and I suspects for his murder?'

'For pity's sake, Jennet.' Rosemary hissed the words at her daughter. 'That's an outrageous question to ask the sergeant. Of course they don't consider us suspects.'

'I don't see why not. We've been told Laurence died from taxine poisoning and either of us could have administered that to him. We were all in each other's company many times in the forty-eight hours before the wedding.'

'Darling, no one could possibly think you murdered your own husband. You were far too happy with him to have done such a dreadful thing.' Rosemary turned to Collinson. 'Please don't pay any attention to this nonsense, Sergeant. You can see how much Laurence's death has unsettled her. She doesn't know what she's saying.'

'I know exactly what I'm saying. Sergeant Collinson' – Jennet fixed him with beseeching eyes – 'please answer me. Are we still suspects?'

Collinson's mouth felt suddenly dry. 'At this stage of the investigation, no one has been formally declared a person of interest. But neither has anyone been formally eliminated from our enquiries.' How else was he supposed to answer such a discomfiting question? 'It's quite normal in an investigation with so many potential suspects – and I'm including all the wedding guests and hotel staff in that tally – for the investigation to begin by focusing on those closest to the victim.'

'Those most likely to have a motive for the murder?'

'Yes, if you want to put it like that.'

'But DI Hall must suspect Marcus Drake?' Exasperated, Rosemary Taylor threw up her hands. 'Why else would she travel all the way to Cornwall? She knows as well as we do that he harboured a grudge against Laurence. You only had to see the way he looked at

Laurence to know how much he hated him.'

20

David Lancefield turned to look over his shoulder at Marcus. 'I'm on my way to the village to see Amber. If you want to talk, you'll have to come with me.'

Marcus hesitated, and then he stepped out onto the path and let the heavy, oak door swing shut behind him. 'Is this about the arrival of DI Hall?' He walked briskly across the turning circle outside the house. 'That was one of the reasons I wanted to speak to you.'

They fell into step, striding out towards the path that led from the estate to the centre of village; some yards ahead of them, Samson was setting a lively pace. 'Poor Inspector Price had no idea she'd invited herself down to Penwithen.' David's tone conveyed a heartfelt sympathy. 'When I told him she'd already called to book a room at The Lancefield Arms, he turned so pale I thought he was going to be sick.'

'I overheard Barbara talking to Kathryn about it. Are we all to be questioned again tomorrow?'

'I assume so. She can only be coming here to talk to us about Laurence's death.' David slipped a hand into his pocket as he spoke, and pulled out Samson's lead. 'Come away from there, boy.' The dog had stopped beside the high, green hedge that marked the beginning of the path and was sniffing furiously at the undergrowth. 'We don't want to add you to the tally of bodies.' He bent down to clip the lead to the dog's collar. 'Can you imagine, that will be her earliest impression of Salvation Hall: a driveway surrounded by taxus baccata.'

'Is that what was used to poison Laurence?'

David winced. 'How did you know Laurence was poisoned?'

'It wasn't difficult to work it out. What else would leave him feeling unwell before he died?' Marcus ran a finger along the hedge as he walked. 'It is poisonous, isn't it? Yew?'

'Yes, it's poisonous if ingested. And I've been told, albeit in confidence, that Laurence died from taxine poisoning. I don't know if they have been able to identify the precise specimen. Ours is Taxus baccata 'Fastigiata'. I have no idea if it's more or less poisonous than other forms.' David set off walking again. 'So much in the natural world is toxic if we don't take care. Of course, they have plenty of their own yew trees up at Liberation Park. The substance that killed Laurence could just as easily have been produced from clippings taken locally.'

'But it couldn't have been Becca, could it?'

'No, it couldn't have been Becca. Even if she knew that yew was poisonous, I very much doubt the poor girl had the imagination to come up with the idea, let alone the patience to investigate the possibilities.'

'Whereas I do?'

David sighed. 'I had hoped we might just have a pleasant walk down to the village, Marcus. Do we have to discuss this now?'

'Yes, I'm afraid we do. Less than an hour ago, Nancy directly accused me of all three murders. DI Hall is coming to Penwithen to question me about them. I'm convinced Inspector Price thinks I'm guilty and you, for all your underlying consideration towards me, have hinted you also think I'm responsible.' Marcus rubbed at his forehead with his fingers. 'Richard thinks I'm guilty but doesn't care, because he doesn't think there is enough tangible evidence to metaphorically hang me with, and Barbara is being kind but non-committal. Only Kathryn seems to be on my side, and even she is showing signs of wavering since Becca's body turned up in the lake. If I'm to be interrogated tomorrow, I'd like to have some idea of whether you still think I'm guilty, and what evidence there is to support the fact.'

'I see.' They had reached a fork in the path and David turned left towards the village. Up ahead in the distance, the tower of St Felicity's loomed like a beacon. 'You say Nancy has directly accused you of all three murders. Does she have any evidence?'

'No.'

'Then why does she accuse you?'

'To deflect attention away from herself.'

'Ah.' David smiled. 'Is this where you tell me you think Nancy is the killer, in order to deflect attention away from yourself?' He gave his stepson a moment to think about it. 'You see the dilemma, Marcus? It's your word against Nancy's. What motive would she have for committing the murders? She and my poor dear Stella could barely stand the sight of each other. I hardly think Nancy would want revenge on Zak for removing a thorn in her side. And would she have murdered Laurence, the man who was her one, tenuous connection to the family? Or Becca? Do you honestly think Nancy would murder Becca and leave Frankie without a mother?'

'So, you cannot bring yourself to think that of Nancy, but you can think it of me?'

'No, Marcus. I cannot bring myself to think it of you. You are the nearest thing I shall ever have to a son and heir, and your mother would be heartbroken if she thought I had such a low opinion of you. The difficulty lies in that I cannot see the alternative. Just because I do not want to believe you capable of these atrocities does not mean you didn't commit them.'

They walked on in silence until Marcus said, 'Have you considered what will happen if I go to jail? Because whether I am guilty or not, that is a real possibility, isn't it?'

'Has my father spoken to you about legal representation, as he did when you admitted to murdering Philip?'

'You mean, has he offered me the moon on a stick to admit to the murders so the family can move on quickly for a second time? Curiously, no, he hasn't. But even if he did, this time I wouldn't be so quick to accept the offer. The last time, I was guilty. I admitted to the murder because it was my crime to admit to. No, this time if I need legal advice and representation, I will take it from Ian Mitchell.'

'You wouldn't accept the family's support?'

'No, I wouldn't. Because I'm not sure I can go on giving my support to the family.'

David stopped in his tracks. 'I don't understand.'

Marcus, just a few steps ahead, turned to look at him. 'The last few months have been hell for me, David. I went out to St Felix with an open mind and an open heart. I was grateful for Richard's support, and I did everything I could to make a go of it. But ever since Eva's death, things have been different. Not just because Eva has gone; if that were the case, I might have been able to thrown myself into my work on the estate and wait for the grief to subside. But I can't do that with Nancy watching my every move from the shadows. I don't understand why Richard decided to banish her back to St Felix. But I can tell you now, whatever the outcome of the investigation into these murders, if Nancy is going back to St Felix for good, then I have no intention of going back there with her.'

*

'I've been keeping busy. And staying out of your way, so as

not to impede the investigation.' Kathryn stared down into the murky water of the lake. 'I spent the afternoon helping Barbara to dispose of the last remnants of Lucy's belongings. I don't know what the family would have done if she hadn't been prepared to take on the task.'

Ennor knew the possibilities were limited. 'It wasn't really in your remit, was it? And I guess it wouldn't have been appropriate to ask Nancy to do it.' He stepped a little closer to Kathryn. 'What brought you down to the lake?'

'I don't know. Morbid curiosity, probably. I went into the kitchen to make myself a coffee and I could see the lake from the window. The divers had finished for the day and they were taking the barrier tape away. I think they must have found what they were looking for.'

'Could you see what it was?'

'Not very clearly. I think one of them was holding a carrier bag full of something. It looked heavy, judging by the way he was holding it.' She turned to look at him. 'Haven't you spoken to them yet?'

'No. I came to find you first.' He rested a hand gently on her back. 'We haven't spoken all day. I wanted to make sure you were okay.'

'Because the storm clouds are gathering? Or because you thought I might have something useful to tell you?'

Whether intended or not, the suggestion stung. Another reminder he was in too deep with this investigation. He lowered his hand and turned his attention to the water. The ornamental lake hadn't given up its latest victim without a struggle and in the glare of the low, late afternoon sunlight the waterlilies appeared bruised, the once-perfect discs of waxy green now blemished by the exertions of the recovery team and the divers. 'Tom tells me that Sadie and Amber want to come and lay flowers where Becca was found. Will Richard permit it?'

'Of course he will. But he thinks the final decision is yours.' Kathryn folded her arms, hugging her body. 'Am I allowed to ask how your day has been? Or is that still confidential?'

Not as confidential as it probably should have been. 'I've interviewed Marcus, David and Nancy again and the only thing I've got for my trouble is a headache. I feel as though Marcus is hiding something, but I don't know what. And Nancy has changed. She's always been so amiable. Not exactly friendly, but she's always had an easy way of talking to me. But not anymore. She's brittle, defensive.' He shrugged, bemused. 'If I didn't know better I'd say she was angry.'

'That's because she *is* angry. She didn't want to go back to Woodlands. We're all hoping she'll calm down when she returns, because Richard will be going out there to join her.'

'It all hinges on my investigation, doesn't it? Until I find the killer, the family can't move on. And even when I do, depending on the outcome, the family will have to adapt to losing someone it can't afford to lose.'

Kathryn took a step closer to the water's edge. 'It couldn't be Marcus, could it? He would have made a much better job of weighting the body down.'

'But all the ironware has gone from the storeroom, so what would he weight it down with? Maybe he just had to improvise. You know, even a murderer can get tired, sloppy, half-hearted with all the effort and strain of avoiding detection. Murdering one person takes its toll. Murdering two is a strain. Murdering three?' Price shook his head. 'It would drain the life blood out of anyone.' He took a step forward to stand beside her and lowered his head to whisper in her ear. 'Is this going to come between us now?'

'Hasn't it already come between us?' She answered without looking at him. 'We're on opposite sides of the fence, aren't we?'

'We don't have to be. We could go out to Marazion tonight and talk about it over dinner.'

'Just like we did in the beginning? When you wanted to question me about the family and its history?'

It would be pointless to deny it. 'I do want to talk to you about the family and I want to go back to where it all started. Where you first told me about them.' But it wasn't the same. He knew that in his heart, he just wasn't convinced that she did. 'I'm too close to them now, Kathryn, and so are you. They've become like family to you, and I'm…'

'You're too close to me.'

'I'm close enough to all of you to wish the answer lay outside the family. Like you, I don't want to admit one of them is a serial killer. I keep asking myself what it would mean for the family if it were Nancy or Marcus or David. Which outcome would affect the family the most. And that shouldn't matter to me. What should matter is justice for the victims.'

'Then perhaps it's lucky DI Hall is on her way to Penwithen. She might bring a much-needed degree of detachment.' Kathryn finally turned to look at him. 'I told you this place was an enchantment, didn't I? You've been seduced by all of this luxury and history and dysfunction, just as I have.' She turned on her heel and began to walk slowly back towards the house.

Price watched as she walked away from him, his spirits sinking. 'So, you'll come for dinner this evening? You'll still help me with the investigation?'

'Of course I will.' She cast the words carelessly over her shoulder. 'We can call it a professional consultation. Just like the first time you took me out for dinner.'

*

'Richard, you look exhausted. Have you been here in the orchid house all day?' Barbara sat down on the Lloyd Loom chair beside the door without waiting to be invited.

'When did you last eat or have a cup of tea? Didn't Nancy bring something over for you?'

'Tush.' The old man grumbled under his breath. 'I wanted you to come down here to talk about the plants. I am not seeking a lecture on my wellbeing.' Nor to speak about Nancy. He pulled the stool from underneath the potting bench and lowered his bony frame carefully onto it. 'Most of the orchids in here are phalaenopsis and will need relatively little in the way of care. You will just need to pay attention to their watering regime and make sure the roots don't rot. The house will need to be well-ventilated every day, even in winter, though you will need to put the heater on once temperatures begin to drop. And they will benefit from the use of rainwater instead of tap water. There is a water butt outside for the purpose.' He pointed up at the long shelf running along the right-hand side of the glass house. 'The specimens up there are cymbidium. You will need to wear gloves when you handle them, they can irritate the skin.'

'Nancy tells me Amber has asked if she and Becca's mother can visit the lake to lay flowers. I was going to suggest we make it tomorrow, to help them find closure. I'm happy to escort them, if it helps. I'll arrange for them to have tea in the conservatory afterwards. It will give us a chance to express our condolences and reassure Sadie that we're there to support her with Frankie.'

'We were speaking about the orchids.'

'No. *You* were speaking about the orchids. The arrangements for Amber and Sadie are more important. It's high time you had a conversation with Sadie. She's Frankie's grandmother and you are the child's godfather. Don't you think we should begin to build a bridge?'

Richard scowled. 'There has never been any question that we would continue to provide assistance for Frankie. I do not see we have to build a bridge for that.'

'But when you are in St Felix, it will fall to David and myself to be there for her. To be there for both of them.'

'I've never met with Sadie Smith, but I know of her by reputation. I've never had any dealings with her.'

'Then perhaps it's high time you did. Not that long ago you'd never had any dealings with Amber Kimbrall and probably held her in as low regard as you do Becca's mother. Now you hold her in such high esteem you've made her the licensee of The Lancefield Arms. What's to say your opinion of Sadie might not change, once you've met her?'

Chastised, the old man muttered. 'There is a reason I named you Soteria. You seem hell-bent on saving me from myself.' He raised his eyes to look at her. 'You are quite right, of course. I owe the woman the courtesy of my time and my attention. You always have the knack of knowing the right thing to do. Much like Kathryn.'

'And yet you don't agree with either of us when it comes to the matter of Nancy.'

Richard grimaced. 'You are spoiling the moment, Barbara. Do not make the leap from Soteria to Aprillis. The change does not become you.'

'Frankly, Richard, I don't particularly care whether it becomes me or not. I'm not out to make mischief. It just seems to me that your definition of the right thing is very subjective.'

'When it comes to Nancy, I *am* doing the right thing.'

'Are you sure? Are you really sure?' Barbara's eyes widened. 'Why didn't you want David to know about Honeysuckle? She's his sister.'

'You are his sister now.'

'But he would benefit from having both of us in his life.' Barbara stood up and turned her eyes to the shelf of orchids, stretching up a hand to lift one down to the bench. 'What's she like?'

'Honeysuckle?' He didn't want to talk about it. And yet somehow, he couldn't resist. 'She's a delight.' His face softened. 'Kind, witty, and intelligent, just like her mother.'

'Were you very fond of her mother?'

'I wanted to marry her.' The words were out before he could stop them; the truth he had buried in his heart for decades. Suddenly, tears were stinging fiercely at the back of his eyes and he pursed his lips inwards with a sigh. 'There. Now I've said it. I wanted to marry her, but my father forbade it.'

'But I thought it was just an adolescent fling?' Barbara put the orchid down and reached behind her for the chair, pulling it closer to the stool so she could sit beside him. 'Why did he forbid it, if you loved her?'

'He simply didn't understand. My father was never a loving man, not even towards my mother. To him, marriage was a matter of business. Angel was an employee on the estate and in his eyes not worthy to become mistress of Woodlands or Salvation Hall.' Richard wiped a tear away from his cheek with the cuff of his shirt. 'My father had a far more unpalatable solution – that I marry well, and continue a private liaison with Angel.' The old man leaned to the side and pulled a battered wallet from the pocket of his trousers. He flipped it open and took out a small, dog-eared photograph. 'This is Angel.' He handed the photograph to Barbara. 'This is Nancy's grandmother.'

'You carry this around with you? You've carried her with you for all these years?' Barbara looked down at the photograph and let out a gasp. 'Oh, my word. Just look at those beautiful, high cheekbones. And that mass of thick, dark curls. How old is she in this picture?'

'She had just turned seventeen. I was only eighteen at the time.'

'And is that why you've always kept Nancy close? Because she looks just like Angel?'

Richard turned his head away. 'They may look alike. But Angel had a sweet and loyal disposition. I used to think the same of Nancy, but there is a belligerence about her of late; a quarrelsome streak that comes from her father's side of the family. Oh, don't get me wrong. I have a lot of time for the man. He's a foreman on a neighbouring estate and a hard worker. But his people came from another island. They don't have the gentle ways or loyalties of St Felix.'

'But that's no reason to disadvantage Nancy.'

'No. But perhaps Nancy manages to disadvantage herself by choosing to display some of his harsher, less appealing qualities.' Richard stretched out a trembling hand and pulled the photograph from Barbara's fingers. 'It will be enough for Nancy that I am to see out my days at Woodlands. She and I will work together on the foundation until my end comes. As soon as DCI Price gives the word, she is to return to St Felix without delay.'

'But…'

'There is no "but", Barbara. There are aspects to this matter which you do not understand, and which I do not need you to understand.' He pushed the precious photograph back into the safety of his wallet. 'Nancy will not be acknowledged publicly and she will not inherit any part of the estate. And that is my final word.'

21

'Thanks for picking me up from the station, I do appreciate it.' DI Hall fastened her seatbelt with a firm click as Parkinson's Mazda moved smoothly away from the kerb. 'Is DCI Price is indisposed?'

'He's still at Salvation Hall.' It was probably the truth. 'The divers were going into the lake this afternoon to see if they could find whatever Becca's body was attached to when it was put into the water.' Parkinson smiled and kept his eyes on the road. 'You must be tired after such a long journey.'

'It was easier than driving. And it gave me time to do some research while I was on the train. I take it The Lancefield Arms is actually named after the family?'

'It isn't just named after them, it belongs to them. They own most of Penwithen village. Lords of the manor, and all that.'

Hall nodded and turned her head to look out of the window as they made their way out of Penzance. 'I've been reading up on them while I was on the train. They settled at Salvation Hall in 1726, is that right?' She didn't wait for an answer. 'According to what I've read, they were wealthy to start with but made most of their fortune in the Caribbean. It's a very similar story to Liberation Park, isn't it?'

'It's a very similar story to a significant proportion of grand houses and businesses right across the country. I had no idea until I started working on this case. They keep it very quiet, of course. The Lancefields have always been reclusive. But you'll find them helpful. Richard – the old man – and his son, David, are old-school country gents: painfully polite and endlessly accommodating. I can't say I have anything against them as human beings.'

'David was in the party that came up to Liberation Park for the wedding, wasn't he?'

'Yes. Along with Nancy and Marcus.' They were approaching a roundabout, and Parkinson slowed the car. 'DCI Price is planning to take you over to Salvation Hall first thing tomorrow. He said he'll pick you up at nine. It's only a few minutes by car to the estate. You can walk it by using a path from the village, but it makes more of an impact if you enter by the long drive.'

'More of an impact?"

The sergeant chuckled as he took his foot off the brake, guiding the car eastwards towards Penwithen. 'Price is a great believer in "context". You'll see what he means in the morning.' They were almost out of the town, moving swiftly along the shoreline. 'I suppose finding Becca's body in the lake here blows your theories about Jennet out of the water.'

'Pretty much.' Hall frowned. 'On the surface it looks as though Laurence was murdered by someone in that wedding party, but I want to see the Lancefield family for myself. I want to make up my own mind. That's why I'm here.' She turned to look at Parkinson. 'I know DCI Price is a senior officer of long standing, and I'm a rookie by comparison. But Laurence's murder happened on my patch and I can't let things drift.' She folded her arms. 'Has anything happened here during the day that I need to be aware of?'

'We attended the post mortem on Becca this afternoon. We've had confirmation she died by the same MO as Lucy Lancefield.'

'But I thought Lucy's killer was already dead?'

'He is. And everyone knows how Lucy died, so it could just be a copycat killing. But it also opens up the slim possibility that Philip McKeith wasn't the killer after all.' Parkinson wasn't sure how much to share with her. Strictly speaking, the investigation into Becca's death wasn't anything to do with her. But it might help her to form a picture of the family. 'We've also had confirmation she was murdered on Thursday morning, so we're working on the assumption she was murdered by a member of the household before David, Nancy and Marcus made the trip to Liberation Park. We're currently trying to establish where the body was stored before it went into the lake on Saturday evening.'

Hall's brow puckered and she sank deeper into the passenger seat. 'Can you see any of those three people murdering a girl on Thursday morning, driving up to Yorkshire, poisoning Laurence Payne, and then driving back to Cornwall to put a two-day-old body in the lake?'

'You're talking about a family that made its fortune from slavery. What do you think they're capable of?'

'But they're not all true family members, are they? Marcus is only related by marriage and Nancy isn't a relative at all. Or have I got that wrong?'

'Who knows? Nancy was born on St Felix and my understanding is that she's descended from the original slave population, though there has been so much intermarriage over the generations that you wouldn't necessarily know it to look at her. I guess she could somehow be distantly related to the family, but then so could everybody else on the Woodlands estate.' Parkinson glanced across at his passenger. 'I thought you said you'd been reading up on the family and how they made their money?'

'I have, but I didn't dig that deeply. You have to remember I come from Wilberforce territory, Sergeant Parkinson. We were abolitionists up in East Yorkshire. We're taught in school that slavery was an abomination and William Wilberforce almost single-handedly wiped it out. I'd never question that he played a significant role, but it's a lot more complex than that, isn't it? I've seen a few glass cabinets in a museum with chains and branding irons in them, and been disgusted by the sight. And I've seen the horrific pictures of how slaves were transported from the African continent to the Americas. But the subtleties of life on a plantation? Questions about intermarriage and how things worked after abolition? Nah, that's all passed me by, I'm afraid.' She pondered another question. 'Does Nancy consider herself to be a member of the family?'

'I think so. Officially she was Richard Lancefield's secretary, and for a number of years she was resident here at Salvation Hall. But she returned to St Felix after Eva McWhinney was murdered. Marcus had already been living out there for a few months. The old man encouraged him to go out there and make a fresh start.' They were on the approach to Penwithen village and Parkinson lowered his speed. 'That's The Lancefield Arms, up ahead on the right. I'll come in with you and introduce you to Amber. She's the landlady.'

'You're on first name terms with the landlady of the Lancefield's pub?'

'You haven't got very far with your research, have you, DI Hall? Amber was Zak Smith's girlfriend. And at one time Becca Smith's best friend. She identified Becca's body for us this afternoon.' He caught the inspector's look of incredulity from the corner of his eye, and smiled. 'Despite her previous involvement with Smith, Amber is as decent a human being as you could wish to find. Once you've checked in, I suggest you order yourself a meal in the bar and invite Amber to have a drink with you. You might find that DCI Price's lack of availability this evening is a blessing in disguise.'

*

'I'm afraid it rather took the wind out of her sails.' David leaned over to the coffee table and picked up a playing card. 'Poor Nancy. It had never occurred to her I might already know what she was so determined to tell me.' He examined the card, holding it close to the others in his hand. 'I don't know what she expected to achieve by betraying your confidence.'

Richard licked his thin lips and kept his eyes turned downwards. 'How did you know?'

'I can't say that I did know for certain. But I have often suspected.' David added the card to his hand and selected one to discard. 'I remember once on a visit to St Felix when mother was alive, she made a cryptic comment about Angel. Something about the art of seduction: it's no good being practised in the art of seduction if you can't pull off the end result. It sounded rather a cruel thing to say.' He dropped the nine of diamonds onto the table. 'She turned to look at you as she was saying it, and then she turned back to look at Angel and started stroking my hair. I felt like a trophy.'

'We were all in the same room?'

'Mother and I were on the terrace. I think Angel had brought some paperwork over from the estate office and she had just given it to you. You were sitting at your desk in the library and we could see you through the open window. Mother made the remark as Angel came out onto the terrace, and I thought the poor woman was going to burst into tears. She almost ran off down the steps back to the office.' David frowned at his father. 'Are you going to take a card?'

'In good time.' Richard lifted his eyes to look at his son. 'Was that the only thing that made you suspect?'

'No. A couple of days later I witnessed an argument between them. Angel accused my mother of not loving you, of only marrying you for your money. It was so out of character, so disrespectful, that it made me vigilant to the way the three of you interacted. I noticed how you looked at Angel, and how my mother looked at her; you with affection, and my mother with loathing.'

'You must have only been about seven or eight years of age.'

'I was a child at the time. Not a fool.' David watched as his father bent forward to lift the next card from the pack. 'Did Angel marry Addison before or after Honeysuckle was conceived?'

'After.' The old man was growing uncomfortable. He stared blankly at the cards in his hand. 'Do we have to have this conversation, David?'

'Oh, I think so. Now that Nancy has opened Pandora's box we might as well see what's in there.' He leaned back in his chair. 'Addison was incredibly kind to me when I was a boy. He used to take me down to the rock pools in Quintard Bay, to look for crabs and sea snails.' David rested his cards face down against his chest. 'How did my mother find out about Honeysuckle?'

'I told her. I didn't want to hold that kind of secret from my wife. She had a right to know.'

'But you didn't mind keeping it from me? Or from Honeysuckle or Nancy?'

Richard growled softly under his breath. 'It wasn't about keeping it from you. It was about respecting Angel's wishes. She didn't want anyone to know.'

'And yet she told her daughter and granddaughter when she was dying?'

'She didn't want to carry the secret to her grave. And I won't judge her for that. She told me what she'd done and asked my forgiveness, but there was no forgiveness necessary. I spoke to Honeysuckle afterwards, and she wanted to keep it quiet for her own dignity. She doesn't want the whole island to know she was my "mistake".' Richard eyed his son over the top of his playing cards. 'Those were her words, not mine.' He reached out to take David's discarded playing card from the top of the pile. 'Did Nancy tell you what she hoped to achieve by betraying her mother's confidence?'

'She wants to be publicly acknowledged.'

'And she can go on wanting. Nancy will return to St Felix as planned when DCI Price gives us the nod. She will have to understand that the secret must be kept.'

'But not from Barbara and Kathryn.' David gave a wry smile. 'They both know, don't they? And they've kept your secret well. Neither of them has mentioned it to me.'

'That is because they respect my wishes.'

'Is Marcus to be told?'

'No. At least, not yet. I fear he would choose never to return to St Felix if he knew the truth. He and Nancy need to make their peace first.' Richard slipped the playing card he had selected into the hand, then fanned the cards out to lay them on the table. 'Rummy.' He looked up at David. 'You're not angry with me?'

'Why? Because you won the hand with my discarded nine of diamonds, or because you kept me away from my sister all these years?' David's smile was gentle. 'No, I'm not angry with you. I always knew, if my suspicions were correct, that you would have good reason to keep it from me.' He dropped his own cards onto the table. 'Did Lucy know about Nancy?'

Richard flinched. 'I don't know. I've asked myself that question many times, but I can never come up with the answer. And she can't tell us now.'

'Would it make any difference if she could?'

'Yes.' His father pursed his lips. 'I am terribly afraid that it would.'

*

Ennor returned the bottle of Chenin blanc to the wine cooler on the table. 'You're sure it's not too cold to sit outside? We can ask to go to the table now if you'd prefer.' He knew he was making a fuss, but it was unusual for

Kathryn to be so quiet, and the unexpected formality between them was making him nervous. 'There's quite a breeze coming off the sea this evening, and it's only going to get cooler as the evening wears on.'

'Ennor, I'm fine, really.' She sounded anything but. 'I'm just a little tired, that's all. And there are blankets to use if we need them.' She stretched out a hand to her glass. 'I've been thinking about what you said to me this afternoon: that you might be too close to the family now to conduct the investigation without bias. And that you keep thinking about what it would mean for the family if it were David or Nancy or Marcus who committed the murders.' She sipped on the wine. 'But you have to do what's right. We both know that.'

Even if it meant their own relationship would be changed irrevocably by the outcome? He could hardly bear to think about it. But there was no denying the truth: if he *didn't* do the right thing, the consequences would hang over the two of them for a lifetime. 'I don't know if it helps, but I want to discount David from the equation. I have an enormous amount of sympathy for him. In the last nine months he's lost his daughter, his wife, and the cousin he thought might fill the void left by Lucy's death. And he's borne all of those losses with a calm and self-possessed dignity. I'll admit I used to think he was just a vacuous, henpecked little rich boy. But when I spoke to him this morning, I realised he's a quietly determined individual with a growing sense of duty and a decent set of values.' Ennor shook his head. 'David isn't a killer. I saw the horror on his face when we discovered Becca's body in the lake. I think he would find the whole question of taking a human life totally abhorrent.'

'So you've narrowed the field to Marcus and Nancy? Do you truly think Nancy capable of killing someone?'

'It's a stretch, isn't it?' Ennor's eyes crinkled at the corners. 'I told you the case was finally getting to me.' He put down his glass and lifted his hands to his face, rubbing at his temples to ease a growing tension. 'Like David, Nancy has changed. Only in her case, not for the better.' There had been an arrogance about her that afternoon which he'd found hard to take. 'Is it really just because she was angry to be sent back to St Felix?'

'Perhaps not. The murders have affected her too, you know. She might not be a member of Richard's immediate family, but…' Kathryn stopped, and turned her head away. She seemed to be weighing up whether or not to speak further, and when she turned back to look at him her eyes were troubled. 'When we spoke this afternoon, you said you wanted to go back to where it all started. It's why we're here in Marazion, isn't it? Why we've come to the place where I first told you what I knew about the family?'

'Yes.'

'Were you also referring to Lucy and Philip?'

'Yes, I think so.' Ennor frowned, remembering. 'Lucy's body was found barely an hour after you arrived at Salvation Hall. Becca found it, Nancy ran to see what the trouble was, and you and Richard followed behind.' He paused, but Kathryn had turned away again. 'What is it?'

'I…' She hesitated, and then leaned down to the large, soft leather bag at her feet. 'I don't know if I can say it, so I'll have to show you.' She pulled something out of the bag, something slim and square and rigid, wrapped in a thick, white cloth. 'You asked me about this the first time we had dinner together.' She handed the object to him. 'Barbara was clearing out Lucy's room today, and she asked me what to do with this. Initially we hung it back on the wall. And then I thought you might like it as a keepsake.'

He studied her face as he took the item from her, but her expression gave nothing away. Except, perhaps, her discomfort. 'What is it?' He loosened the covering. 'It feels like a picture frame.'

'It's the print of Elizabeth and Dido Belle. The picture Nancy gave to Lucy as a gift.'

'The gift Lucy hung on the wall of her suite, even though she hadn't wanted it?' The image was all too familiar to him: two young women exquisitely dressed in Georgian silks and satins; nieces to the Earl of Mansfield; one born into a privileged British life, the other born into slavery but claimed by her father, a British naval officer, and raised as a British gentlewoman. 'You're giving this to me as a keepsake?' He stared at the picture and slowly, painfully, the penny finally began to drop. 'You know why, don't you?' The muscles in his gut began to tighten. 'You know why Lucy didn't welcome this?'

'Please don't judge me, Ennor.' Kathryn's voice was almost a whisper. 'Richard asked me to keep this in confidence, and I didn't want to let him down.' Her mouth twisted. 'I've kept the secret all this time, but I just can't do it anymore. I didn't think it mattered, but now I think I might have been wrong.'

'Kathryn, you're not making any sense. Try telling me from the beginning.'

She stretched out a hand and placed it on Ennor's arm, struggling to hold back tears. 'Nancy is Richard's natural granddaughter. Lucy was her cousin.'

'Why the hell didn't you tell me this before?' The words came out in a growl of dismay. 'I knew there was something about this damn picture. Every time I tried to picture Nancy and Lucy together, I saw them as the girls in the painting. Dido and Elizabeth: Nancy and Lucy.' He placed the picture down on the table, unable to look at her. 'Why didn't you tell me?'

'Because I discovered the truth by accident and at first I wasn't sure of the facts. Her mother is Richard's illegitimate daughter. I found out... well, it doesn't matter, does it, how I found out? I asked Richard about it and he didn't deny it, but he did swear me to secrecy. And it's such a personal thing, isn't it? Especially as Nancy wasn't supposed to know.'

'But she did know, didn't she? Or else why give the

picture to Lucy? She was trying to tell Lucy they were cousins.'

'We don't have any evidence of that.'

'Unless we ask her.' Ennor pursed his lips. 'Who else knows about this?'

'As far as I know, only Barbara. We've both asked Richard to speak to David about it, but he refuses.' Kathryn's face had grown pale. 'Even Nancy didn't know until quite recently. She only learned the truth just before her grandmother died.'

'Does this mean she will inherit the estates when David has gone?'

'No. Richard flatly refuses to acknowledge her.'

'You mean he's spent the last nine months trying to dredge up distant cousins to support David, and all the time he could have just brought Nancy and her mother into the fold?' Ennor shook his head. 'There's no damned wonder she's angry.'

Kathryn took hold of Ennor's hand and squeezed it. 'This is nothing to do with the case, though, is it?'

Nothing to do with the case?

If that was true, why was he beginning to panic inside? It was nothing to do with the case, but it was everything to do with the case. It didn't explain why Zak or Becca, or even Laurence, had to die. But it raised more questions than it answered. He drew his hand away from Kathryn's and stood up from the table. 'I'll go inside and ask the waitress if they can delay our table by half an hour, and bring us another bottle of wine. Somehow I don't think this one is going to be enough.'

22

Jim Collinson's early morning call to Tom Parkinson was unexpected, but not unwelcome.

'I know Steph is going to be tied up for most of the day, so I wondered if we could keep a communication channel open.' Collinson sounded hopeful. 'She has a habit of turning off her phone and not being too quick to answer a message.'

'Worried she'll keep you in the dark?' Parkinson was amused by the notion. 'If it's any consolation, Price has asked me to stay in the background while they talk to the family. But I'm not too sorry to be surplus to requirements. I've got plenty to keep me busy.' He settled back into his seat. 'Have you spoken to DI Hall this morning?'

'Yes, just before she went down for breakfast. She was grateful you stayed to have a bite to eat with her last night, by the way.'

'I thought it was the least I could do, after she'd travelled all that way.' Truth be told he'd felt almost sorry for her. 'I can't say the wife was impressed though, when I rolled up at home and said I'd already eaten.' And even less impressed when he reminded her a detective couldn't always work office hours. 'Anyway, I left your guvnor chatting to Amber Kimbrall. She's the landlady at The Lancefield Arms and knows just about everything there is to know about the family, so hopefully there was a good exchange of information.' Parkinson rocked gently in his chair. 'I'll be honest with you, Jim, I'm feeling pretty nervous this morning. Price looks like a condemned man. I've been working with him for four years now and I've never seen him so despondent. I know he was out for dinner with Kathryn Clifton yesterday evening, to talk about the Lancefields, but I don't know what was said.' And it felt too personal to ask.

'What's the story with Price and Kathryn? Did they know each other before she went to work for the Lancefields?'

'No, they met the day Lucy Lancefield was murdered. She isn't a member of the family, so she was able to provide us with some unbiased information about the workings of the household. Things have changed a bit now though. She's been working for them since last September and has pretty much become a permanent fixture at Salvation Hall. The old man, Richard Lancefield, wanted to document his family's history and she came to help with that. But she's more of a secretary and assistant to the family now.' Parkinson frowned. 'She and Price have become friendly over the last nine months, and she's still a useful source of information.' Though not quite as useful as she used to be. 'Things haven't been quite so rosy between them since Smith's body turned up in the Lancefield's potting shed. I don't know all the details, but there's definitely some area of disagreement between her and Price.' And whatever that disagreement was, it was hurting Price. But Collinson didn't need to know that part. 'Are you going to be kicking your heels today? Only I got the impression DI Hall is fixated on Marcus Drake as her prime suspect.'

'Tell me about it.' Collinson groaned. 'She sent me back to Liberation Park yesterday to tell Jennet Payne that attention was shifting to the Lancefields. The thing is, while I was there something made my nose itch, but I can't get Steph to talk to me about it.' He gave a sniff of disappointment. 'I spoke to the hotel's manager first, and she set me straight about the nature of Jennet's relationship with her mother. Then when I spoke to Jennet and Rosemary together, it was clear they're just not on the same page about something. I wanted to speak to Jennet on her own, but it's like her mother has her on a tight leash and never lets her out of her sight.' Collinson paused, and then added, 'And Rosemary also seems particularly keen for suspicion to fall on the Lancefields.'

'Maybe she just wants the crime solving, so they can heal and move on.'

'Maybe she does. But my nose is still itching, just the same.'

'Well, you know there's only one thing to do with an itch, Jim.'

'Go back to Liberation Park and scratch it?' Collinson chuckled. 'I'm planning to go back later this morning. Jennet wanted to talk to Steph today, but she'll have to make do with me.'

'Do you still think it's possible Laurence was murdered by someone much closer to him than the Lancefields?'

'Without a doubt.' Collinson clicked his teeth. 'Do you think it's possible Steph is wasting her time down there in Penwithen? That the discovery of Becca's phone at Liberation Park and the brochure that turned up in the post were just a clumsy attempt to deflect attention from her murder at Salvation Hall, rather than putting her in the frame for Laurence's murder?'

Parkinson looked up at the ceiling and sighed. 'Without a doubt.'

*

'Barbara has taken DCI Price and DI Hall over to the Dower House, to see my father. Then, as I understand it, they will come back over to the main house to speak to me.' David turned his head to look over his shoulder at Kathryn. 'It will be the third time I have been informally interviewed in the last three days. I am at a loss to know what else I can tell the police and I'm almost past caring who committed these damn murders. I just want the misery to stop so we can return to some degree of normality.'

Kathryn murmured under her breath, a sympathetic hum of solidarity, and lifted the freshly brewed pot of tea from the kitchen counter. The events of the last nine months, the gains and losses he'd endured since last September, were beginning to wear David down. And yet they had almost been the making of him. 'Do you have any idea where Marcus and Nancy are this morning?' She set the teapot down on the table and sat down beside him. 'Have either of them had breakfast?'

'I've no idea. There were no dirty dishes in the kitchen when I arrived, but that doesn't mean much.' He cast a furtive glance towards the kitchen door. 'As we are alone, might I ask your opinion on a rather sensitive matter? My father tells me you are already aware of Nancy's true relationship to the family.'

'You mean he's finally told you?' Kathryn exhaled, a long slow breath of relief. 'There have been so many times I've wanted to talk to you about it, but I couldn't betray his confidence.'

'And I wouldn't expect anything less of you. Your loyalty, as always, does you credit. But I do want to bring this thing out into the open.' David's shoulders sank a little. 'Actually, it wasn't my father who told me. It was Nancy herself.' He pulled a face that suggested it wasn't an uplifting experience. 'I've discussed the situation with both my father and Barbara, and I plan to call Honeysuckle today. I'm quite aware she wants to keep her relationship to the family under wraps, and of course we must respect her wishes.'

'It's possible she might change her mind in the future.'

'Indeed she might. Perhaps a part of me even hopes she will. But at the moment, in the big scheme of things, I don't think it will make a great deal of difference to either of us. We have always had a good working relationship, and now we have the reason and the opportunity to get to know each other a little better. When Inspector Price finally brings his investigations to a close and we are permitted to travel, Barbara and I will go out to St Felix to spend some time with her.'

'So, you and Barbara intend to travel to St Felix, Richard already plans to return with Nancy, if she is given permission to go, and Marcus is thinking of moving to Edinburgh. Who will be here to mind Salvation Hall? The business side of things can be managed remotely, but someone will have to take care of Samson and look after the orchid house.'

A sheepish smile tugged at David's lip, and fleetingly his spirits appeared to rally. 'I rather hoped that would be you. But in the meantime, I wondered if you could shed any further light on Marcus and Nancy's falling out? He tells me now that he won't return to St Felix if she is there permanently.'

'She's making things difficult for him, isn't she?'

'So he says.' David's smile evaporated. 'It's coming to a head, isn't it? This boil that has to be lanced? I don't want to lose my stepson, Kathryn. He means a great deal to me. But I have to face the truth. He may be guilty of these murders. And even if he isn't, he is so disenchanted with the life we have to offer him that he would prefer to walk away from us. Whichever the situation, I feel we have failed him.'

'Has any evidence come to light yet to suggest Marcus is guilty?'

'No. I simply cannot see an alternative.'

Couldn't see one, or wouldn't? 'You must have been shocked when Nancy told you of her relationship to the family.'

'Not at all. As I explained to my father, I already had my suspicions. I think she was very disappointed by my reaction. She looked very deflated. And then she became sullen and said I should think about what it really means.' He frowned. 'What do you think she meant by that, Kathryn? Do you think we brought her to this place? That my father's insistence on searching for distant cousins has brought her to this?'

'Are you suggesting that she, rather than Marcus, might be responsible for the murders?

'Good heavens, of course not. Her relationship to the family has nothing to do with Zak or Becca, does it? Laurence, perhaps.' David appeared to consider the idea, before dismissing it with a shake of the head. 'But I rather thought she liked Laurence.'

'She didn't appreciate his reaction when she tried to tell him they were distantly related. He had no difficulty accepting the idea, but he couldn't see the relevance of it. To him, Nancy was still just Richard's secretary.'

'But it would be ludicrous to suggest Nancy could have murdered him.'

'She had the opportunity. She had access to the yew hedges here, and it's conceivable she could have slipped something into his food or drink while we were at Liberation Park.'

'But his dismissal of their distant relationship was such a small thing.'

'Not to Nancy.' Kathryn could still remember how angry it had made the girl to be discounted. 'What do you think she'll do now? Will she go meekly back to St Felix and resume her work with the foundation?'

'My father isn't giving her any other option.' David hesitated, and then he laughed. 'For heaven's sake, Kathryn, this is Nancy we're talking about. Could you imagine her doing anything meekly?'

'No, perhaps you have a point.'

In any case, Kathryn thought as she set about filling her cup from the teapot, what Nancy might do now was nowhere near as troubling as what Nancy might have already done.

*

Richard watched as Barbara led DI Hall out of the Dower House lounge, and as the door closed behind them he turned to DCI Price with a knowing smile. 'Detective Inspector Hall is quite charming, and I'm sure she's very capable. But do you think she is up to the challenge of flushing out Laurence's murderer?'

'I suspect we'll know the answer to that question by the end of the day.' Just as they would know whether Price was up to the challenge of flushing out whoever murdered Zak and Becca Smith. 'Why did you want to speak to me alone?'

'Because things are coming to a head, Inspector Price. And I think today will be a difficult one for all concerned.'

And wasn't that the truth. Price felt the muscles in his jaw begin to twitch. All through his investigations he'd given Richard Lancefield the benefit of the doubt. He'd taken the old man's willingness to give him free access to Salvation Hall as a sign he was fully supporting the various murder investigations; an indication that Richard was on the side of justice rather than the side of self-interest. And all the time he'd been keeping the secret of Nancy's birth line to himself.

Price looked down at the coffee in his hand and then drained off the aromatic dregs in an attempt to steady his temper. 'I don't deny it's going to be a difficult day.' The delicate china cup rattled noisily against its saucer as he placed them down on the small table beside his chair. 'And I do appreciate you giving us the use of the drawing room again, for DI Hall to conduct her interviews.' He wanted to call out the truth: that Kathryn had revealed to him the secret of Nancy's birth line; how disappointed he was she had chosen loyalty to Richard Lancefield over what he perceived as loyalty to himself; how his trust in Richard was waning. But he couldn't; not just because Kathryn had pleaded with him not to reveal her indiscretion to the family. But because he knew, despite his frustrations, it was in his own best interests to keep that particular powder as dry as he could until he was closer to nailing the killer. 'Was there something in particular you wanted to discuss with me?'

'I understand DI Hall has come to interview the family in regard to Laurence's murder. But I wanted to ask if you think that Laurence's killer, and the person responsible for the deaths of Becca and her brother, are likely to be one and the same?' Richard's brow furrowed. 'I have never before faced the possibility that one member of my family may have been responsible for killing another. Somehow Eva's and Stella's deaths were easier to bear, knowing Zak was responsible. But the idea that one of us may have murdered Laurence...'

'Smith didn't murder Lucy.'

'No, that's true. But I thought it was understood that Philip was responsible. Are you suggesting you might reopen the investigation into Lucy's murder?'

'Do you think I should?'

Richard stared at the policeman. 'I've thought long and hard over whether my poor friend Philip was the subject of a miscarriage of justice. Perhaps not a technical one, given that a dead man cannot be tried. But morally?'

'Are you questioning the version of events Marcus gave at his trial?'

'Sometimes, Chief Inspector, we old men are apt to make the mistake of thinking we know best. We do what we do with the best of intentions despite knowing all too well that the road to hell is paved with them. But it doesn't stop us from following through with our own particular folly.' Richard sighed. 'Mine, perhaps, has been… not necessarily to try to see the good in everyone. But to hope everyone is deserving of another chance, a chance of redemption. I didn't judge Philip for his relationship with Lucy, and I have striven to support Becca and Frankie in his memory.' Richard turned his eyes downwards to the cup in his hand, and sipped on his coffee. 'I know very little about Zak, and I never had the opportunity to talk to the man and fully understand his grievances. But I hope I would have listened to his side of the story had the opportunity presented itself. As to Becca, I was deeply disappointed in her behaviour towards the family, but I freely own that I misjudged the girl. When she tried to warn me about Jason Speed, I wouldn't listen. She did not deserve what happened to her, and I do not want the person responsible to go unpunished.'

Price lowered his head. 'I'm sorry, Mr Lancefield, I'm confused now. I thought you were concerned that a member of the family may have murdered Laurence. But now you're talking about Becca's murder.'

'I am confused myself. I'm ashamed to say I didn't much care who murdered Zak Smith. That I didn't much care who had taken their revenge on him for killing our beloved Eva and Stella. But I care who murdered Laurence, and I care who murdered Becca and left little Francesca without her mother.'

'Even if it were a member of the family?'

'Even if.' Richard nodded. 'You will have my full backing, whatever the outcome. If it is one of us, Inspector, and you can prove that and see justice done, I will do everything I can to support you.'

Except admit that Nancy is your granddaughter? Price bit back the desire to blurt out the words. 'I suppose it goes without saying you will fully fund the legal representation of that person, to ensure they receive the lightest possible sentence.'

The old man smiled. 'As I said, DCI Price, I want

justice to be done. But I still believe that every man deserves another chance.'

23

'Taxine? But I thought his death was a medical issue?' The news had come as a shock to Riley Gibb. 'Jennet, I'm so sorry. If there's anything I can do to help you, anything at all?' She sat down on the edge of the bed next to Jennet and took hold of her hand. 'Why didn't you tell me before?'

'How could I? I'm still trying to come to terms with it myself. That's why I keep coming back to the gatehouse. I keep thinking that if I come back to where he died, I might remember seeing something or hearing something that gives me a clue to what happened to him.' Jennet looked down at Riley's hand resting over her own. 'I'm sorry we haven't been more open with you and the rest of the staff. But it's been so difficult. Nothing prepares you for a shock like this. And to cap it all, can you believe my mother still thinks we can go ahead with next weekend's booking?'

'And you don't agree with her?' Riley nodded to herself. 'Of course, I can see how painful that would be for you. But it will be devastating for the bride and groom if we cancel. They don't know what's happened here, they just think everything will go ahead as planned.' She fell silent for a moment and then she asked, 'Do the police have any idea who was responsible for Laurence's death?'

'At the moment they seem to be spoilt for choice. DI Hall has gone to Cornwall to interview his distant cousins, the Lancefields. And in the meantime, Sergeant Collinson is keeping an eye on me and my mother.'

'Oh, now that's just ridiculous.

'Is it?' Jennet wished she shared the girl's confidence. 'Do you think I'm wrong not to let the wedding go ahead at the weekend?'

'It depends what you mean by wrong. I think it would be a shame to let the couple down if we don't have to, and I'm sure the staff would pull out all the stops with a bit of encouragement. Of course, I'll have to confirm all the additional orders today. I've gone ahead with the extra wine order, because there's no risk of any wastage if the wedding doesn't go ahead. We can always put that into the common stock for later use. But the food orders need confirming today and the florist needs to know by Wednesday.' Riley cleared her throat. 'We do need to be mindful of the cash flow situation if we can't use what we order.'

'What cash flow situation? I thought things were back on an even keel?'

Riley hesitated. 'I know Rosemary deals with the accounts, but you must be aware the business is running very hand-to-mouth again. And I know it must have been difficult for you: knowing Laurence could have helped out with an injection of cash. But no one blames him, Jennet. Rosemary was asking a lot of him.'

Jennet's frown deepened. 'I'm sorry, Riley, you've lost me now. What injection of cash? What was my mother asking of him?'

'You didn't know?' Riley's eyes widened. 'Now I wish I hadn't said anything.' She let go of Jennet's hand. 'Rosemary has been worried for a while now. We always seem to be sailing so close to the wind, and the margins have been getting tighter and tighter. And just a couple of weeks ago, she asked Laurence if he would be prepared to make a loan to the business. Just until things turned around.'

'And you were party to this conversation?'

The girl had the grace to blush. 'No. I was on duty at the reception desk, and they were in the small office behind me. They were talking very loudly and the door wasn't quite closed so I could hear what they were saying.'

'Then I can only think that you misheard. I know things have been a little tight at times, but my mother wouldn't let things slide that badly. And I don't believe for one minute she would have asked Laurence for money. And even if she did, I don't believe Laurence wouldn't have mentioned it to me.'

'Rosemary made him promise not to tell you. She didn't want you to worry.' Riley was speaking softly now. 'He didn't refuse to help. But he wouldn't advance any money unless Rosemary agreed to sell him a stake in Liberation Park, and she flatly refused.'

'And you didn't think to tell me this until now?'

'I didn't think it was my place to say anything at all about it. Especially as it was only something I overheard by accident.'

'Riley, just how bad are things for the business?'

'If this wedding doesn't go ahead and we have to refund the deposit, I'm afraid they'll be very bad. I don't see the accounts but I do see the bank statements. Month on month our receipts are going down and our overheads are going up. And we're getting dangerously close to breaching our overdraft limit.'

'How close?'

'A month. Maybe two, if we're lucky.'

'Then perhaps it's time *I* took a look at the accounts.' Jennet stood up. 'Let's go back to the office. You can show me where the latest account files are kept.'

'They're not on the office computer anymore. Rosemary moved them to her laptop.'

'And when did she do that?'

'In April, after we suffered that expensive cancellation.'

'Then we'll just have to look at her laptop. She's gone into town, hasn't she?'

'Yes. To the bank. She said she'd be back by lunchtime.'

'Then we'll have to be quick. She keeps her laptop in her room, in the desk beside the window.'

'But we can't just go in there and take it.'

'Oh, yes we can. If my mother has been hiding something, we need to know about it. I may not be the general manager here anymore but I'm still a joint owner and major shareholder. If anyone has a right to see those accounts and establish just how bad things are for the business, it's me.'

*

'I understand you didn't have a particularly good relationship with Laurence Payne.' DI Hall rested her notebook on her knee as she spoke. 'Would that be a fair statement?'

Marcus cast a wry glance at DCI Price, sitting next to Hall on the drawing room sofa. 'The nature of my relationship with Laurence is old news, DI Hall. I can't believe Inspector Price hasn't filled you in.'

Price met the suggestion with an enigmatic smile. 'I'm sure DI Hall would appreciate hearing it directly from you, Marcus.'

Marcus scowled. 'I didn't dislike him and I didn't resent him. I held him responsible for Eva's death because he failed to keep her safe, but I didn't kill him because of it.'

'Well, you're hardly likely to admit it, are you?' Hall jotted in her notebook. 'Did you feel any resentment about his relationship with Eva in general?'

'Of course not.'

'Even though she didn't tell you she was travelling

down to London to have dinner with him?'

'I didn't resent that. I can't say I understood it, but Laurence was of the opinion she wanted to keep the meeting a secret because she was planning a surprise for Richard.'

'So, she didn't tell you because she didn't trust you to keep the secret from Richard?'

'She didn't tell anyone in the family about the meeting, so clearly she didn't trust any of us.'

'If you didn't like Laurence, why did you fly back from St Felix to attend his wedding?'

'It wasn't a personal decision. It was a three-line whip from Richard and David. I was representing the family, not there in a personal capacity.'

Hall's brow wrinkled. 'You could have refused.'

'I could. And, on reflection, I wish I had. Then I couldn't have been falsely accused of killing him, could I?'

The detective pushed out her lips. 'Has someone accused you, Marcus?'

'Not in so many words. But I know it's what everyone is thinking.'

'Did you spend any time alone with Laurence when you were at Liberation Park?'

'No. I travelled up with David and Nancy on Thursday afternoon; we all checked in and went to our rooms to unpack, then we met for supper. Laurence joined us for a drink afterwards, and Inspector Price and Kathryn were there.' Marcus cast another glance at Price. 'Laurence left to go back to his room at around ten thirty. The next time I saw him was the following afternoon, at the wedding ceremony.'

'What time did you go back to your room on the Thursday evening?'

'Around eleven thirty.'

'And what time did you go down for breakfast the following morning?'

Marcus frowned. 'I think it was eight o'clock. David or

Nancy will be able to confirm that. We all took breakfast together.'

Hall consulted her notebook. 'If Laurence went back to his room at ten thirty and you left the bar at eleven thirty, you'll allow it's possible the two of you might have had an encounter any time after that, and before eight o'clock on Friday morning?'

'Are you suggesting he might have come to my room?'

'Or that you might have gone to his.'

'I had no idea which room he was in. I had no need to know.'

'Very possibly.' Hall tilted her head. 'But as Laurence isn't here to confirm your version of events I only have your word for it.'

'True. But I'll be honest with you, DI Hall. If I'd wanted to poison Laurence, I would have made a better job of it than his killer. I would have made sure the dose of whatever it was that killed him was substantial enough to ensure he died in the night, rather than lasting until the following evening.' Marcus turned his attention to Price. 'What would you like me to say? That Laurence sought out my company for a further nightcap?'

'Are you sorry Laurence is dead, Marcus?' Hall didn't give Price the chance to answer the question.

'I can't say I have any particularly strong feelings one way or the other.'

'He was planning to fly out to St Felix for his honeymoon, wasn't he? Did you feel uncomfortable about that?'

'Why would I? He was just being given the use of a cottage on the Woodlands estate. I wasn't planning to spend any time with him.'

'There wasn't an expectation you would entertain him and Jennet while they were out there?'

'None that I was aware of.' Marcus, growing weary, turned again to Price. 'I think we might be done here, Inspector. If I could give you any further help, I would.'

Hall pursed her lips. 'With respect, Marcus, *I'll* decide when we're done.'

'And with respect, I would remind you that I agreed to a voluntary interview, even though I've already shared the information with DCI Price.' Marcus barely gave her a glance. 'So, Inspector Price, what happens now, in the absence of any hard evidence that would justify questioning me on a more formal basis?'

'DI Hall doesn't need hard evidence, Marcus. Only justifiable cause.' Price put out a hand and touched DI Hall on the arm. 'But I think we're done for now, aren't we?'

Hall's jaw stiffened and she narrowed her eyes. And then, just as swiftly, she smiled; a demure curve of the lips. 'Just about. If Marcus wouldn't mind answering just one more question?' She closed her notebook and rested her hands on the cover. 'How did you feel after you murdered Philip McKeith?'

*

'This is early for you, Sergeant Parkinson. We've barely got the doors open.' Amber smiled as he made his way to the bar. 'The usual?'

'Better make it a tonic with ice and lemon. I've come to speak to you about Becca.'

The landlady sighed as she added ice and a slice of lemon to a small glass from the shelf behind the bar. 'I'm taking Sadie over to Salvation Hall this afternoon, to see where Becca was found. We're going to leave some flowers.' She turned to the fridge behind her and retrieved a small bottle of tonic water. 'It's going to be hard. We've been invited to have tea with Richard and Barbara afterwards but Sadie isn't keen. She's not sure she can keep her thoughts to herself.' Amber levered the top from the bottle and poured the contents into the glass. 'One tonic with ice and lemon. On the house.'

'On the house? How do you know I deserve it?'

'I don't. Yet. Call it a down payment for bringing Becca's killer to justice.' She skirted the bar with a smile and sat down on the stool next to him. 'So, what have you come to tell me?'

'We've had a lead of sorts come in this morning. We've been able to trace some of Becca's movements on Thursday, after she dropped Frankie off at Sadie's. We've had a sighting of her at Hayle bus station, so we know now that she definitely didn't go straight back to Truro. She was seen getting on a bus to Penwithen. More importantly, before she caught the bus she used the post office near the station to post a letter. The postmaster remembered her, because she seemed agitated. The envelope had to be weighed and measured for the postage, because it was quite bulky; he thought it was a long letter, with a number of pages. But he has no idea who it was addressed to.' Parkinson paused. 'I'm guessing it was addressed to one of a handful of people – you, Sadie or Robin.'

'I haven't had anything from her, Sergeant Parkinson. I would have told you straight away if I had. Sadie has never mentioned anything and she would know if Robin had received it.' Amber pouted. 'How do you know it wasn't something completely innocent?'

'A letter to a pen pal?' Parkinson's eyes crinkled at the corners. 'Who on earth would Becca write a long letter to if not you, Sadie or Robin?' He sipped on the tonic. 'The letter went straight into the post bag behind the counter in the post office, and was collected the same day at three thirty. It was posted first class so wherever it was going, it should have arrived on Friday morning.'

'Friday morning? You're living in the past, Sergeant. There's no guarantee of next-day delivery these days unless you pay a premium. And there was industrial action at the weekend. They're probably still clearing the backlog at the sorting office. But I'll double check with Sadie when she gets here. She might have received something this morning.' Amber hesitated. 'I take it we're still no nearer to knowing why Becca died?'

There was a limit to what he could tell her. 'We've narrowed the suspects down to the Lancefield family, but I shouldn't think that will come as any surprise to you.'

'I can't say that it does. I suppose it has to be Marcus, doesn't it? It's a shame, really.'

'Why is it a shame?'

'Well, I didn't know him very well in the early days. You know, when Zak and Becca were always on his case about Philip. But I always thought he had a soft spot for Becca. I mean, they were both in the same boat, weren't they? Philip and Lucy carrying on like that. Both of them were made fools of. It gave them something in common, didn't it? Like each knew what the other was going through.'

'Did Becca ever talk about him?'

'Not particularly. She did tell me about the night she walked into Salvation Hall and started accusing them of not caring about Philip. She said Marcus took her away from the house and back to Holly Cottage, and he sat and chatted to her for hours. She said she was really taken in by him.'

'Taken in?'

'Of course. At the time, she thought he was being genuinely sympathetic. But later she realised it must have been coming from a place of guilt. Because all the time, he'd known they would find Philip's body in the lake – because he was the one who put it there.'

24

If DI Hall had hoped to achieve a degree of rapport with Nancy Woodlands, she was only to be disappointed. The hostile angry creature perched sullenly on the edge of a drawing room armchair was a far cry from the impression Price had given her of the girl. She cast a questioning glance in Price's direction and he gave an almost imperceptible shake of the head. He knew now that Nancy was nursing an undisclosed grievance but, sworn to secrecy by Kathryn, he could say nothing to Hall about it. He would have to explain to her later that Nancy's brittle and bitter demeanour had been more than even he would have expected. For now, they would just have to go with the flow.

He was sitting beside Hall on the sofa and he leaned forward to rest his forearms casually on his knees. 'Thank you for agreeing to speak to us, Nancy. DI Hall just has a few questions she would like to put to you about your time at Liberation Park.' He nodded to Hall with an encouraging smile.

Hall consulted her notebook. 'Did you know Laurence very well, Nancy?'

'Not particularly. I met him when he came to Salvation Hall, of course, but we had very little say to one another.'

Price tilted his head. 'Didn't you discuss your shared

heritage, and the fact you had a distant ancestor in common?'

'An ancestor of mine was sold by the Lancefields to Laurence Payne's family. That ancestor bore a child to the head of the family, and the child was later recognised as his legitimate heir.' She addressed the explanation to DI Hall before turning again to Price. 'I hope you're not going to suggest that as a motive for Laurence's murder, Inspector Price?'

'No. But you do admit you discussed the matter with him. He wasn't particularly interested, was he?'

'Not everyone is interested in the details of their heritage.' She turned her eyes back to Hall. 'DCI Price, of course, is particularly interested in the Lancefield's heritage because he is particularly interested in the person Richard engaged to investigate and document it.'

Hall let the comment go. 'If you didn't have any sort of relationship with Laurence, why did you accept an invitation to his wedding?'

'Marcus, David and I were there to represent the family because Richard couldn't travel.' Nancy frowned. 'Perhaps I could volunteer some additional information that would help to move things forward.' She cleared her throat and rested her hands loosely in her lap. 'I barely knew the man. His friendship with Eva was of no concern to me. And, most importantly, I had nothing to gain from his death.'

'Did you like him?'

'I can't say I've ever thought about it. I considered him rather handsome and he was certainly well educated.'

'Did you spend any time alone with him at Liberation Park?'

'No, of course not. Why would I? I was with David and Marcus most of the time. Inspector Price can attest to that.'

Hall nodded, and scribbled in her notebook. 'What time did you go to bed on Thursday evening?'

'Some time before midnight. Laurence had joined us

for drinks, but he left around ten thirty.'

'You didn't encounter him at any time between leaving the bar at midnight and going down for breakfast the following morning?'

'No.'

'Do you have any evidence of that?'

'No. Do you have any evidence I am lying?'

Hall smiled. And then she rested back against the sofa's cushions, folding her arms and fixing the girl with a shrewd gaze. 'Becca Smith's phone was found at Liberation Park, Nancy. Would you have any idea how it got there?'

The question was unexpected and Nancy's eyes flashed towards Price. 'What does this have to do with Laurence's murder?'

Price could only think he wanted to know the answer to that question too. But he wasn't going to humiliate Hall by challenging her in front of a suspect. 'This is only a voluntary interview, Nancy, but if you would prefer not to answer the question I might have to ask myself why.'

The girl scowled. 'I have no idea how Becca's phone made its way to Liberation Park. Perhaps Marcus took it with him.'

Hall turned to look at Price, but Price just smiled. 'Do you have any evidence to back up that suggestion?'

'I rather thought that procuring evidence was your responsibility, Inspector, not mine.'

The atmosphere was growing tense. There had never been a possibility Nancy would be fully cooperative, but unless he could pull Hall back from the brink she might shut down on them altogether. 'To be clear, DI Hall has only come to question you about Laurence's death. The discovery of Becca's phone at Liberation Park means she has to consider whether the person who murdered Becca might also be the person who murdered Laurence.'

Hall stiffened, annoyed by the intervention. 'Thank you for explaining that.' She turned a firmer face towards

Nancy. 'Did you have a good relationship with Becca? Did you know her well?'

'She worked at Salvation Hall for a time, and lived at Holly Cottage. Our paths crossed in the way of work. I have already discussed this with DCI Price.'

'So, you wouldn't consider her a friend.'

'No, I wouldn't.'

'And what about Lucy Lancefield? Would you have considered her a friend?'

The unexpected question stunned both Nancy and Price in equal measures. Nancy raised herself up in her seat, her face a mask of indignation. 'Are you going to let her question me like this, Inspector Price? I cannot see Lucy's death has anything at all to do with Laurence Payne.'

Price, himself still reeling, stared at DI Hall. 'Would you be good enough to explain to Nancy how that question is relevant to your investigation?'

Hall smiled, her confidence growing. 'I'm interested to know whether Nancy was on friendly terms with anyone in the Lancefield family. Or whether her indifference towards Laurence was just a reflection of her indifference towards the family in general.' She turned back to Nancy. 'How did you feel when Lucy died?'

Nancy's lower lip began to tremble. 'If you must know, I was heartbroken. Lucy and I had known each other since childhood. We had played together on St Felix when she came to visit for holidays, and when Richard invited me to Salvation Hall to work as his secretary, I was delighted to be working alongside her. We spent a lot of time together, not just working but in our free time, and she confided in me about her relationship with Philip McKeith. And I knew how fond Philip was of her. There isn't a day goes by that I don't wonder why Philip murdered her. I can only think they must have argued. That perhaps she told him she was going to break off their affair before she married Marcus.' A single tiny tear made its way down

Nancy's cheek and she brushed it away. 'There, are you satisfied now, both of you?'

Hall softened her tone. 'I'm sorry if I upset you. And I promise that I only have one more question for you.' She kept her eyes fixed on Nancy's face. 'When Becca Smith disappeared, a search of her home turned up a brochure for Liberation Park. I don't suppose you have any idea how it got there?'

*

'Kathryn has taken Samson for a walk. She is not in good spirits this morning. I thought some fresh air might lift her mood and she didn't object to the suggestion.' David looked ill at ease at the library desk. 'I asked her if I might take a look at the Liberation Park Bible while she was gone, I thought it might take my mind off things.'

'And heaven knows we all need something to do that.' Barbara sat down on the chair beside the desk. 'She doesn't consider it to be a true Bible, does she?'

'No, and I can see why.' The book was open on the desk in front of him and he slid a fingernail under the right-hand page, turning it over carefully. 'Still, it was very kind of Jennet to loan us such a valuable item. In an ideal world I would drive back to Yorkshire to return it in person. But I can see it wouldn't be appropriate at the moment.'

'Perhaps DI Hall would be good enough to take it back with her, when she leaves Salvation Hall.'

'Yes, perhaps she would.' He turned another page and ran his eyes slowly down the text. 'Kathryn tells me the original owners of Liberation Park were a plantation-owning family like ours, and that it passed into the hands of an abolitionist who was also from a plantation-owning family. It makes one think, you know. I've long been aware some abolitionists were born into slave-owning families through accidents of birth, much like myself. Though I've never been able to fully reconcile the fact.' He frowned, a deep furrow of thought across his brow. 'I suppose the rivers of hypocrisy run still and deep. They most certainly do in this family.'

'You're thinking about your father.'

'And the bigger picture. I've often thought if there was any saving grace about our heritage, it was that the Lancefields were known to be tolerant and enlightened masters when it came to their slave population. Kathryn's research shows our workers were well fed and well housed, and given good clothing and time off; they were encouraged to embrace Christianity and attend church, and given a degree of education. Some were allowed to work for a wage outside of their work on the plantation, and earn enough to buy their freedom. And no request for freedom in return for payment was ever refused.' He slumped back in the chair. 'But none of it excuses the deprivation of liberty, does it? None of it gives any of us the right to claim mastery over another.'

'And now you're thinking about Nancy.'

'How well you have come to know me in the last few months.' David's soft grey eyes crinkled. 'Nancy is refusing to speak to me this morning, though I understand from Inspector Price that she has agreed to meet with DI Hall.' He straightened his back and stretched out his neck. 'I was rather dismissive of her claims yesterday evening. But I suppose, having slept on it, she has a point. The girl is my niece, and whether my father will acknowledge her or not she has a far greater claim to a role in running the Woodlands estate than Marcus.'

'Perhaps. But I don't think you can underestimate the privilege she has already been given. Setting up and running the foundation for the family raises her profile on the island as a whole, doesn't it? It's giving her the opportunity to open up the history of both the Woodlands estate and St Felix, the opportunity to make sure the story is told by someone who is bound hand and heart to the place.'

'It's the fact that she is "bound" to it which causes me the most grief.' He couldn't rid himself of the fear his father viewed her as a possession, rather than a granddaughter. And, however much he trusted Barbara, he couldn't share that fear. 'Would it make a difference, do you think, if I could persuade him to change things around? If he could be persuaded to give Nancy the management of the estate and Marcus responsibility for the foundation?'

'Assuming Marcus could be persuaded to return to St Felix?' Barbara pushed out her lips. 'I don't think it would be wise to consider changing anything at the moment. Perhaps a better approach would be to plan for every eventuality?'

'Who will look after the foundation if Nancy is found guilty of murder, and who will look after the estate if it's Marcus?' The answer escaped him. 'I fear we should already be considering a contingency for the loss of Marcus. He has pretty much washed his hands of the family in the last twenty-four hours and tells me that when he is cleared of any involvement in the murders he plans to leave the family for good and make a fresh start of his own choosing.'

'He's angry. And probably afraid he might go to prison. But he may feel differently if he *is* cleared. After all, if he is innocent then it's likely Nancy is guilty. So she would no longer be there to provoke him.'

'It's falling apart, Barbara, isn't it? All of my father's dreams to build a family to support me and to carry the family's heritage forward? All the time there was family there for me, Honeysuckle and Nancy, but it wasn't enough for him.'

'Perhaps it has to fall apart so we can rebuild it on a stronger footing.' Barbara placed a hand on his arm. 'And we will rebuild it, David. Whatever happens, I'm not going anywhere. If Richard hadn't found me, I wouldn't be here now. And as long as I'm needed, I will be here.'

For a few moments, they sat in silence. And then David leaned slowly towards her. 'When you came in, you were looking for Kathryn. Is it something I can help with in her absence?'

Barbara hesitated, and then looked down at the leatherbound book she was holding in her free hand. 'I found something amongst Eva's belongings that I think DCI Price needs to see. I wanted to ask Kathryn's opinion before I shared it with him. I was worried about the impact it might have on the family. But now we've spoken, I can see he must be given it.' She squeezed David's arm. 'I don't want you to give it another thought. If it means what I think it means, we won't have to wait much longer for the investigation to be over.'

'Who on earth said that Liberation Park is having cash flow issues? I suppose it must have been Riley. You know, she only gets to see a snapshot of the situation. She can't possibly hope to understand the position by looking at a few bank statements.' Rosemary Taylor pulled a small cut glass tumbler from underneath the bar and waved it towards her daughter. 'If it were true don't you think I would have told you?'

'Not necessarily. You knew I had a lot on my mind with the wedding coming up. And you knew how happy I was to be marrying Laurence. It would be like you to keep it to yourself until we returned from our honeymoon.' Jennet drew in a silent, steadying breath. 'But now there isn't going to be a honeymoon, you might as well come clean about it. Nothing you could say could possibly make me feel any more wretched than losing Laurence.'

Rosemary turned away towards the row of bottles on the wall behind the bar. 'Darling, everything in life happens for a reason.' She rammed the glass up against the gin optic. 'I know how painful the loss must be but life goes on, and you're young enough to meet someone else.

You just need to give yourself time. The right man is out there somewhere.'

'Laurence was the right man. I don't understand how you can talk about him as if he was so inconsequential.' She watched as Rosemary set about pouring tonic into her gin glass, unsurprised by her mother's familiar coolness and yet suddenly riled by it. 'I know you didn't want me to marry him, but I loved him. I loved him because he wanted me to be happy.'

'*I* want you to be happy.' Rosemary swigged on the gin. 'Did I ever say I thought you shouldn't marry him? Did I make any attempt to stop the wedding from going ahead?'

'Not openly.' Jennet felt her pulse begin to quicken. 'But then I suppose it must have been a very delicate balancing act: weighing up my marrying a man you didn't approve of against the fact that he was wealthy enough to invest in Liberation Park.' She watched her mother's face as she spoke. There was no question the barb had hit its mark. 'Oh, I know all about your suggestion that Laurence might like to invest in the business. But he wasn't interested, was he? At least, not on your terms.'

A flush of angry crimson made its way across Rosemary's neck. 'He promised me he wouldn't say anything to you.'

And he didn't break his promise. But Jennet wasn't about to reveal that the indiscretion was Riley's. 'Did you actually think Laurence naïve enough to just hand over a wedge of cash with no say in how the business would be run?' Jennet shook her head. 'You really didn't know him at all, did you? You know' – she rested her elbows on the table –'the irony is that Liberation Park's financial troubles are over now. With the money I stand to inherit from Laurence, I can put the place back on its feet. And despite all of your efforts, you won't be here to see it.'

'Why on earth not?'

'Because they'll be putting you away for a very long time.'

'Putting me away?' Rosemary frowned. 'Darling, whatever are you talking about?'

'Pre-meditated murder.'

Rosemary's face contorted. And then she laughed. 'Who on earth am I supposed to have murdered?'

'Laurence, of course.'

'Is that honestly what you think of me? That I would break my daughter's heart by murdering the man she wanted to marry?'

'You didn't want me to marry him, but you wanted his money. I made the mistake of telling you he'd made a will in my favour after we became engaged, so you knew if he died, I would inherit his fortune whether the marriage went ahead or not.'

Rosemary drained off the remaining gin and rammed the glass under the optic for a second time. 'Marcus Drake murdered Laurence. Why else would DI Hall travel to Cornwall to interview him?'

'Just because she suspects him, it doesn't mean that he did it.' Jennet licked her lips. 'I realise now that was my other mistake – telling you there was bad blood between Laurence and Marcus. I suppose that gave you the idea of framing Marcus; he was bound to fall under suspicion if Laurence died while the Lancefields were at Liberation Park.'

'And what about that poor girl, Becca Smith? Marcus must have murdered her before he left Cornwall, just so he could throw suspicion on her. He brought her phone to Liberation Park, murdered Laurence, and then planted the phone near the gatehouse to throw everyone off the scent. He killed that girl just to make her a scapegoat.'

'Why did you go to such lengths to research the Lancefield family?'

'I have no idea what you're talking about.'

'I've seen the internet search history on your laptop. I've seen the evidence you searched for information on the Lancefields.' Jennet lowered her voice to a whisper. 'And that you searched for information on taxine, and how effective it can be as a poison.'

The colour drained from Rosemary's face. 'Who the hell gave you permission to look at my laptop?'

'Your laptop is an asset of the business, as is the data it holds. I've every right to look at it. I took it from your room when Riley told me about the hotel's financial issues. I wanted to see the accounts for myself. I wanted to see what you'd been keeping from me.' A sob caught in Jennet's throat. 'I wanted to see how much of a liar you are.' She let out a wail. 'What the hell am I supposed to do now? You've taken Laurence from me, and now I'm going to lose you.'

'Darling, you're not going to lose me.' Rosemary put down her glass and stepped forward to sit beside her daughter. 'Whatever I did, I did for you. I knew you didn't want to leave Liberation Park, and he was going to take you away. Now you can stay here, with me. And we can use his money to put the business back on its feet.' She took hold of her daughter's hand. 'This is just our little secret, isn't it? All we have to do is stay strong. I'll go up to my room now and take a copy of the business files on the laptop, so that we don't lose them. And then I'll take the laptop out into the countryside and destroy it. I'll bury it where no one will ever find it. The police will go on looking at Marcus Drake, and we can get on with our life here at Liberation Park. No one need ever know.'

Jennet recoiled, and pulled her hand slowly away from her mother's grasp. 'I'm afraid it's too late for that now. People already *do* know.'

'What on earth do you mean?'

'You've robbed me of the man I loved, and I wasn't going to take the risk of you getting away with his murder. So I put your laptop where I knew it would be safest.' Jennet's mouth twisted and she turned her head away. 'I gave it to Sergeant Collinson.'

25

DI Hall cast a withering glance around the small housekeeper's room. 'Well, I've worked in worse places. At least they've given you a space to call your own.' She sat down at the table opposite Price, wincing as her body made contact with the stiff, unyielding wooden chair. 'I'll need to put a call in to Jim soon. I've had four missed calls and a text saying he needs to speak to me urgently.'

'I'll raise your four missed calls with another three from Tom, and two text messages. He's on his way to Salvation Hall.' Price settled back in his seat. 'Why did you veer off script and start talking to Nancy about Lucy Lancefield's death?' He tried to sound curious rather than irritated. 'I would have appreciated a bit of notice on that one.'

Hall scrunched up her nose. 'She got my hackles up. She's as guilty as hell about something and I can't help wondering whether you've just grown too sentimental about this entire Lancefield set-up to see it. That crack she made, about you being interested in Kathryn Clifton, doesn't that bother you? Can't you see you've crossed a boundary there?'

'My friendship with Kathryn was built on her willingness to share information about the family. She provided me with valuable insight after Lucy and Philip were murdered. And she did the same when Jason Speed and Emma Needham came to Salvation Hall.'

'And after that?'

'After that she...' He hesitated, suddenly reluctant to discuss it. But he couldn't shirk the question. He knew that now. 'She was a link to Eva McWhinney as well as the rest of the family. And to Laurence Payne. You know that's how I came by an invitation to his wedding.'

'But by then, she wasn't independent anymore, was she? She was part of the Lancefield household.' Hall's eyes narrowed behind her spectacles. 'Just like you.'

The accusation hit him like a punch in the gut. 'Are you calling my professionalism into question here, DI Hall?'

She let out a sigh. 'No. I'm asking you to call your own professionalism into question. These people have become friends to you, whether you realise it or not. I saw it when you were speaking to Marcus, and again when we were interviewing Nancy. When I asked any question that might ruffle their feathers or suggest they were somehow involved, they turned to look at you to see if you would intervene and fight their corner.' Hall slipped her spectacles from her nose and pretended to examine them. 'You don't want to believe that either of them is a killer, do you?' She breathed on the left-hand lens, pulling a tissue from her pocket to rub at an imaginary smudge. 'Why is that, Price? Is it because you don't want to pull the trigger? Because you don't want to shatter this rarified little world you've got yourself embedded in?'

'I thought you weren't challenging my professionalism?' Price slumped back in his seat and the hard wooden spokes dug into his flesh. 'These bloody chairs are so uncomfortable.' He was rattled now, defensive against her rebukes; worse still, enraged with himself for falling into the trap. 'Hall, I ...' The words wouldn't come and he clamped his lips together and looked away across the small, cramped room.

Why the hell had it taken a newly promoted,

inexperienced detective inspector to call out his mistakes? To confront him with the truth? To hint at what he knew to be the biggest mistake of all? He sucked in a breath. 'What do you think Nancy is guilty of?'

'Ah, well, that's the sixty four thousand dollar question, isn't it?' Hall placed the spectacles back on her nose and peered through them at Price. 'It could be Laurence's murder, it could be Becca's. Right now, the important thing is that you agree with me; she's guilty of *something*. And you can accept that, and we can move forward with the investigation knowing that she's going to end up charged with something.'

'You saw through her straight away, didn't you?'

'It would have been difficult not to. You originally described her to me as beautiful, efficient, witty and easy-going. What I saw was sullen, glib, and obstructive. She's beautiful, alright, even with that face on her. But it's only skin deep. There's something rotten on the inside eating away at her, that's for sure.'

'She hasn't always been like that. I won't deny she's changed, but…'

'For pity's sake, Price, just listen to yourself. You're still defending her.'

And he was.

He swallowed hard. This was the point at which he had to tell the truth. He had to betray Kathryn's confidence and tell Hall the reason for Nancy's obvious belligerence. 'Please keep to yourself what I'm about to tell you. I'm telling you because I know it's the right thing do to, but I have to break a confidence to do it.' He lowered his voice. 'I have to betray the trust of a person I hoped I would never betray.'

*

The lounge at The Lancefield Arms was quiet and

Kathryn's favourite table in the window had been vacant when they arrived, as if it were waiting for them.

'Marcus, you look exhausted. Are you sure you don't want something to eat?'

'I don't want to stay in Penwithen any longer than I have to.' He wrapped a hand around the pint of ale on the table in front of him. 'I'm happy just to have a drink.'

Except he wasn't happy at all. 'Are you really planning to leave Salvation Hall and turn your back on the family?' She'd found him in the hallway, his bags already packed, and it had taken some cajoling on her part to persuade him to leave the luggage where it was and join her for a walk down to the inn. 'I know things are difficult at the moment, but I don't think running away is the answer.'

'Is that what I'm doing? Running away? I thought I was making a conscious decision to put myself first for once.' He stared hard at Kathryn. 'Why did you want to speak to me?'

'Because I wanted to ask you about something that happened last year, before you confessed to Philip's murder.' Something that had troubled her for some time. 'There was an evening when we all had dinner together, and after we'd eaten you went outside with Nancy to get some fresh air.'

He gave a shake of the head. 'I don't remember that.'

'The dinner, or going outside with Nancy?'

'Does it matter?' He was growing impatient. 'Kathryn, what does this have to do with the mess I'm in now? You're talking about something that happened almost a year ago.'

'I overheard your conversation. I'd gone out into the hall and the window was open. The two of you were sitting on the bench outside, talking very quietly. But I still heard what was said. I heard Nancy say, "No one must ever know." And I asked you later if she was talking about the fact you gave each other a false alibi.' Kathryn lowered her voice. 'She didn't keep to her side of the bargain, did she?

She admitted the alibi she gave you was false.'

'You already know the answer to that question.'

'I know. But there's more to it than that, isn't there? That alibi wasn't the only secret she was asking you to keep.'

A faint tinge of colour made its way into Marcus's cheeks. 'I don't know what you're driving at.'

'I'm suggesting that you're hiding something. And I think if you could find a way to talk to me about it, it might help to clear your name.'

'Why on earth would I hide something that would clear my name?'

'Because you gave your word. But that was before more people died.' She took hold of his free hand. 'When Ennor and DI Hall spoke to you this morning, did Ennor tell you he was thinking of re-opening the investigation into Lucy's death?'

Marcus recoiled, and drew back his hand. 'Why the hell would he do that? Philip murdered Lucy. Everyone knows that he did.'

'No one knows for certain who murdered her. You were the only witness to what happened, and you claim she was already dead and Philip was leaning over her body. Based on your testimony, the assumption was that Philip murdered her. That was the reason you gave for killing him. You believed he'd murdered her, and you lost control and lashed out at him with the spade.' Kathryn drew in a breath. 'But what if your assumption was wrong? You said yourself that Philip was crying. You said he looked terrified.'

'You haven't answered my question. Why is DCI Price thinking of re-opening the case?'

'Because Becca was murdered in the same way as Lucy. She was strangled with a scarf, and her body was put into the lake.' Kathryn took hold of his hand again and this time held it tightly. 'I don't believe you want to leave the family, or that you want to make a fresh start at Hemlock

Row. I think you believe you've been backed into a corner and you can't see a way out.' She squeezed his hand. 'But there is a way out, Marcus. You just have to tell me the truth.'

'You make it sound so easy.' He slumped back in his seat. 'I look back now, and I can't help thinking if I had told the truth about the night Lucy died then Geraldine Morton, Eva, and Stella all might still be alive. And I might not be under investigation for murders I didn't commit.' He bit his lip. 'But I can't say anything. I gave my word and I can't break it.'

It might have been stalemate. And then Kathryn, her voice barely audible, asked, 'Did Nancy help you to put the bodies into the lake? Is that the secret you were bound to keep?' She watched intently as Marcus turned his head away. 'You know, Marcus, much as I'm fond of Richard, I don't think he has been completely honest with you. And I think you might find it easier to speak if I share one of Richard's secrets with you. It's a secret I promised to keep. But I'm going to break my word, because I want you to know sometimes promises have to be broken in order to do the right thing.' She leaned closer to him, her eyes still fixed on his face. 'Nancy isn't just Richard's secretary. Nancy is Richard's natural granddaughter.'

Her words hung dangerously in the air. And then Marcus slowly turned his face towards her, his eyes suddenly wide with understanding. 'Before I confessed to Philip's murder, Richard asked me to tell him everything that happened that night, just as I remembered it. I told him I took one look at Lucy lying on the ground, and flipped. That I took hold of the spade and lashed out at Philip.' The young man hesitated, the words still sticking in his throat. 'I heard Philip say something about Lucy not breathing; he begged me to help him. And as I swung the spade he screamed "I didn't kill her".'

And that was when I realised there was someone else there, standing close to the bushes, no more than a few feet away.'

*

Price was standing at the edge of the lake, his eyes fixed firmly on the spot where he'd discovered Becca's body, and Barbara Gee's arrival barely registered.

'Dare I ask what you've done with DI Hall?' She gave his arm a gentle nudge. 'Will we find her going through the linen cupboards in search of clues, or has she gone back to The Lancefield Arms to write up her report?'

The attempt at humour fell on unreceptive ears. Price gave an unconcerned shrug and kept his eyes fixed down upon the murky, rippling waters. 'I've left her in the housekeeper's room. She wanted some privacy to put in a call to DS Collinson. And she's only doing her job.'

'Well, I suppose we should be thankful for that.' Barbara took the rebuke in her stride. 'You look troubled. Is it something I can help with?'

'I doubt it. Though I appreciate the offer.' He knew he sounded ungracious. 'You know, I've spent months accusing Kathryn of being beguiled by Salvation Hall and the Lancefield's heritage, and it's just been pointed out to me that Kathryn isn't the only one who's been seduced by it.'

'Ah, I see. Well, it's never too late to put things right, is it?'

'It's too late for Becca. Too late for all of them. All of those victims, they all deserve justice for what happened to them, but I don't feel worthy of the task.'

'Don't blame yourself unnecessarily, Ennor.' The casual use of his name seemed to slip so easily off her tongue. 'For what it's worth, I think we're all culpable in a way.' She took a step closer to the lake and peered down into the water. 'Does your desire for justice extend to Philip McKeith? Because I believe he is just as deserving of it as the Lancefield victims.'

'Richard sacrificed the man's reputation on a whim, didn't he?'

'Oh, hardly. He did it for love. He made a choice between his friend's reputation and his granddaughter's life.' She heard Price utter an audible gasp and she turned to smile at him. 'Oh, I know Kathryn told you about Nancy. It's a pity it didn't all come out sooner. I suppose we were all taken in by her. But then, that's the skill, isn't it? Plausibility.'

'Do you think she knows it's just a matter of time?'

'Before you come up with the evidence you need? I should think so. I think that's what's making her so objectionable today. That, and David's brusque reaction to her plea for family unity.'

'So, David also knows the truth?'

'Nancy made sure of it, though he says he's always suspected something of the sort. It would be exquisitely funny, if it weren't all so tragic. Kathryn, Richard, and I all whispering in corners, keeping the secret of Nancy's birth line from each other and from David, when all the time he'd worked it out for himself.'

Tragic was certainly the word. 'What will happen to the family?'

'If you find the evidence to lance the boil? I suppose that like all boils, it will heal in time. I'll speak to Marcus about coming back into the fold. He doesn't really want to leave, and Richard and David are very fond of him. As am I, for that matter.' Barbara sighed. 'I think Richard will return to St Felix, as long as Marcus will go with him. David will stay on here to run the estates, as planned, and I will be here to support him, along with Kathryn.'

'You think Kathryn will stay?'

'I think Kathryn will stay in Cornwall as long as you're here, Ennor. So please don't think of falling on your sword, or whatever policemen do when they're trying to be noble, and leave the area when the case is over. We don't want to lose her.'

And neither did he. But he couldn't think about that now. 'Why does Richard continue to deny Nancy?'

'I think he's torn. I think he cares very deeply about her, but he's always known she was flawed. I think bringing her to Salvation Hall as his secretary was a way of not just keeping her close, but keeping an eye on her.'

'Then why send her back to St Felix?'

'Isn't that obvious? He suspected that somehow she had a hand in Eva's death. I don't know how. There is an obvious answer, of course, but with Zak and Becca both dead I doubt you would ever prove it. I think Richard wanted Nancy out of the way in case you discovered the truth.'

'And leave poor Marcus to be the scapegoat again? There's no wonder he wants to leave the family behind him.' Price turned to look at her. 'All of this is conjecture, of course, isn't it? It isn't enough that Nancy is sulky and belligerent, and we all suspect her. We need evidence to prove she was behind any of these murders.'

'Which is why I came out here to find you. I think I've discovered something that might help.' Barbara looked down at the slim, leather-bound book she was clutching loosely to her chest. 'I found this amongst Eva's possessions in Hemlock Row, but I didn't look closely at it until today.' She held it out to him almost reluctantly. 'It's her journal. And I've marked the page at the appropriate entry.'

Price took the book from her and pulled on the slim, blue ribbon marking the page. He ran his eyes across the neat, handwritten entry. 'It isn't concrete evidence.'

'No, but it might give you a fresh line of questioning. Now' – she turned to look back at the house – 'isn't there something you need to do?'

26

Tom Parkinson rubbed at the back of his neck with a weary hand. Information on the circumstances of Becca Smith's death was coming in thick and fast now, the hastily-read emails piling up in his inbox faster than he could share the details with DCI Price.

Not that Price was picking up any of his messages or returning any of his calls. He could only imagine what might be going on at Salvation Hall.

He reached across the desk for his mobile phone and tapped on the screen with his thumb. The call to Price's mobile connected to voicemail almost immediately and he let out a sigh of frustration. 'Boss, it's me again. I've got another update for you.' He squinted at the computer screen in front of him as he spoke. 'I've had confirmation that the email brochure request sent to Liberation Park in Becca's name was sent from an IP address in the Penzance area. We haven't nailed it to the exact location. But we have confirmed the email address used was only created the day before the email was sent, and it hasn't been used to send or receive any other communications. The account is still open, but dormant.' He tapped a finger on the desk. 'Anyway, give me a call back if you want to discuss any of the updates further. I'll focus on information gathering here until I hear from you.'

He ended the call, dropping the phone onto the desk, and turned his attention back to a page of handwritten notes. There was no doubt in his mind that all roads in the search for Becca's murder led back to the occupants of Salvation Hall, and not just because her body had been found in the lake beside the house. A forensic examination of the rope that had been tied around her wrist had confirmed it as a match for a reel of cotton cord discovered under the bench in the Lancefield's potting shed. The bag of stones fished out of the lake, assumed to be the means of weighting Becca's body in the water, were a match for the granite rocks that underpinned the alpine garden beside the south-facing terrace. And a search of the grounds had revealed a large patch of disturbed earth in a damp, secluded spot beneath the rhododendron bushes close to the rear gate of the Salvation Hall estate: the most likely spot that Becca's body had been hidden.

The question uppermost in his mind now was how she came to be in that spot on the morning of her death, and which member of the household had put her there. He'd already established that she'd caught the bus from Hayle to Penwithen at eight minutes past ten and would have arrived in the village at around ten forty-five. The newsagent in Penwithen had confirmed that Marcus Drake collected the morning papers on Thursday morning, as he claimed, and that he had the Lancefields' dog with him. But the man had thought it was around ten fifteen. That was half an hour before Becca would have arrived in the village, though the newsagent admitted he didn't see where Marcus had gone when he left the shop. The bit that troubled Parkinson was the presence of Samson. If Marcus had intercepted Becca on her way to Salvation Hall, wouldn't the dog have kicked up a fuss? What would you do with a wire-haired fox terrier if you wanted to commit a murder halfway through his morning walk?

As to Nancy's alibi: there was no question she had parked up in the harbour car park in Penzance at around nine thirty, and both the tailor and the florist in Chapel Street had confirmed she'd visited them sometime between nine thirty and ten o'clock. If she'd walked straight back to the car park, a walk of around ten minutes, she could have left the town by ten fifteen and easily been back in Penwithen by the time Becca's bus arrived. But, unlike Marcus, Nancy didn't have an obvious motive to murder Becca.

Did she?

He was about to ponder the conundrum when the mobile phone on his desk skittered into life and he scooped it up to press it to his ear. 'Tom Parkinson.'

The voice at the other end of the line was both unexpected and hesitant. 'Sergeant Parkinson? It's Amber.' She sounded uneasy. 'I'm sorry to bother you, but I've just got back to the pub after visiting Salvation Hall with Sadie.'

No wonder she sounded unsettled. But it wasn't a reason to call him. 'You sound upset. Is everything alright?'

'It depends on what you mean by alright. The letter Becca posted from the bus station... it's turned up.'

Parkinson felt his pulse begin to quicken. 'So she did send it to Sadie?'

'No, she sent it to me. The post was delivered while I was at Salvation Hall, so I've only just seen it. I wasn't sure what to make of it at first... there was another envelope inside it, and a covering letter. Perhaps I should start with that.' Amber cleared her throat, and began to read. *There's something I have to do and the letter enclosed is my insurance policy. I don't want you to open it. If all goes well, I'll collect it from you on Friday. But if you don't hear from me, give it to Sergeant Parkinson. He'll know what to do. Becs.* The envelope inside is addressed to you, but I opened it. I know it was wrong, but I wanted to know what happened to her.' Amber paused, and all he could hear was her breathing. And then, in a voice he could barely hear, she said, 'I think you need to collect it from me, and take it to Salvation Hall.'

*

DI Hall was still in the small housekeeper's room when Price returned. She was sitting at the table, arms folded and head bowed, and she looked up as he approached. 'There's something I need to tell you.' And whatever it was had brought a sheepish note to her flat, northern vowels. 'I've spoken to Jim, and he's as certain as he can be that Rosemary Taylor murdered Laurence Payne.'

It took a few moments for the words to sink in. And then Price sat down at the other side of the table and put his hands up to his face. He could hardly believe what he was hearing. 'Has Rosemary actually confessed?'

'Not directly to Jim. But she has admitted it to Jennet. Jim's asked her if she wants to make a voluntary statement to begin with, but she's asking for a solicitor so he's taking her in for questioning.' Hall picked up her pen and twizzled it around between her fingers. 'Jennet's handed Rosemary's laptop over. There's evidence she searched for information on the Lancefields and Marcus Drake, as well as how to use taxine as a poison.' The detective paused, and then tapped the pen on the desk. 'She doesn't deny the laptop is hers, by the way. So I don't think we need to worry that the searches might have been carried out by someone else using it.'

'But what on earth made her do it?'

'On the surface, some argument over money. She wanted Laurence to hand over fistfuls of cash to shore up the business but didn't want to give him a share of the place in return for it.' Hall dropped the pen and it clattered onto the table. 'Jim thinks there's a bit more to it than that.

He thinks she'd come to rely very heavily on Jennet after her marriage broke up, and she didn't want her to leave. As she saw it, Laurence was taking Jennet away from her. But Jennet felt suffocated; she didn't want to leave Liberation Park, but she didn't want to go on being controlled by her mother. Rosemary's solution was to remove Laurence from the equation. That way she could keep Jennet close and benefit from his fortune at the same time.'

'Does Jim have any idea when she administered the taxine?'

'No, but there are no shortage of possibilities.' Hall pursed her lips. 'We could do to find some actual taxine, of course. It would have been easy for her to take some leaves or berries from the trees at Liberation Park, but she doesn't seem inclined at this stage to talk about how she made the decoction and what she did with any that remained. She might have just disposed of it by now, but Jim's organising a search. Given she's made an admission to Jennet, a good brief could persuade her it would be in her own best interests to tell us exactly how she did it.'

'Then you've had a result.'

'A result?' Hall snuffled a laugh. 'I dropped the ball spectacularly, though, didn't I? My original hunch was that Rosemary or Jennet was responsible for Laurence's death. But when Becca's phone turned up at Liberation Park I jumped to the wrong conclusion. I thought Marcus Drake was trying to frame her for the murder.'

'It must have muddied the waters for Rosemary Taylor when that phone turned up. She knew she hadn't planted it.'

'Maybe. But it didn't derail her overall plan to blame one of the Lancefields. If anything, it added weight to the idea one of them was responsible.' Hall leaned towards Price. 'You know what this means, don't you? I'm here in Cornwall under false pretences because I followed the wrong lead.'

Price shook his head. 'You're here because fate led you

here. Becca's phone was still planted at Liberation Park, and now we can be pretty certain Marcus or Nancy planted it to make it look as though Becca was in Yorkshire, not in the lake at Salvation Hall. And… well, I needed to hear I was in too deep with Kathryn and the family. I'd lost perspective. And I'll always be grateful to you for pointing that out. It needed doing.' He ventured a smile. 'Not necessarily in the way you did it, though. That was a bit rough around the edges. But you'll learn.'

Hall blinked, and then she jabbed playfully at his arm. 'It's called plain speaking, DCI Price. It's the one thing us northern girls are good at.' She sighed. 'I suppose I'd better get out of your way now, and let you get on with your own investigation.'

'Actually, I'd be pleased if you'd stay. Can Jim Collinson take things forward at Liberation Park until tomorrow? Tom's on his way to Salvation Hall to join me while I speak to Nancy. I think we'd appreciate some unbiased support in the background. This isn't going to be easy.'

The question brought a faint blush to Hall's cheeks. 'I'll have a quick word with my DSI to explain the situation. But given Jim's had a result with Rosemary Taylor I don't think he'll object. After all, the background information you gave me on Laurence was the starting point for our investigation. I'll just tell him that we owe you one.'

*

Familia Super Omnia.

Kathryn shivered as she passed the burgundy-painted board beside the lichgate, her eyes skimming over the prophetic gold lettering as she turned in through the gate to walk slowly down the path past Lucy Lancefield's resting place. A fresh bouquet of roses, verbascum and gypsophila had been placed atop the black marble gravestone, and that was all she needed to see to know she would find what she was looking for inside the church.

She pulled firmly on the heavy metal door ring and passed through doorway into the knave. Inside, afternoon sunlight was pouring through the stained-glass window at the rear of the church, scattering tiny flecks of green and red and blue across the stone floor of the aisle.

Richard Lancefield was sitting silently at the end of a pew in front of the altar, Samson by his feet, and she made her way quietly towards them. The dog lifted his blue-grey head to greet her, his wise eyes searching for a sign of reassurance, and she smiled at him. 'It's alright, Samson, it's only me.' She hesitated beside the pew, waiting for Richard to speak, but when no acknowledgement came she placed a hand gently on his shoulder. 'May I join you?'

He shuffled his gaunt frame farther along the seat. 'By all means.' He waited as she eased into the seat beside him and then turned his eyes towards an elaborate carving on the wall. 'Some of these relics go back as far as the seventeenth century: Lancefields, their distant cousins the Silvers, generation after generation; and all for what?' He turned sorrowful eyes to look at her. 'What was the point of it all, Kathryn? If this is how it must end?'

'Perhaps it isn't an ending. Perhaps it's a beginning. Your family weren't the original landowners in Penwithen, were they? They came here when another line died out. And life went on.'

'And will life go on now, when Nancy is brought to book?'

'Are we talking about Becca's murder here, or Laurence's?'

'Lucy's.' His eyes filled with tears. 'I've always suspected Nancy was responsible for Lucy's death. And foolish enough to think it would all just go away.' The words seemed to be sticking in his throat. 'How could I see my beautiful girl incarcerated in a prison? How could I put her through that?'

'But so many more people have died.' Kathryn could hardly believe what she was hearing. 'If you truly believed she was responsible, you could have ended it. Even if you couldn't bring yourself to surrender her, all you had to do was recognise her, and all of those deaths might have been prevented.'

'I know.' His voice had sunk to a whisper. 'So many have died, and ultimately it is all my fault. I suspected right at the beginning she had betrayed us by murdering Lucy. And when Marcus was persuaded to confess to killing Philip, it gave me the opportunity to place the blame for Lucy's death on my poor Philip's shoulders. He wasn't here to defend himself. And I thought, if I could save her from what she'd done…' His voice trailed away. 'I see now she was beyond saving. She is beautiful, efficient, capable – but she is cold. When I look at her, I see Angel, but it's only skin deep; there is no love in her eyes. No warmth.' He nodded to himself. 'Humour, intelligence, wit, but any compassion she shows, any pretence of empathy is simply an intellectual exercise. She says what she knows is expected of her, not what she feels in her heart.'

'Do you think she murdered Lucy because Lucy wouldn't accept they were cousins?'

'I think it's highly likely. Though I doubt she would ever admit it.' The old man's shoulders sagged. 'I had hoped to return to St Felix and see out my days with her close by, but I see now that I cannot go on protecting her at the expense of others that I love. I have tried to build a family of sorts for David, to support him when I am gone, but he will have to make do with Barbara and Marcus. And Honeysuckle, now the truth is out.' Richard tilted his head towards Kathryn. 'And yourself, my dear, if you can be called upon to go on giving him your support.' His words dripped with regret. 'I had hoped for Eva and Laurence to be there for him too. And poor, dear Stella.' His face began to crumple. 'Dead, all of them, Because I wouldn't see the truth.'

'Are you truly convinced of that?'

'Of course. Who else could it possibly be? I have kept my feelings in check for so long, but I cannot suppress them anymore. I must accept what has to happen, and pray to God that David and Marcus will forgive me for my blindness.'

Kathryn stretched out a hand and took the old man's thin, gnarled fingers in her own. 'There is no evidence yet to support any of these suspicions.' She squeezed his fingers gently. 'Don't you always say that you can't hang a man on circumstantial evidence?'

'Wisest of friends.' He turned to look at her. 'She should never have learned she is my grandchild. I did the best I could for her, before the truth came out. But it would never be enough. I see that now. Lucy's rejection would have wounded her ego, and Eva's relationship with Marcus posed a threat to her position in the family. I cannot think what Laurence might have done to deserve her rage.'

'She didn't murder Dennis or Emma.'

'No, but perhaps if I had acknowledged her and accepted there was no need to reach out in search of a broader family…'

'Why would she murder Becca?'

'My only thought can be that Becca was in some way a threat to her.' Richard's lip began to tremble. 'Kathryn, will Inspector Price do what has to be done? I do not want anyone else to lay charges against Nancy. I know he has come to understand us well enough to treat her with respect and dignity, whatever her crimes. If the axe must fall on my beautiful girl, then let it be Price who strikes the blow.'

27

Nancy turned her head as the kitchen door opened. 'My goodness, I am honoured. Not just one detective, but two in the kitchen this afternoon. Have you both come in search of coffee?'

'No, Nancy, we've come in search of you.' Price, growing weary from the battle, pulled a chair away from the table and sat down without waiting for an invitation. 'I'm afraid this isn't a social event. We have something we need to discuss with you.'

She frowned in DS Parkinson's direction. 'Have you brought dispatches from the battlefield, Sergeant Parkinson?' She walked slowly towards the table and took the chair opposite Price. 'Have you finally discovered who murdered Laurence? I see DI Hall isn't with you.'

'As it happens, we *do* know who murdered Laurence.' Parkinson dropped a large manilla envelope onto the kitchen counter. 'DI Hall has just been speaking to her counterpart in Yorkshire and the killer is local to the area.'

'You see, I told you it wasn't me.' Nancy looked almost triumphant. And then the penny dropped. 'But I would hardly call Marcus local to the area, would you?'

Price answered the question with a faint, inscrutable smile. 'We'd like to speak to you again about the murders of Eva McWhinney, Geraldine Morton and Stella Lancefield.'

'They were all murdered by Zak. I was there with Eva when he confessed to murdering Stella and Geraldine. And I thought it had been confirmed he was responsible for Eva's death in London?'

'No one is disputing that the murders were committed by Zak. What we still have to establish is *why* he committed them.'

Nancy sucked in her cheeks. 'He murdered Geraldine and Stella by accident, didn't he? And as to Eva… well, he always claimed that Marcus offered to pay him to get rid of her. Perhaps you should be asking your questions of Marcus.'

'Why would Marcus want to get rid of a girl he'd never met, and whose existence posed no possible threat to him?'

'I don't understand.'

'Well, when Zak went up to Edinburgh to make his first attempt on Eva's life, he had a description of her and an address where he could find her. Someone must have given him that information.'

'Again, you should speak to Marcus.'

Price turned to look at Parkinson and the sergeant lifted the envelope from the counter. 'This letter was sent to Amber Kimbrall by Becca Smith last Thursday morning, with an instruction to hand it to me if anything happened to her. She posted it at Hayle bus station before she caught the bus to Penwithen.' He pulled the folded letter from the envelope and opened it up. 'I won't bore you will all the details, just the salient points:

If something happens to me, speak to Nancy. I think she murdered Zak. On his way to Salvation Hall he sent me a letter – I should have given it to you straight away but Zak told so many lies I didn't know what to believe. And I couldn't bear to admit that Marcus might be innocent. I've enclosed Zak's letter. Please do what you can to make things right.'

Parkinson pulled the top sheet of paper to one side and read from the page underneath.

'*Becs – I'm sending you this letter as an insurance policy. I'm on my way to meet Nancy Woodlands at Salvation Hall.*'

Nancy rolled her eyes. 'Surely an intelligent man like yourself isn't going to fall for such a simple piece of misdirection. I can't imagine Inspector Price has fallen for it.'

Price held out a hand to Parkinson and took the letter from him. 'The letter goes on to say it was you, and not Marcus, who offered Zak money to murder Eva; that you told him where she lived; you sent him cash when he was on the run; you kept in touch by unregistered mobile phones; it was your idea for him to change his appearance; you provided him with the information he needed to make the Obeah garland…' Price swallowed hard. 'And that you told him where to find Eva in London.'

'The letter is a forgery, of course.' Nancy's voice was unnervingly calm. 'I had no idea Becca felt such animosity towards me. I couldn't say we were friends, but I always tried to do right by her.' She turned her head to stare out of the window, and then looked back at Price. 'You seem to forget that only three people knew where Eva was going to be that evening: Eva herself, Laurence, and Jennet. Unless Eva did reveal her plans to Marcus, and he chose to lie about it.'

'That's almost true. Eva did reveal her plans to a fourth person, and that fourth person certainly chose to lie about it.' Price held out his hand to Parkinson a second time and the sergeant pulled a smart leather-bound journal from the envelope. ' Did you know Barbara brought a collection of Eva's personal belongings back to Salvation Hall, so she could decide what should be done with them?' He took the journal from Parkinson's outstretched hand. 'She found this earlier today, while she was going through Eva's things.' A thin blue ribbon marked the page he wanted, and he pulled on it to open the book and began to read.

'Laurence has agreed to meet me on Friday. Had another call with Nancy to let her know. Have told her where I'm staying and where I'm meeting Laurence for dinner, and that I'll call her afterwards to let her know how it went.'

Price dropped the journal onto the table, his eyes still fixed on the girl's face. 'You set her up, Nancy. You knew Richard didn't want her to go to London, but you also knew it would be too risky for Zak to make another attempt on her life in either Edinburgh or Penwithen. So you put the idea into her head: go ahead and meet with Laurence as a surprise for Richard.'

Nancy pointed to the journal. 'Does Barbara know what's written in the journal? Did she read it?'

'Of course. Why else do you think she gave it to me?' He cast a sideways glance at his colleague and Parkinson took his cue.

'Why don't you tell us about Zak, Nancy? Why don't you tell us exactly what happened when he came to Salvation Hall to collect his payoff?'

*

Nancy's face lit with a sudden fury. 'Zak Smith was a fool. An arrogant, overconfident fool. He didn't just want the money. He was deluded enough to think I would be interested in him. In *him*, for pity's sake.'

Price felt a sudden surge of adrenaline. Was she actually going to confess? He shot an incredulous glance at Parkinson, but the sergeant was transfixed, his eyes directly on Nancy. 'So, you agreed to meet with him?' If he trod carefully, there was a chance he could lead her softly to the truth. 'You must have known the risk you were taking by letting him come to the estate?'

'He wanted his money, so I told him I'd leave it in the potting shed. He said he wanted me there too, and if I didn't meet him he would tell the family what I'd done. He said he would give them the SIM cards he'd used to keep in touch with me, and they would show a trail of all the texts and conversations that we'd had. How could I take the risk?' Her mouth was twisting and she looked at Price with eyes that pleaded to be understood. 'He said he would try to screw more money out of Richard to keep it quiet, and I couldn't let that happen. It wouldn't have been fair to Richard.'

Price murmured under his breath. 'It's okay, Nancy. I understand.' He just hoped that Parkinson would keep his cool. 'What happened when Zak came to the potting shed?'

'I knew I'd have to shut him up, so I hid behind the door and waited for him. I wasn't sure if I could overcome him unless he was facing away from me so I had to plant something to attract his attention. I put a bundle of banknotes on the floor but it was dark in the potting shed and they weren't really visible, so I put my gold bracelets on top of them. It was the best idea I could come up with, something glittering enough to catch his eye and valuable enough for him to bend down and take a closer look. I knew he was greedy, and probably fool enough to fall for such a simple device. But then he wasn't renowned for his brains, was he?'

'No, I don't suppose he was.' Price laughed softly, as if to share the joke. 'So, he walked in and the gold caught his eye. And when he knelt down to look at it, you hit him with the spade?'

'He had no idea I was there.' Nancy gasped, a tiny, tortured breath of dismay, as if the enormity of her actions had only just struck her. A single tear made its way down her cheek. 'I thought if I hit him with the spade, everyone would think that Marcus was responsible, because that was how Marcus murdered Philip.' She licked her lips. 'I thought it was really rather clever of me.'

'Clever?' Tom Parkinson pushed himself away from the kitchen counter and stepped forward to place his hands on the table. 'And what about Becca, Nancy? Was that clever?' He bent his neck to stare into her face, growling the question under his breath. 'What the hell did Becca ever do to you, that she had to end up in the lake?'

The spell broken, Nancy shrank back. 'She tried to blackmail me. When she heard I'd returned to Penwithen to visit Richard and David, she sent me a letter – handwritten and delivered by hand. She said Zak told her it was me who offered him money to get rid of Eva. She told me she'd had a letter from him, confessing everything, and that he posted it before he came here to meet me. But the letter had no stamp on it, and it took weeks to be delivered. She didn't receive it until after Eva's funeral; until after I had returned to St Felix.' Nancy scowled. 'He said he'd earned the money I owed him, and that if anything happened to him he wanted her to have it. That she and Frankie should benefit from it, and she should demand I hand it over. And that's just exactly what the grasping, money-grabbing little bitch did. She wrote to me, demanding the money in return for Zak's letter. If I didn't pay, she would hand his letter over to the police.'

'Was that when you decided to kill her?'

'Yes. But I knew I had to divert suspicion away from Salvation Hall, and Laurence's wedding gave me an idea. I went to the public library in Penzance and used one of their computers to set up an email address in Becca's name, so I could request a brochure for Liberation Park and have it sent to her home. I found her address amongst Richard's papers. And then I told her I needed time to get the cash together, so she would have to wait until Thursday morning for it.'

'Did you get the cash?'

'No, of course not.' Nancy flashed a withering glance at Parkinson. 'I had no intention of paying her.'

'But you picked her up on your way back from Penzance on Thursday morning?'

'She'd already got off the bus and started to walk

towards the hall. I pulled up beside her and told her it would be more private if we spoke in the car.'

'And then you drove her to the rear of the estate, and you killed her.'

Nancy's face contorted. 'I…' A sob made its way to her lips and she suddenly wailed. 'Leave me alone.'

'You killed her, didn't you, Nancy?'

Nancy's mouth opened, her lips working but no sound emitting. And then her shoulders heaved and she drew in a steadying breath. 'No comment.'

The words cut the air like a knife.

'No comment?' Parkinson, enraged, lunged at her. His fingers clawed at her dress and he yanked on the soft woollen fabric to drag her to her feet. 'No comment?' He was yelling into her face. 'Is that it? Is that all you have to say for taking Becca's life? For making Frankie an orphan?'

'Tom, for pity's sake, let her go.' Price pushed back his chair and stood to grasp at Parkinson's shoulders, pulling him roughly away. 'I said let her go.'

Shocked, the sergeant released his grip, and both detectives watched as Nancy stumbled back onto her chair. She was breathing heavily, her shoulders rising and falling with each breath, her body trembling. And then she sighed. 'You know, it's wrong of you both to ask me these questions without representation. I really don't think I can speak about this anymore at the moment. I need to speak to Richard.'

28

'You've left her alone with Tom?' Kathryn looked up at Ennor as he sat down beside her on the bench. 'Was that a good idea?'

'They're not alone. DI Hall has gone in to join them.' It was cold on the terrace and Ennor folded his arms against the rising breeze. 'We're going to give her a few minutes to speak to Richard, under observation, and then she'll be taken over to Truro for formal questioning. We'll start with the murders of Zak and Becca. There will probably be a delay while her representation is arranged, especially if Richard decides to send to London for his expensive brief again.' Ennor shivered. 'I'm going to arrange for another officer to sit in with Tom while he questions her. I'm far too close to it now. DI Hall was right. I let myself be blinded by what I wanted to see, and not what was there.' He took hold of Kathryn's hand and was relieved when she didn't pull away. 'I take it Richard will go on protecting her? She was quite right to call out that we shouldn't have been questioning her without a caution. There is a chance she could wriggle off the hook, at least for the Smith murders.'

'But not if you question her formally over Lucy's murder?'

Ennor frowned. 'Has any evidence come to light that

would help us to make a case?'

'No. But Marcus has admitted to me that it was Nancy's idea to put Philip's and Lucy's bodies in the lake, and she helped him to do it. And he has always suspected it was she, and not Philip, who murdered Lucy. She was there when he struck the blow that killed Philip, but she claimed to have just arrived. It's only now that he's beginning to realise she might have set the whole thing up. He thinks she might have told Philip that Lucy wanted to see him down by the lake, and when Philip arrived Lucy was already dead.'

'Why has he never spoken up before now?'

'Partly because he couldn't be sure. And partly because the night they put the bodies in the lake, he promised Nancy he would never speak of it if she helped him, not just with the bodies but with an alibi. She only agreed on condition they keep it a secret between the two of them. Unfortunately, Richard also suspected Nancy was responsible. That's why he asked Marcus to confess to Philip's murder and bring your initial investigation to a speedy conclusion. He thought if Marcus could be persuaded to blame Philip for Lucy's murder, knowing Philip couldn't defend himself, you would accept the explanation and not look any further at the family.'

'So, when Nancy originally gave Marcus what she later claimed was a false alibi for the time of Philip's murder, it wasn't false at all. She actually was with him. Only they were disposing of the bodies. And then she stitched Marcus up by telling us the alibi was false.' Ennor shook his head. 'What an idiot I've been.' He chewed on his lip. 'Do you think she told Lucy they were cousins?'

'Probably. And either Lucy didn't believe it, or she was distinctly unimpressed by the idea. That's why the gift Nancy gave her was so unwelcome. One way or another, she couldn't reconcile herself to the idea of Nancy as an equal. So Nancy got rid of her.'

'And Eva was just Lucy in another form, come to take

her place in Richard's affections and stand in the way of what Nancy believed was her own rightful inheritance?'

'I suppose so.' Kathryn sighed. 'Do you remember how Becca received texts from Philip McKeith's phone when everyone thought he was on the run? And how you found that phone under Marcus's bed? He had no idea Nancy had that phone. He can only assume she planted it there. And because of the agreement he'd struck with Richard – confess to Philip's murder, and take full responsibility without implicating anyone else – he wouldn't tell anyone what she'd done.'

'Then she probably did the same with the burner phone she'd been using to contact Zak. She was constantly trying to point the finger at Marcus, wasn't she? Because she knew he was the one person who could point the finger at her for Lucy's murder.'

'She's going to go away for a very long time, isn't she?'

'Without question. It's going to hit the old man very hard.'

'It's going to hit the whole family very hard. Not just here, but on the Woodlands estate too. David is going to wait until you confirm she'll be charged, and then he'll let Honeysuckle know what's happened.' Kathryn rested her head on Ennor's shoulder. 'I still can't believe all those people died just because the family wouldn't recognise her. I keep thinking that if only Lucy had welcomed her into the family, or David had voiced his suspicions, or Richard had acknowledged her publicly as his granddaughter, those people would still be alive.' She turned her eyes up to his face. 'Is there really a possibility she could get away with murder?'

More of a possibility than Ennor liked to admit. 'There is very little evidence that isn't circumstantial. We have Eva's journal and the letters from Becca and Zak, and we could take witness statements from the family. But a solid legal team could pick holes in it all.' He frowned. 'Do you think she might confess?'

'I would think that very much depends on what instructions she receives from Richard and whether she will agree to follow them. She was a clever adversary, you know. Richard confided to me that he'd always know she was intelligent, but he made no allowance for her cunning. She was always one step ahead, wasn't she? Always ready with a false trail or a piece of deflection. And all the time turning up as amiable, reliable Nancy. Looking after everyone, taking everything in her stride…'

'And she might have got away with it, if only Becca hadn't decided to brazen it out and challenge her.' Ennor frowned. 'It was clever of Becca to use the same insurance policy Zak had deployed.'

'Sending a letter to Amber, in case something happened to her? Poor Becca. She had so much to be thankful for, and in the end she was just too greedy.'

'No, she wasn't.' Ennor wouldn't believe it for a minute. 'Zak might have wanted Becca to have the money if anything happened to him, and Becca might have used that to get under Nancy's skin. But I think what Becca truly wanted was justice. She wanted to confront Nancy, to tell her that she knew Philip had been framed and Zak had been sacrificed. But we'll never know the truth because it's too late for Becca to tell us.' He would never be able to understand why Becca didn't just bring Zak's letter to himself or Tom Parkinson.

But it was too late for Becca to tell him that too.

29

The sitting room at Holly Cottage was the sanctuary David needed. He leaned back in his chair with a sigh and lifted his feet up onto the small velvet footstool in front of him. 'I wonder how long it will take before the enormity of the day's events finally hits me?' He dropped a hand down the side of the chair, to where Samson was quietly dozing, and ruffled his fingers into the dog's wiry coat. 'My newly discovered niece was probably responsible for my daughter's death, and indirectly responsible for the death of my beloved Stella. And yet I feel unreasonably calm.'

It was probably the shock. And it would take some days, at least, for him to grasp not just that Nancy was responsible for the deaths, but that she was unquestionably a dangerous serial killer and his father had aided and abetted her by turning a blind eye to her crimes. Until then, Barbara reasoned, the best she could hope for was to keep David's mind occupied with mundanities. 'Do we know where Kathryn has gone this evening? Has she returned to The Zoological?'

'Yes. She offered to drive my father to the hotel in search of Marcus, and then she was going to shower and change and meet up with Ennor for something to eat.'

'David, you called him Ennor.'

'I did, didn't I?' He smiled to himself. 'Perhaps, now, I feel that I can. I always said he would be Inspector Price until this whole sordid matter was resolved.'

'And now it almost is.' There was a small gin and tonic on the side table beside Barbara's chair and she reached out to retrieve it. 'Do you think the time has come to speak to Kathryn about moving onto the estate? I know she's always felt the need to keep a professional boundary in place, but things will be so different now.'

'Speaking for myself, it would be a godsend if she would consider moving into the main house. It will be a lonely place on my own in the evenings once my father returns to St Felix. Though I suppose I would have to get used to Ennor cluttering up the place. It's probably just as well I've overcome my aversion to using his name.'

Barbara sipped on her gin. 'I do hope Richard can persuade Marcus to return to the family fold, and not just so he can run the Woodlands estate. We've all been living a nightmare for the last few months, yourself and Marcus most of all; we need some time together to get used to the fact that it's over.' Or, at least, that the truth was out. 'If and when Ennor brings charges against Nancy for whatever crimes she has committed, we're going to have to be strong for each other.'

'And I have every confidence we will be.' David settled deeper into his seat. 'What do you suppose made her do it, Barbara? Did she hate us all so much?'

'I don't think she hated us at all. Although I've asked myself more than once today how I managed to escape her madness. There was a point at which I'd convinced myself I was going to be the next victim in all of this, but for some reason she let me be.'

'Perhaps because you were a comfort to her, and not a threat.'

'And yet I'm the one who gave Eva's journal to Ennor, and showed him that Nancy knew Eva planned to go to London.' Why did doing the right thing have to feel like a betrayal? 'I suppose if Richard had seen the journal, rather than me, he would have destroyed it to protect her.'

'Lucky for us then, that it was you.' David turned his

head to look at her. 'You did the right thing, Barbara. But even if you hadn't brought the journal to Ennor's attention, the letter Becca sent to Amber would have sealed Nancy's fate.' He puffed out a heartfelt sigh. 'Even if we can be strong for each other, do you think we will manage to ride out the storm?'

'Oh, yes, I'm sure we will. I think Richard will still travel to St Felix to see out his days, and you and I can manage the estates here. Kathryn might be persuaded to take over the foundation. There is still little Frankie to consider, but I'm sure Amber will help us to build a bridge with Sadie to secure her future.' Barbara stared into her glass. 'I suppose it's a small comfort that Nancy wasn't responsible for Laurence's death.'

'Indeed. Though my heart still breaks for poor Jennet, having to face the truth about her mother. Perhaps I should make a trip to Liberation Park after all, to return her Bible and to offer the hand of friendship. She is my cousin's widow, when all's said and done.' David closed his eyes. 'My poor darling Stella had the measure of Nancy all along, didn't she? I thought it was rather cruel that she always referred to her as The Girl. But she must have seen something in Nancy that the rest of us failed to pick up on. When I told her we planned to invite Eva to visit Salvation Hall she asked me how I thought Nancy would react. She said that since Lucy's death, Nancy had achieved the privileged position of being the only young woman in Richard's life, and that when she set eyes on Eva she would begin to rock the boat.' David's lower lip began to tremble, and he bit it to stem the rising tide of emotion. 'I didn't listen to her, Barbara. If only I had listened to her, if only I had believed her instead of jumping to Nancy's defence, then both Eva and my beloved Stella might still be with us today.'

*

'I can hardly believe that it's over.' Kathryn slipped her hand through Ennor's arm as the taxi pulled away from the kerb. 'Are you sure this is okay? You're definitely not needed at the station?'

'I'm definitely not needed at the station.' He could hardly believe it himself. 'We have twenty-four hours to get the truth out of Nancy: at least for Becca's murder. Tom is taking the first watch, I'll be picking up the reins in the morning.' Always assuming Tom hadn't managed to extract a full confession from her by then. 'I can tell you now that he won't be going easy on her, but after what she did to Becca you wouldn't expect him to, would you?'

'No, I don't suppose I would.' Kathryn followed his lead as Ennor turned on his heel, setting a course for the Marazion shoreline. 'Earlier today, Richard confided in me that he hoped you would deal with Nancy yourself. He was sure you would treat her with dignity and respect.'

'Tom will treat her with dignity. But in a situation like this there can be a fine line between showing respect and being lenient.' A line which Price wasn't sure he could even trust himself to observe, let alone Tom, given their past encounters with Nancy. 'He'll be fair, but he'll be firm.'

'Well, I hope you're right.' Kathryn pulled gently on his arm. 'You know I failed in my task, don't you? You challenged me to flush out the killer. But it wasn't me that brought it home. You did it yourself.'

If only he could confidently take the credit. 'Actually, it was DI Hall who brought it home. She went out on a limb and rattled Nancy's cage so hard even my teeth began to jangle. She began to question her about her relationship with Lucy. It didn't get her anywhere, but it was pretty obvious Nancy was on the backfoot. And so was I, to begin with. I was furious that Hall had crossed the line and start to poke into my investigation. But it gave me the push I needed. She took an instant dislike to Nancy and couldn't understand why I couldn't smell the guilt on her.

She called out that I was far too close to the situation. So, when Tom and I went back to question Nancy again, taking Eva's journal and Becca's letter with us, I wasn't prepared to give her the benefit of the doubt. And neither was Tom.'

'Did Nancy admit to requesting the brochure for Liberation Park?'

'Yes. But there are plenty of things she hasn't admitted yet: telling Zak that Eva would be out on the terrace the night he broke into the grounds of Salvation Hall; what she's done with the various burner phones they used to keep in touch; planting one of those phones under Marcus's bed to make us think he was the killer.' They had reached the low stone wall that separated the pavement from the beach and Ennor halted in front of it to stare out across the sea. The craggy outcrop of St Michael's Mount was a ghostly outline in the moonlight and the castle at its peak was bathed in a glow of golden lights. 'Do you think Richard will still travel to St Felix, now Nancy won't be there with him?'

'Yes, if he can persuade Marcus to return.' Kathryn frowned. 'And always supposing no action will be taken against him for not sharing his suspicions about Nancy.' She took a step backwards, away from the wall, gently pulling Ennor in her wake. 'Is there any danger of that?'

'We're back to that fine line again, aren't we?' He unhooked his arm from Kathryn's and rested it around her shoulders as they began to walk back towards the village. 'If Richard had known for certain that Nancy murdered Lucy, and that she was party to a joint enterprise with Zak for the murders of Geraldine, Eva and Stella, then yes, he could be charged with assisting an offender and perverting the course of justice. But as things stand, he didn't know for certain. And hiding the fact that she was his granddaughter isn't a crime. It's a private family matter. However brutal the outcome of keeping that secret, he couldn't have foreseen the consequences.'

'He does blame himself, Ennor.'

'And I can't say that surprises me.' They had reached the entrance to the restaurant and he lowered his arm to usher Kathryn through the open doorway.

But she halted in her tracks and turned to face him. 'I'm sorry for the way I behaved when you brought me here yesterday evening. And I'm sorry I didn't tell you sooner that Nancy was Richard's granddaughter.'

He lifted his hand and gently touched her lips with his fingers. 'Don't say any more. I know you gave your word to Richard to keep the secret, and I know how much it must have cost you to break that confidence.' If she said any more he might have to admit to her that he'd broken his own word, and shared that information with DI Hall. 'It's over now. And we have much better things to talk about this evening.'

'Do we?'

'It isn't a question of whether we bring charges against Nancy, so much as how many charges we're going to bring. And as soon as we charge her, I'm going to be drowning in paperwork. But my SIO knows I'm running on empty thanks to the Lancefield murders. I haven't had any time off since last September. He's encouraging me to take the leave I'm owed before I lose it, so I can come back to the table in peak condition. If Richard and David can spare you, I thought we might take a holiday together.' He lowered his head until it was touching hers. 'I know it's a little late in the season, but I wondered if you might know somewhere we could get away from it all? Maybe somewhere in the Caribbean?'

ABOUT THE AUTHOR

Mariah Kingdom was born in Hull and grew up in the East Riding of Yorkshire. After taking a degree in History at Edinburgh University she wandered into a career in information technology and business change, and worked for almost thirty years as a consultant in the British retail and banking sectors.

She began writing crime fiction during the banking crisis of 2008, drawing on past experience to create Rose Bennett, a private investigator engaged by a fictional British bank.

Liberation Park is the fifth and final Lancefield Mystery.

www.mariahkingdom.com

Printed in Great Britain
by Amazon